FEALDER'S CHOICE

To Ron + Carole

Live well & read lots of mysteries!

Pete

Peter Swan

ISBN: 1533582637
ISBN 13: 9781533582638

To Joyce

1

The Mariners game was in the top of the four-teenth inning when Parkinson Fealder's phone chirped. He sighed, stood, stretched his arms over his head and ambled into his kitchen.

"Yeah, Fealder here."

"Fealder, it's Matson. There's been a death at the university. Sounds like a jumper from the big office building, Bracknell Hall. James wants you to get over there."

"They know who it is?"

"No. Campus Security called it in. They said a 'white male'. They know not to touch the body."

"OK. I'll be there in ten minutes. What did James say about a partner?"

"He said he was assigning Berbieri. She's the wom-an from Property Crimes. Just transferred to us. You know her?"

"Met her, yeah. She'll be called to Bracknell?"

"Yes. I'm calling her next."

"Right. I'm on my way."

So he was still on James's shit list, Fealder thought. Sent out in the field in the middle of a dark Portland night for a suicide verification where making the call would probably be a no-brainer. And James partnered him with a rookie who had never before worked in homicide. Well, she would *have* to be better than Dick Nabors. He guessed that Nabors was likely to be promoted before him since the guy was more than willing to play the married-to-the-chief's-niece card. Nabors, who screwed up the chain-of-custody on a piece of evidence last month and implied to the D.A. that it was Fealder's doing! Fealder had not fingered Nabors. He had succinctly denied that the lapse was his. All he said to his immediate boss, Lieutenant James, was that it was counterproductive to have Nabors and him on the same team. He had added that he wanted a new partner as soon as that could be arranged. Not that James was going to cut Fealder any breaks. But what the hell! That was then and this is now. He had a stiff to check out and a green-as-grass partner. He wondered, as he strapped on his shoulder holster, whether James was setting him up as an on-the-job trainer to slow his upward progress in the unit. He threw on his sport-jacket, slipped into loafers, and headed for his garage without remembering to record the rest of the game.

Fealder turned off the city streets and thread-ed his way along the lanes of the campus toward Bracknell. Even at this time of night, he saw that sev-eral floors of the campus landmark were fully lit. He guessed those must be the floors where custodians were working. Closer to Bracknell, the lane widened to allow diagonal parking. Fealder eased his silver Corvette to a stop at the curb and strode across the dew-covered lawn to join the group standing in darkness at the narrow end of the ten-story brick building. He recognized the police officer assigned to the campus and spoke to him first.

"Evening, Mel. Looks like I'm handling this one. Detective Berbieri will be arriving soon to work with me."

The officer grinned and said, "Glad you're here, Detective. I'll introduce you." He turned to the oth-ers and in a louder voice said. "This is Dougherty, a Campus Security Officer and Satino here is a student patrolman. It was Satino who discovered the body." He gestured toward an older man not in uniform. "Paul Stranglund is University Counsel. This is Detective Fealder from the Portland Police Bureau's Homicide Unit."

They acknowledged the introductions with nods except for Stranglund who shook Fealder's hand. Fealder turned up the collar of his jacket as he felt a light, but chilling, breeze.

"Mel," said Fealder, "maybe you can start isolating the area with tape. The rest of us should stay back here while he secures the area. So what have we got?"

Satino wore a simple uniform jacket with the emblem of Campus Security to show his official status as a student employee of that office. He shuddered as he answered. "I was doing my walk around the building about midnight. I thought I saw one of the ground-floor windows open. That quarter moon was behind those high clouds so I turned on my flashlight. Before I reached the building I saw this body off to my left, half underneath one of those large rhodies."

"Was the window open?" asked Fealder.

"No, actually it wasn't. It must have just been the shadows that made it look that way. Anyway, at first I thought he was a drunk, but I couldn't rouse him." He shuddered again. " I... I haven't taken the CPR training yet so I just used my radio to call in."

"That was the right thing. Did you touch him?"

"Well, yeah, but only on the wrist. I tried to find a pulse. But I didn't move him or even roll him over."

"Had you made an earlier round past here this evening?"

"Yeah. It was probably about nine-forty-five. My shift starts at nine. But I didn't get close enough to notice him, if he was there by then. It was only that thing about the way the window looked that..."

"I understand." Turning to the others, Fealder asked, "Do we know who he is?"

"Not yet," said the police officer. "I confirmed that he was dead and felt a wallet in his pants, but I told them to wait moving him or fussing with the body until Homicide arrived."

A Ford Explorer braked to a sudden stop at the curb. A raven-haired woman in her early thirties wearing charcoal slacks and a gray sweater got out and approached the group. Dougherty moved to meet her. She displayed her badge to the police officer and identified herself as Detective Berbieri. Fealder motioned her aside as soon as introductions were finished. He remembered her as a very attractive woman and he could see this was true even in the middle of the night when her face was without makeup. She looked a lot more energized than she had been at their very brief meeting as she was being shown around the office earlier in the week.

"You've got a lot of names to remember. I'm Park Fealder. It looks as though we're going to be working together on this one." He hesitated to affirm that she was probably going to be his permanent partner. "I'm sorry we have to get to know each other's approach in the middle of the night with the corpse barely cold."

"Oh, I remember you. I've heard you're damn good, so I'm glad we're working together."

"That's good news," said Fealder. He had heard the men in Property Crimes had tagged her as ambitious. Well, aren't we all? he thought. Anyway, she sounded confident and sincere. "Let's get at it," he said as they rejoined the group.

Fealder used his radio to reach the police dispatcher. "Sergeant Matson, it's Fealder. Have the crime scene techs been dispatched?"

"Yeah, the Lieutenant alerted them. They should have a crew there in another five or ten minutes."

"Fine. How about an investigator from the Medical Examiner's office?"

"They already had someone in the field and he's on your side of the river. He just finished up where he was so they're sending him straight to your scene."

Fealder clipped the radio back on his belt. "OK, Berbieri and I will check him out," he said to the others.

They played their flashlights on the body which lay face down. A blot of blood marked the mulch beside the man's head. A branch broken from the rhododendron lay two feet away. Fealder put on latex gloves and slid a wallet out of the man's back pocket. Berbieri aimed her Mini Maglite at the cards Fealder extracted. "Driver's license says he's Adam Warburton," he said loudly enough for the others to hear.

Stranglund spoke up, "He's faculty. I met him last year at a reception for the new College of Arts and Sciences dean.. He's in the Psychology Department. Their offices are in this building."

Fealder turned to Berbieri. "Can you see his watch without moving him? Is it still running?"

"Yes. Yes it is."

"So much for an easy way of suggesting the time of death."

"Look at this. His left shoe is missing."

"He was wearing loafers. Huh! It should be right here."

Berbieri swept her light around the immediate area.

"Nothing," affirmed Fealder.

At that moment, the M.E.'s investigator arrived followed by the criminalists in their van. Fealder met them at the line of tape. He recognized the investigator, Bob Tramell, and introduced Berbieri. "Bob, the deceased was a faculty member. His office is in this building. The body was discovered about midnight. Gerri, get your photos and then, as soon as you techs have finished around the body, we'll let Bob get to work. In the meantime, can one of you start looking for his left shoe? A brown loafer."

The photographer set up her lights and the rest of the forensic team laid out a search grid extending from the building to thirty feet beyond the body. Fealder was eager to take a closer look at the body, but contented himself with having Satino flesh out the details of how he approached the body and examined it. Berbieri spent time talking with Officer Dougherty to learn something of the layout of the building. When the photographer had finished the "in situ" pictures, Tramell began his examination. Less than a minute

after that, one of the criminalists who had been searching the shrubbery bed with the aid of her powerful
flashlight reported, "I've found the shoe!" She marked
the exact location of where the shoe was found on a
"map" of the grid after using a surveyor's tape to mea-
sure the distance to two points on the building and
from the body. Another member of the team helped
with the tape and used a compass to determine the
angles to salient fixtures on the building as seen from
the shoe. They repeated the process for the body itself.

"So, Andy, the shoe must have been a good twenty-
five feet from the body?" Fielder asked the leader of
the forensic team.

"Well, we measured just over twenty-seven feet.
We'll also do the trigonometry back at the lab and get
it that way too, Park."

Tramell looked up from his kneeling position and
spoke softly. "Park, he died of a fractured skull. Very
probably from the fall, but the autopsy will look at
everything."

"Any idea on the time of death?"

"Very recent. Possibly within the hour. But almost
certainly within the last two hours since there's no
rigor."

The criminalists were wrapping up their grid search
and Fealder turned to the team leader. "Anything turn
up besides the shoe?"

"Well, we found a cigarette about half smoked. It was
about eight feet from the body. We'll see if we can get a

DNA sample from it. Until then, could be anyone's. You know, pitched from one of those balconies up there," said the criminalist pointing straight overhead.

"What's the brand?"

The technician glanced at the plastic bag in his hand. "Kool."

Fealder turned to Berbieri. "Tami, we'll need to find out if Professor Warburton smoked and, if he did, what brand."

They walked back to the group standing beyond the yellow tape. Fealder saw that the local television stations' camera crews were already on the scene and knew they had been monitoring the dispatcher's radio messages. Stranglund introduced Fealder and Berbieri to the University's Director of Community Relations who had also arrived. "So, Detective Fealder," the director asked, "is this a suicide?"

"Ma'am, it's way too early to answer that. There'll be an autopsy and that will shed some light on the immediate cause of death, presumably the fall. But we have to get a lot more information before we'll have any indication whether it's an accident, a suicide, or a homicide."

"A homicide?"

"It was a violent, unnatural death. At this stage, nothing should be ruled out." He turned to Stranglund. "Do you know which floor Warburton's office is on?"

"Well, I've never been in his office," said Stranglund, "but the Psych Department is housed on the sixth and seventh floors so it's almost certainly on one of those floors."

"Thanks, Mr. Stranglund. I'd like to speak to the wife and his Department Head as soon as possible this evening."

The General Counsel looked shaken, but replied, "I think he's divorced so there is no wife. The Department Head's name is Mortinsen. David Mortinsen. I'll arrange for him to meet you here, outside the building, as fast as he can get here."

"Thanks. Here's my card with my cell phone number on it. Now can you get us inside that building?"

"Well, I can't, but Officer Dougherty can. I'll tag along if that's alright with you."

"I'll respect that request, but please don't touch anything, not even a light switch or a doorknob."

They entered the building and verified from the lobby register that Professor Adam Warburton's office was on the seventh floor, room 714. Berbieri asked to be shown the fire stairs and how the doors opened. "I'll take these stairs up to seven and meet you there. When we're done, I'll take the other stairway back down."

"Right. We'll see you up there," replied Fealder. He turned to the Campus Security Officer as they entered the elevator. "Dougherty, is there a lock-off on these elevators at night or can anyone use them?"

"My understanding is that Campus Security has recommended that a lock-off capability be added and be used after six in the evening, but they don't have it on this elevator at this time. I've heard the Physical Plant is hoping to include retrofits like that in next year's budget."

Fealder punched the seventh-floor button with the tip of his pen. They emerged from the elevator to a long, vinyl-floored hallway with offices on each side and fluorescent lights overhead. They stopped in front of the door to room 714. Fealder, still wearing his gloves, gingerly tried the doorknob. "Locked. Do you have a passkey Dougherty?"

"Yes. Give me a second to be sure I've got the right one."

They could hear the faint sound of classical music from behind the door. Dougherty flipped keys back and forth on a large ring, then selected one and used it to unlock and turn the knob. Fealder and Berbieri entered a modest-sized office. A dozen or more academic journals were stacked on one of the two chairs in front of the desk. Bookshelves covered one wall and were filled with works on Psychology. An imposing leather executive chair was behind the steel desk. A draft document of some twenty pages was spread on the desk with editorial corrections on the visible pages. A personal computer sat on a wheeled caddy to one side of the desk.

"Better make a note, Tami. Door was locked, but lights and radio were on."

Fealder studied the papers on the desk. Berbieri had her notebook open. "I got it, Detective Fealder. What's on the desk?"

"Some kind of a write-up of an experiment. Looks like a work in progress." Using tweezers, he checked the last page. "It seems to end in the middle of a section. We'll have the crime scene techs take it for analysis." He looked at Stranglund standing in the hallway. "I want our techs to go over this office so it and the elevator and stairways and this corridor will have to be off-limits to everyone for the next few hours." He turned back to Berbieri. "We need to make sure our computer guy gets copies of all the files on his computer."

Berbieri nodded and was about to use her radio when Stranglund spoke up. "Well there are privacy issues we have to consider before going into an employee's computer. I'd want..."

"Mr. Stranglund, we're investigating a death here. If there's nothing of interest to us regarding the death, whatever we see stays confidential with us. Let's not stand on niceties here."

"It's more than niceties, Detective. The university has rules. And if there should be student information or federal grant information on there, there will even be federal rules to follow."

"Here's the deal," said Fealder. "My people will copy out the files and the cache memory and then we'll unplug the computer and seal the room. If we have other evidence to make us sure that this is an accidental death or a suicide, we return the disks without printing anything out. If it looks at all like a homicide, we get a search warrant and go from there."

Stranglund looked uncomfortable, but nodded. "That's reasonable. We'll rely on those assurances."

Fealder nodded. "Now we need a look at that balcony."

He started for the door but stopped when he saw a calendar pad on the corner of Warburton's desk. "Look at this, Tami. The top page on the calendar is for today, the day that has just begun, There is no page for yesterday. It has been torn off."

Berbieri bent over to check the wastebasket. "Wastebasket's empty." She checked the pages on the calendar back to the start of the month and said, "Two other pages are also missing. Perhaps the torn-off page is not significant."

"Maybe not, but find out from the custodians when they last emptied the wastebasket. And make sure they know not to enter the corridor or this room so long as the tape is up."

When they reached the threshold, Fealder paused and studied the door knob. "Can be set to 'unlocked' from the inside, but otherwise the door locks when shut," he said to Berbieri. "Okay, Officer Dougherty, now you can show us the balcony."

2

The detectives saw cartoons, course assignments, and notes pinned to the professors' small exterior bulletin boards as they walked down the hallway. Fealder noted that Warburton's board was relatively sterile compared to most of his colleagues': only a statement of office hours and a notice about rescheduling a lab session. They passed the elevator and kept walking to the balcony door at the end of the corridor. A sign beside the door indicated it was a fire exit. Dougherty again fished among the keys on his ring to find the key to unlock the door. Before he inserted the key, Fealder reached in front of him and satisfied himself that the door could not otherwise be opened.

"Dougherty, how come the sign says 'fire exit', but you have to have a key?"

"Good question, Detective. These locks are automatically overridden if any fire alarm or smoke alarm is triggered. Some kind of a solenoid connected to the alarm circuit, I suppose."

Dougherty again turned the knob with the key and Fealder and Berbieri walked onto the balcony enshrouded in stygian darkness. It was surrounded by a solid concrete wall which rose almost to Fealder's belt. Using his flashlight, Fealder measured its dimensions and Berbieri recorded them.

"The wall is thirty-eight inches high." She held one end of his tape for him as he walked toward the far end. "The balcony measures twenty-two feet long." He retracted the tape and got the width. "And... four feet wide. The metal fire stairs at this end have a railing and are... twenty-six inches wide and take up eleven feet into the overall length. The door is three feet wide and begins about thirty inches from the .... is this direction East, Dougherty?"

Dougherty stepped onto the balcony long enough to see which way Fealder was pointing. "Yeah, that's East."

"Okay, Tami. Thirty inches from the east end of the balcony. And there's a cylinder full of sand with a few cigarette butts near the wall in those thirty inches. Get Gerri to take photos of this place and have the criminalists grab those butts."

Berbieri nodded and turned to Dougherty. "Is the layout of each balcony identical?"

"Yeah, they're just stacked one above the other, all the same. Oh, wait a minute, the top one has no upward fire stair and the lowest one has a vertical ladder to the ground that's winched up when not in use."

"Could someone reach up to that ladder at the bottom?"

"Well, maybe, if they were a great basketball player, they could jump for it. Anyone else would need a boost or a ladder of their own."

"And the doors? Do they all have the same lock and override system?"

"Yes. I'm not sure, but I'd guess everyone in the building should have a key that fits all the doors."

Fealder turned to Stranglund. "Is smoking allowed inside the building?"

"No. I imagine a few people sneak a smoke inside their offices from time to time, but they're not supposed to. So they have to go outside ... or to a balcony like this."

Fealder leaned over the edge and saw men from the morgue loading the bag holding Warburton's body onto a gurney. He left the balcony, but stopped to study the door-closing mechanism. It was a hydraulic device that gently, but surely, drew the door shut. "So you need a key to open this door from either side once it closes?" he asked Dougherty.

"Yes. Of course a person who used their key to get out here would have it to use coming back in. But we had a situation about eight or nine months ago where a guy came out with some other folks, then stayed after they left. Then he realized he'd forgotten to bring his own key and was stuck out there for a while until he decided to use the fire-escape stairs. Made a bit of a stink about it. Said we shouldn't have the locks. But my Director and the Administration wanted the security, so the locks stayed."

Fealder spoke quietly into Berbieri's ear. "When you have a moment, check with the crime scene techs on their inventory of Warburton's personal affects. See if his keys were on him. If they were, have them find out if one of the keys opens this door."

One of the criminalists radioed Fealder from outside the building to say that the Department Head had arrived. As they emerged from Bracknell Hall, a short, stout man wearing a dark pullover and jeans approached them. "I'm David Mortinsen, the Head of the Psychology Department," he said. "This is terrible! Paul Stranglund called me. He said you wanted to speak with me."

Fealder introduced himself and Berbieri and said, "Thank you for coming at this hour, Professor Mortinsen. We appreciate that because we need to learn all we can about this situation as quickly as possible. Can we do this in Detective Berbieri's car?"

They reached the car and Fealder sat with Mortinsen in the back seat. Berbieri, in front, opened her notebook as Mortinsen said, "What can I tell you?"

"Everything you know about Professor Warburton," said Fealder. "Who were his friends? Did he have enemies? Was his research or his teaching controversial? What was his role among the faculty? Things about his family, his interests, his vices if you know them."

Mortinsen sighed. "He was very intelligent. Not brilliant – few of us actually are, you know – but definitely intelligent. He had somewhat of an aggressive personality. No close friends in our department, but he had several friends elsewhere in the University, I believe. He was divorced and had not remarried. So far as I know, he was not living with anyone. And he had no vices that I know of. Well, of course he smoked, but I'm sure that's not what you meant."

"Sometimes even the smallest details end up being important, Professor. Do you happen to know what brand he smoked?"

"No, can't say that I do. I'm a non-smoker, so I don't pick up on things like that."

Berbieri looked up from her notepad. "Can you give us the names of the outside-the-department friends and of the ex-wife?"

Mortinsen frowned in concentration. "The only friend I can think of by name would be Faraday, Bruce Faraday in Education. Adam's ex is Kate Warburton. I'm pretty sure she still uses her married name. When they split, she got the house so I believe she lives in the Raleigh Hills area."

"Did he have enemies in or out of the Department?" asked Fealder.

"Well, 'enemies' is a loaded word if you're investigating a possible killing, but, yes, there are a couple of people who blame him for things... who definitely dislike him."

Fealder looked at his watch and frowned. "Can you tell us the details?

"Yes, I understand that you need specifics. I suppose I'm just reticent to shine light on our internal bickering. Every Department has some of that from time to time and, of course, it's the Head's job to smooth things over and help the Department continue to carry out its program." Fealder glanced at Berbieri and rolled his eyes. Mortinsen paused, then nodded and continued, "Yes. Well. So Howard Callison is an Assistant Professor. He's in his terminal year with us. In other words, he was not granted tenure. Warburton chaired the Departmental Promotion and Tenure Committee last year when Callison's case came up for consideration. The Committee gave him a pretty luke-warm review. They didn't recommend against tenure – they hardly ever do—but when a dossier goes up to the University Personnel Committee, it really needs a powerful recommendation from the Department to stand a chance. Warburton wrote the report from our Committee and Callison accused Warburton of scuttling his case."

Fealder cocked his head. "So let me get this straight. A prof who doesn't get tenure can only stay one more year?"

"Yes. The policy is to allow the person time to find a new position so there won't be a conspicuous gap on the CV."

"The CV?"

"Sorry. The curriculum vitae. Like a resume for an academic: job history, publications, honors, accomplishments."

"Okay. So why does Callison think Warburton was biased?"

"That probably goes back to Callison's first two years in the Department. Warburton was Department Head in those years. He isn't –wasn't—the mentoring type. He apparently made some research suggestions to Callison that Callison ignored. After that, Warburton was a little harsh on him, including once rather publicly in a faculty meeting. And in the Committee's P&T report, Warburton had a rather compromising sentence about Callison's productivity. He also placed fairly heavy emphasis on the one and only referee who was somewhat critical of Callison's publications."

"What does a 'referee' do, Professor Mortinsen?"

"Most universities, including ours, go to outside academics or experts to evaluate the candidate's scholarly books and journal articles."

"Got it. So what was Callison's recourse?"

"There's a promotion and tenure appeals committee, the so-called PTAC. Callison took the case there. I gave some modestly supportive testimony, although I certainly didn't assert there was any undue bias. The

Committee's ruling is final inside the University. They are due to render their decision next month."

"Were you, as Head, involved in the Departmental report?"

"No. At our institution, the Department Head is not involved in the process. The Associate Dean of the College writes a separate report or letter that accompanies the Committee's report in the dossier that goes up. She wrote in favor of promotion and tenure and her letter was a little more positive than the Committee's."

"Is she also on Callison's 'list'?"

"I do think he's become distrustful and embittered about the entire process, but he did not attack her or attempt to impeach her letter during his appeal."

Berbieri said, "You alluded to 'a couple of people who blamed Warburton'. Who's the other one?"

"Yes. There is a doctoral student, Will Mayfield. He worked under Adam until about a year ago. They had a dispute over first-author credit on a research paper submitted for publication. Mayfield contended all the work was his. He was barely agreeable to having Warburton on as second author. But Warburton had the contacts with the journals and sent it in with himself as the first author. It was accepted for publication and Mayfield learned he was listed as second author. Mayfield threatened to take the whole thing to the University Ethics Committee. He eventually backed off and the article was published as submitted, but Mayfield switched to work with another professor and asked that Warburton resign from his dissertation committee – which he did."

Fealder frowned. "So this first-or-second-author business is that important?"

"There is a tradition of courtesy to the senior investigator when writing up the results of joint research. I guess you could say there's a spectrum that runs from deserved credit to the person who had the original concept, designed the experiment, and edited the article ... all the way to rank exploitation of underlings who do virtually all the work, but get only second-or-third-author credit. I like to think we in this department always behave in the upper half of that spectrum, but, obviously, Mayfield felt otherwise regarding Warburton."

"Thanks. This is helpful even if it's awkward for you to tell us these things. What do you know about Warburton's research?"

"He was a good grant writer. You can check with the University's Office of Research as to his exact track record. His specialization was clinical depression. He's published a lot in that area and he mines a lot of experimental data from the Department's clinics. As I recall, he also has some corporate support from pharmaceutical companies... in the area of human trials ... that sort of thing. Some on the faculty haven't been too happy about some of our researchers pursuing that latter kind of research."

"Why is that?" interrupted Fealder.

"Well, there's a feeling that clinical trial work is beneath the dignity of a pure research university. They see the trials as more like just grinding out pre-designated drudge work for the drug companies and not 'pure' research at the frontiers of the field. Of course, running trials is not that simple. There's much to be learned and analyzed, but the researchers have no independence in choosing the subject. In any case, it brings in good money and central administration likes the indirect cost credits that come with it."

"Indirect...?" started Berbieri.

"Sorry. That's the overhead rake off from grants or contracts that goes into the general university budget."

"What about Warburton's attitude? His mental health? Do you think he took his own life?"

Mortinsen paused for a few seconds before replying. "I wouldn't have called him a light-hearted or excessively cheerful person, but no, I didn't see him as suicidal. Not at all. He was too sure of himself. Too into his projects. Righteous, maybe even arrogant at times, but not despondent."

"If a person had a high opinion of himself and then something happened to undermine that... some important defeat or loss of face... could that drastically change such a person's will to live?" asked Berbieri.

"That's a perceptive question. However, please understand I had no clinical relationship with Adam whatsoever. Sure, in theory, such an event could be crushing to certain self-centered personality types but, speaking just personally and informally, I don't see Adam Warburton losing it to that extent. He would certainly have hated to lose even partial control of his destiny, but he was also tough and, I'd guess, plenty resilient."

"Professor Mortinsen, where were you this last evening?" asked Fealder.

Mortinsen's eyebrows arched in mock astonishment. "You mean do I have an alibi? My wife and I were in our bi-monthly Friday-night bridge game with the Tollefsons. We broke it up sometime between eleven-fifteen and eleven-thirty and came straight home."

Berbieri entered the Tollefsons' names in her notebook and Fealder opened the car door.

"Thank you Professor Mortinsen," said Fealder. "Again, we appreciate your coming down here in the middle of the night. It's an unpleasant situation and you've been very helpful."

Fealder turned to Berbieri. "I'm going to have dispatch send out a uniform to secure Warburton's house. Then let's try for a few hours of sleep and get together downtown at eight-thirty. We'll be thinking more clearly and we've got a big day ahead of us."

3

Tamara Berbieri downed a cup of black coffee. Her morning shower and the coffee had not brought back her normal energized state. Three-and-a-half hours of sleep will do that, she thought, as she poached her morning eggs. She had been separated from her husband for six months and their lawyers had nearly completed negotiating the commitments to make the divorce final. Stan had been a very successful realtor and a man with plenty of charm, but he had a zipper problem that she could not forgive. There were days when she still seemed to have some feelings for him, but distrust and hurt had made it impossible to reestablish the emotional bonds of the early years of their marriage. She was through accepting his abject apologies and assurances that it would not happen again.

She had bought her little house with her share of the equity in the house they had shared. Whatever else he was, Stan was shrewd about properties and had helped her find the house on Nineteenth Avenue in the Sellwood district. It was already a good investment. She had chosen the house partly because the kitchen was oversized and could accept the Viking chef's range that she brought with her. Her work on the force carried her past the trauma of her failed marriage and reinforced her natural inclination to be independent. Her gustatory achievements in the kitchen were her creative outlet.

Her thoughts focused on her new partner even before she considered the few details they had gleaned about Professor Warburton's violent death. She had already become aware of Fealder's reputation in the Bureau: easygoing, a bit of a joker when not deep in an investigation, and possessing a great record of closing cases. She felt lucky to work with him because she wanted to prove herself and wanted to do it quickly. She knew that few cops rose in the system without some success as a homicide detective. Something had caused Fealder's breakup with his previous partner, Dick Nabors, but − if people suspected what was behind it-- they were not talking about it. She had already sensed a coldness between Fealder and the Homicide Lieutenant, Doug James. Someday, she might ask Fealder about that, but she had no intention of poking her nose into such matters so early in their working together. Tami wanted to be supportive of her new partner, but she also knew she had to be careful not to tie her career too closely to someone who might be falling out of favor with the police hierarchy. She finished her eggs, set the security alarm and left for police headquarters at Portland's Justice Center.

Fealder had slept fitfully at first as the details of Warburton's death swirled through his brain. A deep, leaden sleep finally overtook him only to be stolen away by the harridan pulsing of his alarm. Shortly after Fealder decided to leave professional baseball, he had inherited a spacious older Portland house on Savier Street from a spinster aunt. That made it easy for him to return to Oregon and its mellow, but urbane, largest city. Two-and-a-half years of his patient efforts in remodeling the house left him with a very comfortable home and valuable real estate close to the eastern edge of Forest Park. He had fully modernized the kitchen but, like many bachelors, he dined in restaurants much of the time. He tied a Navy-blue-and-red rep tie, brushed his collar-length brown hair and headed for his garage.

He stopped on the way downtown for a latte and a Marionberry scone from a neighborhood espresso stand. His fragmentary thoughts during the night had not coalesced into any meaningful theories. He liked this less and less for a suicide. He had learned that his early impressions did not always hold up and, in fact, one of his strengths was his ability to take fresh looks at a case as it progressed. Nevertheless, this morning it felt like murder.

He was hanging up his jacket when he saw Berbieri across the room. She nodded with a half-smile and met him at his desk. "Morning, Tami. Ready to sign off that Warburton jumped?"

She looked at him in momentary disbelief, and then grinned. "Not just yet, partner. There are still a bunch of things I'm wondering about."

"Good. So am I. Why does a guy who's going to off himself leave his radio playing and his office light on? Why wouldn't a guy as pedantic and self-centered as Warburton leave some kind of an explanation even if there's no one he wants to write a personal farewell to? And why kill himself at the University which has been a real important part of his life?"

"Yes," she replied, "and Mortinsen didn't make him sound like the kind of person that would do it. High on my list today is to talk with his physician. Make sure he didn't have some fatal disease."

"Yes, that'll be helpful and anything else he can tell you about the guy's mental health. Did you see the little tear in the seat of Warburton's pants?"

She cringed. "No!"

"I did and Bob Tramell spotted it too. How do you suppose that happened? I'm guessing this guy was 'way too fastidious to be wearing slacks with even a small rip in them. So I'm going to assume he came to campus without the rip, but would he be so clumsy in getting himself off the balcony to have torn his slacks?"

Berbieri pursed her lips. "Probably not, but if they *did* rip as he positioned himself with the intent to go over, he sure wouldn't call it off just to go to a tailor!"

"Point taken," Fealder replied with a grin. "And how about his shoe? I'll have to talk to the criminalists, but, for now, I'm guessing that even if it came off as he fell, it would have landed much closer to the body. That shoe bothers me."

"And they also found that partially smoked cigarette."

'Yeah. We can't draw any conclusions from that yet. If the State Crime Lab can find his DNA on it, that raises an interesting question. Why would a guy who was going to kill himself, smoke a cigarette?"

"Maybe like the classic scene of the man facing the firing squad?" Berbieri suggested. "One last pleasure?"

"Possibly, but in that case, why not finish it? Why jump with it in your mouth or fingers half smoked?"

"Even if it has his DNA, couldn't he have smoked it at some previous time?"

"Yes, he could have. But there were no other butts in the area and there was that cylinder full of sand on the balcony where everyone else seemed to put their butts."

"It looked to me like the bark-mulch between the building and the grass was fairly fresh. Sort of hard to be sure with the light we had last night, but might be worth checking with the Physical Plant... see when they spread it."

"Even if they spread it last week, I concede that Warburton still might've tossed the cigarette the day before he died. But, if the butt we found has his DNA, I'll check it out. Who else are you talking to today?"

"His brother in California for starters. Hopefully, I'll catch both him and the doctor in the next few minutes," Berbieri replied. "We got lucky with the doctor. The University Health Service keeps minimal records on faculty who show up for flu shots and vaccinations. They had recorded his regular doctor's name in their records. When are we seeing the Medical Examiner?"

"He'll do the autopsy this morning so I told him we'll get there right after lunch. His written report with the lab work won't be ready then, but he'll give us his preliminary findings. We have an appointment with Callison at ten at his home. While you're on the phone, I'm going to talk with the crime-scene techs. See if they have anything of interest yet."

Fealder walked down the stairs to the twelfth floor where the police criminalists worked. The receptionist looked at him from behind a low counter. "I'm here to see Andy Delikoff."

After a short wait, a pudgy man with rolled-up shirtsleeves and tousled hair arrived to escort Fealder to his office.

"Nothing like a good night's sleep, eh Park?"

"Right, in some other life! Your people find any prints of interest, Andy?"

"A partial on the shoe. Looks to be Warburton's."

"I want you guys to try something for me. Can you calculate the expected distance from the body the shoe should've landed if it came off as he fell?"

Delikoff frowned. "Well, we probably can. We might even run a couple of experiments with an identical shoe. But I gotta tell ya, if the poor guy was flailing his legs as he fell, that could give it additional momentum that could make our calculations meaningless."

"I see. Well, would you try it anyway?"

"Sure. I'll put Atkins on it. He's our physics geek."

"How about the doors?"

"Well, that's kinda interesting. Warburton's prints were on the inside knob at his office. Likewise the door to the balcony. But the outside knobs on both doors had no prints at all. Appear to have been wiped clean."

"As your people no doubt discovered," said Fealder, "the balcony door has a closer and, once shut, it needs a key to open it from the outside. Did Warburton have his keys on his person?"

"He did … including the keys to his office and to the balcony. So looks as though he was alone?"

"Could've been, yeah. But he could've gone out there with a colleague who had his or her own key. Or someone could've left by climbing down the fire-escape stairs. Did your team see any disturbance on the ground beneath where that retractable ladder was positioned?"

"We did look there. Can't be certain because the surface of the bark-mulch is sort of uneven, but it looked undisturbed."

"How about that missing page from the calendar on his desk?"

"Well, the custodian says he hits the offices on the seventh floor around seven-thirty and no one was in the office then. He dumped the wastebasket into his larger trash bag. I've got someone trying to find the right trash bag and, hopefully, the calendar page."

"Thanks, Andy. There are enough strange little facts connected to this death that I want to stay on this hard until we know a little more one way or the other. Have your guys had time to look at his computers?"

"We have the material from the home and the office computers. I'm going to organize everything by file name and I'll be able to discuss it with you soon, maybe tomorrow. The e-mail is a little more complicated since the office stuff resides on a University server. They'll cooperate, I think, but that's going to take a little longer. They told me they wanted to run that by somebody named Stranglund."

"I met him last night. He's the University's lawyer. We may have to dot our i's and cross our t's, possibly even get a search warrant, but I think he'll come around. How about prints in the stairwells and the elevator?"

Delikoff shrugged. "Elevator doors and buttons were too smudged to be helpful. We did the stairwell crash bars on the second and seventh floors and the hand rails between the sixth and seventh. We lifted dozens of prints. We'll run matches for you when you want."

Fealder looked at his watch. "Thanks again, Andy. Call me when you're ready with the computer stuff. I've got to hurry for an appointment with one of Warburton's colleagues."

Howard Callison lived in a shake-sided bungalow-style house on Knapp just off S.E. 18th Avenue. It was a quiet street of well-kept, but modest, homes. One side of the small front yard was devoted to a rose garden. Callison answered the door and Fealder saw a man of medium height in his early thirties wearing jeans and a rugby shirt. He introduced his wife and showed his visitors to chairs in a living room that featured framed Modigliani prints but, conspicuously, not a television set.

"You asked to speak with me about Adam Warburton's death."

Berbieri took out her notebook and Fealder leaned forward in his chair. "Yes. We plan to talk with several faculty members as we try to get a clearer picture of what happened."

"You're from homicide. That must mean you suspect foul play?"

Berbieri joined in, taking the 'good cop' role. "It's too early to say, Professor Callison, but we cannot rule it out at this stage."

"Are you saying I'm a suspect?"

'Not at all. We investigate any violent death at least until its causes are understood."

"So why do you think I can help?"

Fealder cut in. "We understand you had some animosity toward the man. Could you tell us about that?"

"Sure." Callison lit a cigarette and took a keep draw. "Warburton chaired the department's Promotion and Tenure Committee last year. My case was before the committee and he wrote a report that almost assured denial. Any chance of my getting an objective review was lost when that self-righteous prick was made chair!"

"Can you appeal the decision?"

"Yes. My appeal is pending, but once the departmental committee's report sets the tone, it's hard to change direction. Warburton was no fool. He covered his selective weighting and emphasizing with nice neutral language."

"How many people are on the departmental committee?"

"Three."

"All tenured?"

"Yes. That's a requirement. But you don't understand. Warburton was aggressive... at times, even an intellectual bully. It wouldn't have been that hard for him to steer the others, especially when he was the one writing the report."

"But doesn't the committee's recommendation have to be supported by a College Dean and the University-level committee and, finally, by the Provost to take effect?"

"That's so, but, like I said, once the departmental report has poisoned the well, everybody drinks the same water! The people above may read most of the same documents, but they view them through the lens of those closest to the issues. And Warburton had a reputation for being so principled... sort of a Calvinist on academic standards, if you follow me. So, perversely, those outside the department would likely credit him even if they thought he was a pompous ass socially."

Fealder persisted. "But why are you so sure Warburton had it in for you?"

"Look, Detective, he rejected both of my suggested outside referees. He denigrated my book as a 'rehash' of my dissertation that 'brought little new to the subject area'. He called the number of my refereed publications 'sparse'."

"Did you feel he was against you even before the promotion and tenure process?" asked Berbieri.

"Sure. You can ask others in the Department too. When I first joined the faculty, he was overtly supportive of me. I think he was looking for a young scholar he could mold and shape to his interests and standards.

I ignored some of his favorite research suggestions and, very quickly, he became chilly and critical toward me. At first I didn't feel threatened, but in more recent years, he started floating these little innuendoes around the department about my lack of originality or the relative unimportance of my research."

"I see," said Fealder. "Do you have a key to the balcony at the end of the hall?"

Callison seemed distracted by the change in the line of questions. "Key? Oh, yeah. I think every faculty member on the floor does."

"Okay. May we ask where you were last evening?"

Callison lit a cigarette, took a long draw on it, and scowled at Fealder. "I went to the women's volleyball game. Left the house around six-forty-five and ate a hotdog dinner at the game. It was a close match and lasted a bit longer than usual so it was probably 10:30 or so by the time I got home."

Berbieri turned toward the woman who had been standing behind her husband during the questioning. "Did you go to the game also, Ms. Callison?"

"No. I've spent several days with my sister in Seattle and just returned a few hours ago."

Fealder studied Callison's face. "So you were alone in the house last night, Professor Callison?"

"What's that supposed to mean?" fumed Callison.

"Simply that I don't know your household situation, Professor. Children at home? Roomers? A friend who went to the game with you and came back for a beer?"

"No. No one lives with us. So I suppose that means there's no one to substantiate my 'alibi'. I went to the game alone. I had finished grading some mid-term exams late in the afternoon and Jeanie was away so it was sort of an impetuous decision. We go to a few games each year and this looked to be a good one."

Fealder realized they were not likely to learn more from Callison in his defensive state of mind. He stood up, expressed their appreciation and nodded to Berbieri. In their car, Berbieri said, "He seems to feel pretty persecuted on this tenure business, but, other than that, I didn't get much of a sense of him."

"Same here," offered Fealder. "He's certainly ready to blame Warburton for his career problem, but it's hard to tell whether that could lead to a fixation or hatred strong enough to kill someone."

"Yes. Especially if his appeal is still pending. But I can see him as the sort of person that would let something like that gnaw on him and maybe become consuming."

Fealder covertly appraised the quiet beauty of his partner's face and wondered if her failed marriage gnawed at her. She had shown him a remarkably balanced and calm temperament in the short hours they had worked together. He thought ruefully that he had only been close to marriage once. Early in his baseball career he had been engaged, but the ambitious, road-centered life of a minor leaguer had proven too much for their relationship and she broke it off. He was devastated and in the dumps for weeks, but eventually came to realize that she would not have been happy married to a professional ball player. Today, he was comfortable enough with his bachelor status, but he knew he was missing an important dimension to his life. Braking for a stoplight returned him to the present.

"Professor Callison is a smoker," said Fealder. "Marlboros. It won't prove much one way or the other, but I've asked forensics to get as much DNA as they can from the butts on the balcony. Later, we may want to ask Callison if he uses the balcony on the seventh floor and ask for a DNA specimen. What'd you turn up with Warburton's doctor and his brother?"

Berbieri smiled and flipped a few pages of her notebook. "The brother said they were not particularly close. Tony Warburton said they saw very little of each other, maybe every couple of years is all. He's a commercial insurance broker. Says his brother had a 'difficult' personality. Said he had a bit of a superiority complex and was a bit of an intellectual snob."

"And the brother was in the L.A. area last night?"

"Yes. At a dinner party. He gave me the hosts' names."

"Did he think his brother could've taken his own life?"

"He characterized Warburton's moods as 'a little volatile', but said he'd never been remotely suicidal and it was impossible for him to believe that his brother had killed himself."

"Did he know what brand his brother smoked?"

"He wasn't positive, but thought it was Kools."

Fealder nodded. "And the doctor?"

"He said Warburton was in good health. He had a physical three months ago with everything looking fine. Blood pressure a little high, but not of real concern. He wasn't on medications. The doctor said he had tried to convince Warburton to quit smoking, but only on general grounds. He said there was no record of mental instability and nothing he's seen would indicate despondency. But he emphasized that Warburton was healthy enough that he rarely was in contact with him."

Berbieri saw they were heading for the northern reaches of the city. "Did you set up our discussion with Mayfield at his place?"

"Yeah. I like to see where and how people live. We'll turn on twenty-sixth. I know it's lunchtime, but I want to talk to this kid right away."

4

It was an older neighborhood in the north end where small rental houses were interspersed with larger, owner-occupied houses and apartment complexes. The sidewalks showed numerous cracks and the occasional heave. Many of the lawns were thick with weeds and the shrubs were often overgrown. The homes were close together and had small, stand-alone garages at the rear of the properties that typically shared a common driveway with the adjacent home. The house William Mayfield rented on Farragut Street had a moss-splotched roof and could have used a fresh coat of paint. They produced their credentials when Mayfield met them at the door. He was slender, maybe one-sixty-five Fealder judged, and looked an even six feet tall. The front door entered directly into a living room furnished with a slip-covered sofa, a scarred coffee table, a television and a sound system layered on a platform of cinder blocks and boards. Mayfield offered coffee and led them down a short hall to the kitchen. The door to an unused bedroom was open and, as they passed, they saw bookshelves of unfinished pine crammed with books and a table on which was mounted a device for tying flies. In the kitchen, they saw a stained sink and plates in a drying rack. Mayfield filled their mugs from the carafe of a Mr. Coffee machine and led them back to the living room.

His hand brushed at his goatee for a second before he bagan. "So I guess you've heard how Warburton screwed me," he said more as a statement than a question.

"Well, we know you are no longer doing research under him after a publication dispute," responded Berbieri.

Mayfield raised his head sharply, shaking his light-brown hair tied in a pony tail. He spoke with derision and mock disbelief. "Well I suppose you could call it a 'publication dispute'. The bastard put himself in as the first author on an important paper that I, and only I, wrote."

"Was it a write-up of one of his experiments?" asked Berbieri.

"Only in the sense that he had envisioned the whole research program. He got a small grant to carry it out. I'll give him that. But the experiment he had in mind wasn't going to be conclusive one way or the other. I came up with a refinement of his hypothesis and conceived a whole new experiment that gave us the data to really test it. When it came to running the experiment, Warburton was preoccupied with other things and delegated the entire project to me. And then he takes my article and puts *his* name on it!"

"Did you two ever try to work it out, Mr. Mayfield?"

"You can call me Will. One of the journals we sent it to had an article suddenly withdrawn and they had already accepted my piece to take its place in their upcoming issue by the time I learned how he'd submitted it. I realized he was determined to have his name on the article and other graduate students told me not to fight it. So I just told him that I should be first author. He basically told me to fuck off. I was so frustrated that I went to the Student Advocacy Office and considered filing a complaint with the Research Ethics Committee. But at that point, it seemed wiser not to make an issue of it. So I started looking for a new dissertation committee and a new prof to work under. The Head approved it and now I'm working with Professor Talbot."

"So how would you characterize Warburton?"

"Truthfully? I think he was a manipulative bastard who wasn't above exploiting graduate students to his advantage. I think he could be a vengeful person."

"Did he avenge himself on you in any way?"

"No, but this only happened last year. I'm sure if I'd filed a complaint he would have."

"Had you reconciled your thoughts about him?"

"Is there a safe answer to that question?"

Fealder gave him a steady look. "The truth is always the safest way to go, Mr. Mayfield."

Mayfield's eyes darted from Fealder to Berbieri and back to Fealder. "Alright. I tried to be reasonable and he just gave me that 'tradition and position' crap. Told me it wouldn't have even gotten published without his backing! I felt he was gloating the whole time. At that point, I hated his guts."

"We need to know where you were last evening," said Fealder.

Mayfield launched himself out of his chair. "Do you think I killed him? Sure, I was extremely pissed at him, but I didn't kill him! I told you the truth about my feelings toward him, but I'm *not* a killer."

Berbieri saw fear for the first time cross his angular face with its flaring nostrils. "We're not saying you did, but we do need to know the answer to Detective Fealder's question."

"Deralyn, she lives with me... she had a bad cold and didn't want to go out. It seems like I'm always behind on my dissertation so I decided to spend the evening working."

"Can your friend verify that?" asked Fealder.

"Well... she knows I wasn't home."

"I see. So where were you doing this work?"

Mayfield looked out the kitchen window for a long moment, and then answered. "In my office at Bracknell. Room six-twenty-six."

Berbieri looked up from her note-taking. "How long were you there?"

"I came in after dinner, probably quarter to eight or so. I made pretty good progress so I stayed until a little after eleven."

"And then?"

"I went straight home. Deralyn was asleep by the time I got here. I think she woke up for a moment, but— if you're going to ask can she verify the time – probably not. The bedroom was dark and she just rolled over and went back to sleep."

"Does 'room six-twenty-six' mean it was on the sixth floor?"

"Yes."

"Do you have a key to the balcony at the end of the corridor?"

"I never needed one. I don't smoke."

"At any time during the evening, especially toward the end of the time you were there, did you hear any loud noise? Any screams or shouts?"

"No. Nothing. If you mean did I hear Warburton falling, I did not. Do you understand the office numbers get higher as the hallway goes away from the end of the building where the balconies are? Six-twenty-six is almost at the far end. Besides, I had my door and window shut. When did he fall?"

Fealder ignored the question. "Did you see or speak to or communicate with Warburton yesterday?" he asked.

"No. Absolutely not! We pretty much stayed out of each other's way. Listen, I'm not the only person that disliked Warburton! Have you talked to Susan Gelbhorn's husband?"

Fealder and Berbieri exchanged subtle glances. "Why should we do that, Will?"

"Nobody's told you that Warburton was balling Susan Gelbhorn?"

"So they were having an affair?"

"Yeah! I don't think it was still going on, but earlier this year it was flaming and it wasn't much of a secret around the department. The word was that her husband found out and threatened Warburton."

"Is she on your faculty?"

"Yeah, she's an Associate Professor."

"The husband also?"

"No. I think he's an architect or a designer or something."

"What do you know about this threat?"

"Nothing specific. Rumor just had it that there was a very heated confrontation between the two men right in Warburton's office. The door was shut, but I guess there was loud shouting and the words 'dead meat' were heard a couple of times. I wasn't there, but that sort of thing gets talked about."

"I think that will be enough for today. Thanks for meeting with us," said Fealder as they closed their notebooks and stood.

Fealder started the engine and turned toward Berbieri, "He seemed pretty edgy toward the end."

"Yes. He did seem a little unnerved, but he's only a graduate student. Probably feels pretty powerless around the faculty, let alone the police ... and this is heavy stuff."

"True, but he sure took that authorship business awfully damn seriously. We have to consider that he had motive and opportunity."

"He's sort of slender," said Berbieri. "You think he could wrestle a man of Warburton's size off that balcony?"

"Maybe not easily, but take a man by surprise or trick him into leaning over and it could be done."

"How could he have left the balcony without a key?"

Fealder smiled. "Good question. We should be thinking about that."

"This Gelbhorn business sort of adds a dimension," said Berbieri.

"Yeah. See if you can talk to Professor Gelbhorn this afternoon after we see the M.E. I'll try to run down the husband. No matter how it happened, it doesn't sound like too many people are going to mourn Warburton's death."

Berbieri said she had brought a macaroni salad from home, so Fealder left her at the entrance to the Justice Center and headed for Rory's down the block. He grinned at the woman who seated him.

"Detective Fealder! Pretty late for lunch, aren't you?"

"Hi, Sandra. Yeah. Late and hungry! I'm glad you guys stay open Saturdays. Think I'll have a Reuben."

"You got it! Want today's paper?"

"Thanks, I didn't have time to read it this morning."

Fealder opened the paper to the sports section and started reading a story about Carlos Beltran and the Yankees. His thoughts drifted to baseball. As a teen-ager playing American Legion baseball, he had wor-shiped Ryne Sandberg and Willie Randolph. Fealder had played varsity baseball at Oregon State and, af-ter impressing scouts in the NCAA tournament, was drafted into the St. Louis Cardinals' farm system. His strong arm and aggressive base running propelled him to AAA-level professional ball where he played second base for the Memphis Red Birds. His fielding had been good, but his batting average never got out of the lower two-hundreds. He was in no danger of being sent down, but, by his fourth year, he began to think that he was not going to get a chance to play in the majors. He kept believing that "next year the bat will start working" and stayed in baseball. He was still batting eighth and struggling at the plate two seasons later.

Then came that day in late August. They were play-ing at home and the opposing team had a runner on first with one out. The batter hit a bounding ball to the shortstop who threw to Fealder at second base for the force out. The player running from first came in with cleats high. Fealder had to leap after he touched the bag and pivot in mid-air to make the throw for the double play. He very rarely made throwing errors. But on that day, his throw missed the first baseman's mitt and hit the runner. The man had been batting left-handed and his helmet did not protect the left side of his head. Fealder's throw hit him just in front of his ear and he instantly collapsed. He regained consciousness soon afterwards, but he had suffered some brain damage. The injury ended his career and his chance to live a fully normal life. It was just a freak accident, but Fealder had always blamed himself.

Fealder had asked to sit out the next four games. He then returned to the lineup, but was still shaken to his core by that incident. He even had a few nightmares about it. He quit baseball for good when the season ended two weeks later. He had agonized over his decision to leave the sport he loved and find a new job. A high school coaching job had not appealed to him. He had enjoyed majoring in Geography, but had no stomach for graduate school and he found there were almost no opportunities for geographers without graduate degrees. He returned to Oregon. Besides having inherited the house, he liked the relatively mellow lifestyle in Portland. He even thought it might help that Portland did not have a major league team. He was turning a new page and did not need the distraction of wondering what might have been.

After much thought, he decided to try police work. Fealder liked the teamwork approach in 'major crimes' and bringing villains to justice resonated with his competitive spirit. The brutality and senselessness of assaults and murders had always infuriated him and now he could help hunt down the perpetrators of those crimes. His new career gave him enormous satisfaction and, in eight years, he had ascended rapidly to join the Homicide Unit and become one of its most productive, if somewhat unconventional, detectives. The frustration of not reaching "The Big Show" still haunted him and he was determined not to stall-out in his second chosen profession. So far, so good, he reflected as he finished his Reuben sandwich. Now he had to find out who helped an unpopular professor off that balcony.

5

Their morning schedules had prevented them from being in the viewing room while the autopsy was underway, but Fealder had set up a meeting with the Deputy Medical Examiner, Dr. Philip Westling, at two o'clock. His office was in the building on Southeast Eighty-fourth Avenue shared by the investigators for Multnomah and Clackamas Counties and the State Examiners assigned to work those counties. Westling was a jovial man in his early sixties with rounded features and a trim, salt-and-pepper beard. Fealder stood to tell and act out a doctor joke. Berbieri had not heard it before and she laughed with them. Fealder grazed a hand over his brow. Lunch had given him an energy boost, but he still felt the effects of a short night's sleep. He sat down and addressed Westling in a more serious tone.

"Phil, can you tell us anything more specific about the cause of Warburton's death?"

"Yes. A fractured skull and internal injuries are what killed him."

"So it was the impact from the fall off the building?"

"That's a little harder to say with certainty. Many of his vertebrae were also broken or crushed by compression. Those injuries are very consistent with a fall from a high place. I understand blood was found on the ground beside the body?"

"That's right."

"Since I'm quite sure death was instantaneous, that tells me the fatal impact was where he was found."

Fealder smiled inwardly at the man's conservative approach. "In other words, he wasn't pushed off a *different* building and then brought to the base of Bracknell Hall?"

"That's right."

"Had he been drinking or was he under the influence of anything that would make him crazy?"

"There were no needle marks and no discoloration of the tongue or nasal passages to suggest drugs. But I won't have the toxicology report until Monday earliest, so I can't answer your question definitively right now. I'll let you know."

"There was a small rip in the seat of his pants," Fealder said. "Did you find any wounds or abrasions on his ass?"

"No. But there was a fresh abrasion on his left shin."

Berbieri looked at Fealder and said, "Let's have Criminalistics look at the left pant leg and also ask them if they found any fabric matching his pants on the top of the balcony guard wall."

"Good idea," said Fealder. "Thanks, Phil. Be talking to you."

Susan Gelbhorn agreed to meet with Berbieri at the cafeteria in the Student Union at four-thirty. The low, afternoon sun cast long elongated shadows as they walked across the lawn in front of the Union. They wended their way through the cafeteria dining room to find a clean table in a quieter section. Berbieri offered to buy hot chocolate and bagels and Gelbhorn sat down to save the table. Berbieri returned carrying a tray with their order and opened her notebook on the table. She looked across at the features of a woman in her mid forties. She saw a woman who still had a good figure and who groomed herself carefully and wore nice clothes, but seemed to have angry eyes and a hard edge. "I'll come right to the point. We understand you had a relationship with Professor Warburton at one time."

Susan Gelbhorn stiffened and set her lips tightly. "Yes. So?"

Berbieri continued, "Do you think he could've taken his own life?"

"Adam? Hardly! No. He was a complicated man, but much too full of himself to cash it in."

"Was your relationship ongoing to the time of his death?"

"Well, we're colleagues, so..."

Berbieri interrupted. "I mean your romantic relationship."

Gelbhorn paused and looked down at her coffee cup. When she resumed, Berbieri heard smoldering anger in her voice.

"We had a fling, I guess you'd say. But, no, it was over. Had been for a couple of months."

"What were your feelings toward him once it was over?"

Berbieri thought she saw the woman's eyes moisten and observed that she looked down before answering.

"Those things usually end. I went on with my work and my life."

"Were you the one who broke it off?"

"We just decided it wasn't going to work out."

"Did your husband know?"

She looked at Berbieri for several seconds before answering. "Yes. He knew toward the end."

Berbieri continued, "You are still married?"

"We're living apart. We're talking about a divorce."

"Where were you yesterday evening?"

Professor Gelbhorn's expression tightened. "Do I need an alibi? Is that what you're saying? Well, I was at a dinner party at Jack and Clarise Donovan's home."

"When were you there?"

"I arrived a little after six-thirty and we all left about quarter to eleven."

"And then?"

"I went straight home. I came and went alone. That's a little awkward at a social gathering, but no friends are going to invite Herb and me as a couple right now."

"Do you have a key to the balcony at the end of the corridor in Bracknell Hall, Professor Gelbhorn?"

"I must have somewhere. Perhaps in my desk drawer, but I never go out there."

Berbieri closed her notebook and thanked Gelbhorn for talking with her.

Fealder met with Herbert Gelbhorn at the architect's office in downtown Portland. His firm occupied the entire second floor of a small, older building on Northwest Glisan Street. Fealder left the utilitarian elevator lobby and entered the reception area. He saw nine or ten drafting tables in the open bay and the principals' offices against the wall at the opposite end. A middle-aged woman and a younger man stood in an animated conversation at one of the tables, but otherwise, the room was deserted. Fealder saw a solidly built man in his forties leave an office and walk toward him as soon as he introduced himself to the other two and asked for Herbert Gelbhorn. The approaching man wore his dark hair short, nearly in a buzz cut. His tie was loose at his collar and his shirtsleeves were rolled up to expose powerful, hairy forearms.

"Thanks for seeing me, Mr. Gelbhorn," Fealder said after they shook hands.

"You said it was about Professor Warburton's death," said Gelbhorn.

He gets right down to business, thought Fealder as they entered the office and Gelbhorn shut the door. "Yes. Our investigation so far has turned up indications that your wife and Professor Warburton had an affair."

"And you're wondering if I am a jealous-husband suspect?" asked Gelbhorn who had turned to gaze out the window.

"Well, I need to know your feelings on the matter, yes."

Gelbhorn spun to face Fealder. "How would it feel to you to be cuckolded, Detective?"

Fealder met the man's intense stare. "Did your anger lead to any action on your part?"

"I confronted my wife. She ultimately admitted the relationship."

"Did you take any action toward Professor Warburton?"

"I went to him and told him he had to end the affair... that I intended for my marriage to survive."

"Where did you meet him?"

"In his office at the University."

"Did you threaten him?"

"Threaten? No. He knew I was plenty angry and he seemed a little unnerved that I had explicitly faced him. That's all. I didn't go there to harm him. Just to tell him how things stood."

"What do you mean by that?"

"That I knew about the affair. That Susan's and my marriage was intact. That I was not into 'open marriages' and that I intended to save our marriage."

"What was his reaction?"

"To the best of my knowledge, the affair stopped immediately."

"Alright. But what was his reaction right there in his office?"

"He was surely taken aback to see me at first. I didn't call ahead. I just went over there hoping he'd be in his office. After a minute or so, he became sort of haughty... like he wouldn't stoop to discuss anything like that with the sub-intellectual husband! Then he got very quiet. I don't know whether he started to feel contrite or was just having second thoughts about the wisdom of having the affair, but he was almost meek as I left."

"Was there a yelling match?"

"I raised my voice at some point, I'm sure, but a 'yelling match'? No."

"When was this?"

"I don't remember exactly. Probably two months ago."

"Did you confront him again?"

"No."

"And you and Professor Gelbhorn reconciled?"

"When I first talked with her and then went to see Warburton, I had the impression that was possible... even that we had taken the first steps. That did not turn out to be the case. Susan moved out a week after I saw Warburton. She's retained a lawyer and seems to want a divorce."

"Where were you last evening?"

"I was at home. I fixed my own dinner and then did a little paper work from the office and read a little."

"Can anyone confirm that?"

"No. I was alone all evening."

"No phone calls?"

"Only a solicitation call early in the evening. It was from the Sheriff's Office, I think, wanting to sell circus tickets to benefit their pension fund or something. I wasn't interested."

Fealder made a note about the fund-raising call thinking he might be able to verify that Gelbhorn had been home if the solicitor kept good records. Still, as he reached his car, he was thinking that Gelbhorn had not told him everything. Nothing Gelbhorn told him sounded like an outright lie and Gelbhorn had owned up to barging in on Warburton in his office. Nevertheless, Fealder thought the responses were too lawyer-like: not false on their face, but carefully filtered to suggest a measured discussion instead of a possibly heated and threatening confrontation.

Back at his desk, Fealder saw a message to call Andy Delikoff. The Chief of the Criminalistics Section answered on the second ring. "Delikoff."

"Andy, it's Park. Message said to call you."

"Right. We had a talk with Mr. Stranglund. He agreed that the e-mail server, the ethernet connections, and the office computers all belong to the University and that their own policies state that there should be no expectation of privacy in sending e-mail using the University's system. He said they do have a confidential classification for faculty records, but I told him that all I wanted to look at right away were the e-mails Warburton had sent and received in the last week. He seemed concerned that some e-mails – sounded like he meant communications between committee members or deans evaluating personnel – might be these 'faculty records' and might be restricted even though run-of-the-mill messages would not be."

"Yeah. He seemed reluctant to let us into Warburton's computer last night, too."

"He said that you told him you would get a search warrant if there was reason to believe it was murder."

"Yes, and I *am* going to ask the court for a warrant if we have to. There're enough people who hated this guy to form a club! And no one who knew him seems to think he was suicidal or even had any reason to be depressed. I'll call Stranglund and see if he's still going to insist on a search warrant just for Warburton's e-mail."

He called Paul Stranglund who finally conceded that the e-mails to and from Warburton could be printed out and examined. Stranglund told him whom to contact in the Computing Center and Fealder passed the name back to Delikoff. Berbieri entered the room and came to his desk as he finished the call to the General Counsel of the University. "Hi, Partner! How'd it go with the lady professor?"

She summarized her meeting with Professor Gelbhorn. When she finished, Fealder asked, "Get any sense of who broke up the affair?"

"No, her answer was kind of cagey. Made it sound like it was a mutually-agreed-upon decision. But I think she's a fiery one! I don't know why exactly, given what we've heard about this guy Warburton, but I think she really had the hots for him. And she certainly seems to have lost interest in her husband. I'm going to try to get some more background on that affair and how it ended. What'd you turn up with the husband?"

Fealder recounted his interview with Herbert Gelbhorn and his reservations about the version of the confrontation Gelbhorn had offered him. "He chose his words so carefully, like he wanted to portray himself as really calm and in control the whole time. Will you ask Records to run a criminal history check on him?"

"Sure. I'll do it right after our meeting with James."

"Good and while you're at it, let's get checks on Callison and Mayfield too."

They walked together to their Lieutenant's office. Doug James looked up as they knocked on his partially-open door. "Come in, Detectives." His slender face and angular features with a pencil mustache matched his lean frame. His slightly hooded eyes drilled into those he addressed and smiles were not part of his social repertoire. Fealder and Berbieri took chairs and waited for him to continue. "So what've we got on this Warburton death?"

Fealder answered, "Nothing conclusive at this point, but it certainly looks like a homicide."

"The TV news said he was in the Psych Department. I'd have guessed those guys are as likely to off themselves as anyone I could think of."

Berbieri looked uncomfortable with James' offhanded stereotyping, but held her tongue. Fealder said, "Well there's nothing we've turned up yet that shows he had any suicidal tendencies. On the other hand, he was—to put it mildly – pretty unpopular with certain people on campus and off. And there're some little details that don't add up for me on suicide."

"Fealder, you always add things up different than anyone else."

Fealder suppressed the urge for a riposte and continued the defense of his preliminary conclusion. "The lights were on in his office. His radio was playing. His pants were ripped. He appears to have gone off the balcony smoking a cigarette. Somehow one of his loafers came off. We need to pursue this cause-of-death question a lot further."

James sighed with an indifferent expression on his face. "Alright. Dig some more. But first, tell me who you've talked to so far and who has or hasn't an alibi."

Fealder and Berbieri summarized what they learned from their interviews. As they were wrapping up, James's phone trilled. He waved his hand in a dismissive manner as he reached for the phone. "Okay. Keep me posted."

At his desk, Fealder found his voice-mail light blinking and listened to another message from Delikoff. "Park, it's Andy. Listen, we've been looking at the e-mail and there's an incoming message that you might want to consider. It's from a Bruce Faraday and he tells Warburton that some woman named Patty Lawson has been defaming him big-time as a bigot and an affirmative-action dinosaur. I'm forwarding it to you by e-mail. The rest of the messages, I'll print out and bring up in hard copy with an "eyes only" stamp for you and Berbieri. You should have them first thing tomorrow."

Fealder flipped through his own notes as he tried to remember why the name Faraday sounded familiar. It was growing dark outside and his brain was starting to numb with fatigue. Then he found the notation he had made: Faraday was Warburton's friend in the College of Education. Stranglund had given him a faculty telephone directory and he punched in Faraday's number.

"Professor Faraday, this is Detective Fealder with the Portland Police Bureau, Homicide Unit. I'm calling in regard to the death of your friend, Adam Warburton."

"I see," said Faraday in a barely audible voice. "It's a terrible thing. I never could imagine that Adam would take his own life. I take it that if you're involved, you think it's murder?"

"We're not sure of anything yet, but we too don't think he committed suicide. Was anything bothering him or frightening him that you know of?"

"No. Adam wasn't easily frightened. And I never...."

"Could you speak up a little?"

"Sorry. I said I never saw any indication that he was depressed. We had lunch together at least once a week and I'm pretty confident I would've known if something was troubling him that severely."

"We understand you warned him a few days ago regarding someone called Patty Lawson. Could you tell me about that?"

"Sure. Patty's a radfem and she's not afraid to accuse people of being intolerant of minorities and women and then acting on that intolerance by trying to stymie those persons' advancement."

"A 'radfem' meaning a radical feminist?"

"Yes. It seems that Adam was on a university committee to draft an administrative rule about the hiring of non-academic staff. Patty was on the same committee. There was some disagreement on the committee about how affirmative the affirmative action policy in the rule should be. Adam urged a more balanced and, he thought, more defensible version. Needless to say, Patty wanted stronger, much stronger, language."

"So what was the outcome?" Fealder asked.

"Lawson apparently recruited a bunch of her friends to testify at the hearing held before the committee finalized the rule. Unfortunately for Adam, the Committee Chair was sick the day of the hearing – I think it was about ten days ago --so Adam had to preside. A lot of the testimony was redundant and pretty obviously orchestrated by the radfem group. It got late and Adam declined to adjourn the hearing. He announced it would run an extra thirty minutes and then it would be closed."

"This didn't sit well, I assume."

"To put it mildly. I wasn't there, but Adam told me about it. He said a couple of people didn't get to speak and Patty was fuming at him. He said she even placed a formal objection on the record. Anyway, I was having lunch in the Student Union cafeteria a few days ago and Lawson and some other faculty members from Sociology were at a table next to mine. She started doing a number on Adam. Said he was a Neanderthal, a lackey of the administration, and that he had cut off testimony at the hearing in an effort to 'balance the record'."

"So this is what you wanted to talk to him about?"

"Yes. And as this lunch group broke up, I heard her say to one of her friends that castration was too good for Warburton ... that she'd like to kill the bastard."

"Did you think she meant it?"

"Well, no. Not in so many words, but she sounded capable of flaring up at him if they ever got in a direct confrontation with no one else around. She is an angry person and one of those people who think if you're not her strongest ally, you automatically become her enemy. Besides, she was slandering him to other faculty. I thought he deserved a warning."

Berbieri had come over to stand beside Fealder's desk as he thanked Faraday and hung up the phone. "It looks like we need to talk to a Professor Patty Lawson, Tami."

"Tonight?"

"No. Let's call it a day. Tomorrow I want to poke around more in Warburton's background. See if that leads anywhere. But let's plan on seeing Lawson on Monday."

6

Fealder and Berbieri had agreed to meet at ten-thirty in the detectives' conference room on the thirteenth floor of the Justice Center. Fealder, refreshed after a decent night's sleep, arrived a little early and saw Detective Tom Hokanson in his cubicle. "Tom! What brings you in on a Sunday?"

"Hey, Park! I've got a court appearance on Tuesday and I'm in the field all day Monday so I'm in here going over the file in the court case. Are you working on the Bracknell Hall death?"

Hokanson was known for his love of cheese and Fealder had once hidden a hunk of Limburger behind one of the drawers in Hokanson's desk. The others had ridden the easy-going detective unmercifully accusing him of everything from forcing them to share his favorite smell to forgetting about an uneaten lunch bag. He eventually located the offending morsel and took the prank well. He strongly suspected his old friend Fealder was behind it and implied a fitting reprisal would be forthcoming.

"Yeah. It feels like a killing," said Fealder. "It's the old story: learn as much as you can as fast as you can and the odds of cracking the case go way up."

"I see you've picked up a great looking new partner."

That was true, Fealder thought, but he was not going there.

"She's catching on fast. I could've done wor….," he interrupted himself as he saw Berbieri come through the door.

"Hi, Tami. Ready to hit it?"

She eyed the two men with an intuitive feeling they had been discussing her.

"Hi, Guys. Yeah. Let's get going!"

Fealder's cubicle had pictures of Lou Whitaker, Steve Sax, and Tony Womack tacked to the wall. Berbieri saw a well-thumbed copy of the Baseball Almanac on one of the hanging shelves next to a small trophy from the Multnomah Athletic Club. The trophy had a statuette of a racquetball player on top and "Park Fealder, Men's Champion 2011" engraved on its base. Fealder reached for the Faculty Telephone Directory that Stranglund had given him and jotted down a number.

"My idea for today is to find out what Warburton did on the campus besides piss people off. Mortinsen said the man had some research grants so I'm going to start with the Director of the Office of Academic Research. Maybe you could try to find out if the professor was on any committees... other people who were on them, what they did. And try this Office of Student Advocacy. See if any students filed grievances against him."

Berbieri nodded and reached for the directory. She found the numbers she was looking for and went back to her own cubicle. Fealder reached the Director and persuaded her to go to her office to look up information about Warburton's research grants. She also offered to fax Fealder a copy of Warburton's curriculum vitae which she said would list the titles of his publications. Forty minutes later, she called back.

"He had two smallish grants from the County Mental Health office to help operate the on-campus depression clinic. He had a contract with a book publisher to do a book on "the depressed employee in the workplace". And he was co-PI on a fairly large grant to do a clinical study for Bradley Pharmaceuticals."

"Co-PI?" asked Fealder.

"Sorry. He was a co-principal investigator."

"Is that unusual?"

"Well, it's not too common, but I wouldn't go so far as to say it's unusual. If a couple of established researchers join forces to write a grant, they would most likely ask to be co-PIs. It's easier on the egos, although it creates administrative problems for the rest of us."

"How so?"

"Well, take this grant. His co-PI is a professor in the Medical School. They have their own grants-and-contracts administrators over there so we have to coordinate with each other, divide the indirect costs, figure out how to integrate the human-subjects oversight, and so forth. In fact, if I remember correctly…." she paused and Fealder could hear her flipping pages in a file. "Yes, here it is. They actually were doing the testing in two different clinics simultaneously. Professor Warburton had the smaller clinic here on campus and the other PI had a considerably larger group at the Med School campus."

"So who is the other PI?"

"Professor Townsend. Ralph Townsend. He's a clinical psychologist also."

"Was there ever any difficulty with any of Warburton's grants?"

"Difficulty? No. He almost missed a renewal deadline once on one of the small ones and he fired a grant-supported secretary a couple of years ago for sloppy work. We weren't involved in that directly, but I think it was a headache for Human Resources. Other than those little things, I see nothing out of the ordinary. Good paperwork, no budget overruns. Clean."

"Can you give me the name and phone number of the secretary that got fired?"

"Let me see…" Fealder heard more flipping of pages. "It looks like Harriet Malone. Our records would not have a phone number."

Fealder thanked her and hung up. He noticed that Hokanson had brewed coffee so he stopped by the squad-room coffee pot and carried his steaming mug to Berbieri's desk. "Anything on his campus activities?"

She smiled and answered, "Nothing sensational. The Director of the Student Advocacy Office was just about to leave for church when I called and was not at all keen to go back in to the campus. Lucky for me, she was able to quickly connect to her data base using her laptop. Her records showed one complaint against Warburton for badgering some woman as to her recitation in the classroom. That was four years ago and apparently it was settled through mediation."

"How about committees?"

"Not much there either. He served on the departmental promotion and tenure committee for three years as we already know. The university-level records I could access only go back two years. At the time he died, he was only on the Board of Advisors of the University Art Museum."

"What do you suppose the 'advisors' do?"

"I called the Museum Director and asked him that. He says they do some limited oversight on accessions – acquiring new works of art --, they review the budget and make non-binding recommendations, they help the Director with long-range planning, and they advise on fund-raising campaigns and, occasionally, on some of the issues that arise in capital construction projects."

"Did you find out how long Warburton had served on this board?"

"The Director said he was in his second two-year term."

"Did the Director have any light to shed on Warburton's death?"

"Not really. He said Warburton never seemed depressed although he thought at times the man was 'a bit of a sour apple'. I asked if Warburton had any enemies on the Board and he said 'no' and, to the best of his knowledge, not on the museum staff either.

"Okay. This afternoon, I'm going to try to meet with a professor in the med school who was sharing a grant with Warburton. Why don't you see if you can reach the student who filed the grievance and that secretary, Harriet Malone. That's enough for today. Tomorrow we've got Professor Lawson to see and Phil Westling may have his lab results for us."

"And I have Kate Warburton scheduled for midday."

"Sounds good. I'll see you tomorrow at Lawson's office if not before."

Fealder's first call to Professor Townsend reached an answering machine. He left no message and went home. He called again at four o'clock and Townsend answered. Fealder asked if he could come over to discuss Warburton's death and Townsend gave him directions

to his home. The day had cooled down and a breeze
had picked up. Fealder wondered if the fine September
weather was drawing to an end. Townsend's house was
off of Southwest Sixteenth on Elizabeth Street. It was the
smallest house on a long block of large homes, probably
built in the fifties, most of which had superb views over
downtown Portland and the Willamette River beyond. A
manicured hedge offered Townsend some privacy from
the relatively quiet street. The house had a stucco exteri-
or and appeared to have another story below street level.
Fealder glanced through a window in the garage door
and saw a Lexus 400. He guessed it to be three or four
years old. He rang the bell and was greeted by a man of
medium build and nearly six feet in height. Townsend
wore rimless eyeglasses and had a full head of dark hair
lightly flecked with grey and a well-trimmed black beard.
He wore an Italian sweater, chinos and black tassel-loafers. Fealder introduced himself and produced his badge.
Townsend smiled and nodded, then shook his hand and
showed him to the living room.

Townsend's view was somewhat circumscribed by
the larger house to the right, but quite good enough to
make his property enviable and quite valuable thought
Fealder. He wondered if Townsend, an outlier in the
medical school constellation, felt the need to "keep
up" with his wealthier doctor colleagues. Fealder took
a seat on the maroon leather couch facing the window,
his feet on an oriental rug. Both the couch and the rug
showed some wear, but he was sure they had not come

from any discount-furniture outlet. He had ordered Warburton's house to be secured and he knew it would be guarded for several days. He reminded himself to go through that house. He wanted to compare how the two researchers lived in addition to searching for the helpful information that could sometimes be found in the victim's home. His thoughts stopped drifting as he heard Townsend speak.

"This is a terrible thing. Adam was so productive. He had many more full years ahead of him"

"Do you think he could have taken his own life?"

"The news said he fell from a balcony on the building where he had his office. I assumed it was some kind of an accident."

"Did anything you know about him suggest it could've been suicide?"

"Well I knew him well academically, but not particularly well on a personal level. It's hard for me to understand what could have driven him to take his own life, but one seldom really knows things of that nature."

"So he did not seem depressed or troubled to you?"

"No, not especially. He wasn't an overtly happy person, but suicidal? I just don't know. I can say that he seemed quite involved in our ongoing project. But, since you are investigating, you must be thinking there was foul play."

"We have not ruled that out. How would you characterize your working relationship?"

"Oh, quite good. We each had our own clinics so we somewhat divided our responsibilities along those physical lines, but we wrote the grant together, agreed on the protocols with the patients, and would jointly crunch the numbers at the end of the study. It all went smoothly. He was very competent and ... forthright to work with."

"We've heard he irritated some folks."

"Ah, yes. Well, he could be prickly sometimes, but other than an early bicker over allocating a portion of the indirect cost credits, he was congenial enough with me."

Fealder consulted his notebook, and then asked, "Tell me about these human trials you two were running."

"You probably know that the FDA, the Federal Drug Administration, has to approve drugs before they can be marketed. The testing is extensive and can go on for several years, first with animals then with human subjects. The pharmaceutical companies often have some outside entity carry out the tests. We are testing an anti-depressant tentatively called Zolane for Bradley Pharmaceuticals. It is a Phase One test where the objective is primarily to show that the drug has no harmful effects. The patients are divided into a control group that does not take the drug in question and an equal-sized, randomly-selected group that does take it."

"Did you two PIs – I've recently learned that expression – directly interact with the patients?"

"Yes, to some extent. We screened them all on intake to try to make sure they were each appropriate for our sample. We disclosed and explained the protocol to them, though of course we did not then know or say who would be in which group. We were responsible for clinical oversight since these people were our patients whom we were, over and above the experiment, trying to help combat their depression."

"You used the word 'oversight'. What does that mean?"

"For most of the day-to-day consultations or therapy, we use our doctoral students plus three fully-licensed psychologists. They're involved in almost all of the direct contact. Adam and I would review progress in weekly staff meetings at our respective clinics and occasionally intervene if some crisis occurred."

"So did any of the patients ever turn hostile toward Professor Warburton?"

"To my knowledge, no, but you must remember we each had our own clinic. The experimental data would eventually be merged for statistical analysis and quality control, but I wouldn't necessarily know if any one particular patient was reacting unfavorably toward Adam or his staff. Nor would he necessarily know that about my patients. Of course, he might have consulted with me as a colleague, but even then, there would be issues of patient confidentiality. If there were such hostility and it could somehow have skewed our experimental findings, that would be a different matter. But that never happened."

"How about Professor Warburton and the staff at either clinic? Any bad relations there?"

"No. Adam was hardly the sort of person staff would greet with a hug. He was a little distant... a scholar... all business, but no issues of that nature that I was ever aware of."

"Professor, may I ask where you were last Friday evening?"

"Where I was?"

"Yes. We need a sense of where all Professor Warburton's associates – in fact anyone with whom he crossed paths – were at the time of his death."

"I went to a movie at the Pioneer Place Theater."

"Alone?"

"Well yes. I'm widowed and I'm not seeing anyone at the moment."

Fealder closed his notebook and stood. "I think that does it, Professor Townsend. I appreciate your seeing me on a Sunday."

Berbieri called the University Registrar trying to locate the young woman who had filed the grievance. She caught the Registrar at home in the middle of doing a load of washing, but the woman was able to use her laptop to connect to the University's computer system. She called Berbieri back to say that the student had dropped out two years ago without graduating. She suggested calling the Alumni Director. Berbieri left a message on the man's home answering machine and he called back an hour later. She gave him the former student's name. The Director surprised Berbieri with his willingness to help and accessed his records as they talked. He told her that the last address they had for the student, Cathy Burgoyne, was in Rock Springs, Wyoming.

Berbieri heard a very tentative voice answer the phone. "Yes?"

"Do I have Cathy Burgoyne?"

"Yeah. Who are you?"

"I'm Detective Berbieri of the Portland Police Bureau. I need to ask you some questions."

After a lengthy pause, Burgoyne said, "Well, Okay, I guess."

"Ms. Burgoyne, we understand you filed a student grievance against a Professor Adam Warburton about four years ago. Can you tell us about that?"

"Jesus! That was a long time ago. Why are you asking me about that?"

"I'll try to explain in a minute, but could you let me know what that was about?"

"Well that asshole of a professor would pick me out to recite in class almost every week. At the start, I would raise my hand, but after a couple of humiliating exchanges I never did *that* again. We had classes of fifty, sixty students, but he'd still call on me much of the time. He'd lead me down some tricky string of questions. I'd get the first one or two right and then I'd get confused or he'd ask something so hard nobody could figure it out from the readings or the lecture. He'd chortle and essentially tell the class how far off I was! I took it for three or four weeks. I don't know why he did it, but I hated him! At the mediation, he said I was 'a good foil, an excellent instrument' to help him explain the tough points to the class! What a bastard!"

"You mentioned mediation. Did that resolve your grievance?"

"I guess you could say that. He agreed to write me a letter saying he 'regretted' that his Socratic technique had offended me. It wasn't really an apology, but I just wanted to get it over with. I still hated the man, but I was no longer in his class by then."

"Have you been in Portland recently?"

"No. Not for nearly four years! What's the matter? Why are you asking me these things?"

"Professor Warburton is dead. We're looking into his death."

"Oh. My God! Well, I didn't mean that I hated him in that way! I can't say I feel great sorrow, but that's too bad."

"What are you doing in Rock Springs?"

"I'm working at a child-care center, The Bumble Bee. I've been with them for three years."

"Were you working this last Friday?"

"Yes. You can check with my boss, Mrs. Baswell."

"May I have her phone number and The Bumble Bee's address?"

Burgoyne provided them. Berbieri asked, "Did Professor Warburton have anything to do with your leaving the university?"

"In one sense, maybe. I dropped his class which was required for Psych majors and I was thinking of majoring in Psych. It would've been a whole year before the class was offered by a different professor. But I dropped out mostly because I couldn't get deeper in debt. By then, I was considering a different major anyway."

"Well thanks for speaking with me. I may need to call you back, but you've been helpful today."

Berbieri finished her notes from the conversation with Burgoyne and called Ms. Baswell who confirmed Burgoyne had been at work on Friday. Berbieri leaned back in her chair. She had pinned two of her favorite flies on her bulletin board and, as her eyes caught them, she was transported to the Sandy River. She had spent lots of happy days casting into riffles on the Sandy. By association, her thoughts jumped to William Mayfield and the fly-tying equipment she had glimpsed in a corner of a room as they passed on their way to his kitchen. A fly fisher can't be all that bad, she thought wryly.

Her thoughts of sporting recreation then flashed to her new partner. She had noticed the racquetball trophy on Fealder's office shelf. He was a hard man to read. He was laid back as they moved about in the field, but utterly professional and driven when they did interviews or reviewed the evidence. He was a nice looking guy, too … he had a great smile and brown eyes with greenish flecks … eyes that were kind but, she thought, eyes that had a certain sadness from seeing more than their share of evil doing. Berbieri's attention snapped back to the case file on her desk. She reminded herself that she had a case to work on and a chance to prove she belonged in the Homicide Squad. Their working together had been easier than she had expected, but she knew it was early days yet. They had possibilities and suspects aplenty, but no hard evidence. The real test of their teamwork would be whether they could deliver a murderer to the District Attorney.

Berbieri called the University's Director of Human Resources who said she faintly remembered Harriet Malone, the secretary Warburton had fired. She said the records for former employees were on microfiche, but that she had a couple of work-study students re-organizing the fiche collection over the weekend. She would ask one of them to check and to call Berbieri back directly. Twenty minutes passed before a work-study student called to give her Malone's last known address and phone number. Berbieri touched the number into her smartphone and a woman answered. She identified herself as Donna Helton, Harriet Malone's sister. She told Berbieri that her sister had passed away from cancer six months ago. Berbieri offered her condolences and asked, "Did your sister get another job once she left the university?"

"Yes," the woman replied. "She worked for an insurance company until she became ill."

"Did she find that job fairly quickly?"

"No. It took her quite a few months. She was pretty distraught to have been let go. She was much happier once she was back at work."

"Was she married?"

"'Was', yes. But she'd been divorced for ten years."

"Did you know her boss at the university?"

"No. Not at all."

"Did you know his name, at least?"

"I may have heard Harriet mention it, but I don't think I ever really knew it."

Berbieri thanked her and crossed Malone's name off her list. She locked her files away and put on her coat. There was a Spanish recipe for game hen in wine sauce that she had wanted to try for over a month. There was a game hen in her freezer. Her kitchen called her.

7

Patricia Lawson had majored in Women's Studies at the State University of New York, Buffalo. Iconoclastic and occasionally abrasive, she ran for a student body office as a protest candidate and surprised lots of people by getting elected. She and her cadre of student activists did not endear themselves to the SUNY Buffalo administration, but they did manage to get concessions on a few governance issues. After getting her Ph.D. in Sociology from New York University, she was offered an Assistant Professorship at the university in Portland. It was the only tenure-track position she had been offered. She would have preferred to stay in the East, but the prospect of becoming an academic "gypsy" bouncing from school to school was not appealing. She decided the prospective stability and prestige of a tenure-track position was worth transplanting herself to the terra incognita of the Pacific Northwest.

Two years later, she had published her first article and adjusted to the demands of college teaching. A year after that, she had networked her way into the most progressive circles of intellectual life at the university. She had also developed a small, but loyal, following of graduate students and professors.

She had heard of Warburton, but had never met him before they were both appointed to the same ad hoc committee to help draft the employment rule. She almost instantly identified his haughty formalism as a badge of "up-tight conservatism". Their relationship had been strained from the start and deteriorated even further as the drafting process got under way.

Lawson would not agree to meet the detectives at her home, so they went to her office in Bracknell Hall after she finished teaching her eight-thirty class. Fealder had asked Berbieri to conduct the interview. Berbieri was proud that Fealder had enough confidence in her to let her handle the interview though she suspected it was partly because a woman might have an easier time establishing a rapport with this reportedly difficult female. She knocked on Professor Lawson's office door. A large woven mandala hung from the ceiling in one corner. A computer monitor dominated Lawson's desk and shipping cartons were stacked against one wall.

The lid was off the top box and Fealder saw it was filled with labeled file folders. Berbieri began her questions.

"Professor Lawson, we understand you served on a committee with Professor Warburton."

"Yes I did. What does that have to do with anything?"

"Well the circumstances of his death force us to talk to every one with whom he was involved. We need to know if he could have committed suicide. We need to understand if he had enemies ... how he got along with people."

"About suicide, I don't know. I doubt it. He wasn't a fragile person. As for enemies, I suppose someone has told you that he and I were at cross purposes on that rules committee."

Berbieri let the statement hang in the air hoping the pause would induce Lawson to continue. It did not. In a moment of silence, she studied the unflinching face: pursed lips and stern brown eyes framed by straight black hair falling just below the shoulders.

"What were your feelings toward him?"

"He was a bigoted SOB ! I couldn't stand him! He was impossible to work with and a supercilious ass."

"When was the last time you saw him?"

"There was a hearing on the administrative rule our committee was helping draft. That must have been about a week ago. The committee is due to meet to-morrow to finalize the proposed wording."

"Had you communicated with him since the hearing?"

"No. I had nothing to say to him."

"Can you tell us what you were doing and where you were Friday evening?"

Lawson eyed them warily. "You think I had something to do with his death!"

"Please answer Detective Berbieri's question, Professor," said Fealder.

"Listen. I was with a friend all evening. I did *not* kill Warburton. It's that simple!"

"Please understand," said Berbieri. "We've asked everyone we've talked with where they were that evening. But we must have a way of verifying what you've told us. We need a place and your friend's name."

"Screw you, Detective. That's my business, not yours. However that creep died, it had nothing to do with me. I'll ask you to leave now."

Fealder and Berbieri took a diagonal walkway across the grassy quadrangle on their way back to their car. The tops of stately firs and cedars quivered in an early-autumn breeze. Students with backpacks strolled nearby in animated conversations. Berbieri grinned at their innocence and said to Fealder, "Lawson's a piece of work. I really had to bite my tongue when she got insulting! And she certainly had it in for Warburton."

"You're right about that. And, with her office in the same building, she had a key to those balconies."

"And just her word that she was elsewhere."

"We'll need to revisit that. She goes on our list, but I have some trouble seeing her contempt leading her to kill him."

"I rescheduled my visit with Warburton's ex, to fit in Lawson," said Berbieri as they reached their cars in the campus police station's parking lot. "Now I've got to hurry to make it. See you later."

Berbieri wondered if Kate Warburton had "moved on" since her divorce. She herself had been angry and crushed as she tried to come to terms with Stan's infidelities. Once she had decided to start divorce proceedings, her mood improved. She definitely had moved to a happier place in her own life, although she did not yet feel ready to trust herself in a romantic relationship. She wondered if she ever again would be able to trust in that way.

Kate Warburton's house was a small colonial with a whitewashed brick front and twin dormers in Raleigh Hills just outside the Portland city limits. The picket fence surrounding the small yard gave the property a quaint, forties look. Kate Warburton was a tall woman with dark blond hair that Berbieri guessed was dyed. She was handsome, but not glamorous. She wore simple make-up and a bulky sweater with slacks. Berbieri smelled liquor on her breath as they shook hands. They sat in the living room and she could see a decanter on the side boy in the dining room.

"You're here about Adam's death," Kate Warburton said more as a statement than a question.

"Yes. Had you seen him recently?"

"No. Ours was a rather nasty divorce. We occasionally have to talk about property matters or taxes. But I haven't seen or spoken to him for months."

"Do you think he took his own life?"

"Adam? No, I don't. Whatever else he was, he wasn't a person of doubts or weaknesses. It's a terrible thing. I'd had enough of the man, but it's awful when anyone has a fatal accident or is killed and that includes Adam."

"Can you think of anyone who would want to kill him?"

"I'm afraid there are a few people who weren't fond of Adam, but kill him? Certainly not! I can't think of anyone."

"May I ask where you were Friday night?"

"I had a date, believe it or not. We went to a movie at the Fox and had milkshakes afterward."

"May I have the name of your escort?"

"Dan Castanow. He owns a construction company."

"When did you get home?"

"We went to the nine o'clock movie so it was rather late. Midnight, I think. Dan did not come in."

Thankful that the woman's answer saved her from having to ask that question, Berbieri finished with, "Did you ever have a key to Professor Warburton's office or to Bracknell Hall?"

"No. I don't now and I never did."

"Thanks, Ms. Warburton. I appreciate your talking with me," said Berbieri as she stood and closed her notebook.

In her car, Berbieri called Fealder and said she had finished the interview of Warburton's ex-wife. Fealder proposed they lunch together and said she could give him the details then. They met at the Elephant Delicatessen on South Park Street and each ordered a bowl of Mama Leone's chicken soup. Fealder studied his partner across the table and mentally affirmed his impression of earlier that morning:she was turning out to be very capable. Out loud, he said, "you handled the interview with Lawson very well. Neither of us believe she gave us the whole truth and we likely will have to question her some more. You'll take the lead again when we do."

Berbieri's cheeks took on a tint that complemented the dusty rose blouse she wore with her navy pant-suit. Berbieri broke out of the moment by telling Fealder that although Kate Warburton seemed to be relieved to be free of her ex, she did not appear to have borne him any obvious malice and she did have an alibi for the night of his death. Berbieri assured him that she would verify the movie date by calling Castanow. They finished their soup and started the walk back to the Justice Center. They passed an outdoor store and Fealder asked her how she got started fly fishing.

"My dad was an avid fisherman. On vacations or holiday weekends, we'd go camping and from the time

I was ten, he would invite me to fish with him. My mother wasn't interested. She would take short hikes or stay in camp and read. My younger brother was more interested in building lean-tos out of fir boughs or climbing on boulders. But I liked the sport from the beginning. When I was married to Stan, he was always showing homes on weekends and he wasn't interested in fishing anyway. I had a woman friend who liked to fish so sometimes we went together. Other times, I went by myself. It takes some skill choosing the flies and a little practice to cast and to learn the water, but it's also very relaxing ... calming."

"That sounds nice, Fealder rejoined. "Guess I've kind of gone for the more urban sports."

"Yes, I noticed the racquetball trophy."

"Yeah. That's a sport where I can satisfy my competitive urges, have fun, and get a good workout all at the same time."

Back in the squad room, Berbieri hovered over Fealder's shoulder as he called Delikof and clicked on the speaker-phone. "It's Park. Anything else of interest turn up on those e-mails?"

"You'll have to decide for yourself, of course," answered the criminalist, "but I noticed one odd incoming message at the start of last week. It was from a Norman Plaget. I'll read it to you: 'I have thought over what you said, but just can't bring myself to do it. Find some mercy in your soul and look at the bigger picture. Please understand what the consequences would be!'."

"Will this be included in the printouts you've sent?" asked Berbieri.

"Yes. I segregated them by day, so this would be in the Monday batch."

"That'll be worth looking into," said Fealder. "Anything else?"

"Nothing that jumped out at me as unusual. The rest all seemed to be routine communications."

"Did your guys find anything on the balcony wall where he went over? Were there any threads from his pants or blood from the scrape?"

"On the wall, no. But we did find some dried blood on his slacks in a spot that corresponded to the abrasion I described on his leg."

"Did it show from the outside?"

"Well, not much, but if you happened to see it in the right light ... yeah, you could tell there was a stain of some kind."

"How about that cigarette butt?"

"The State Crime Lab says the DNA looks to be Warburton's, but they said they need more tests before they'll stand behind that as their definitive conclusion. Knowing how backed up they are, it could be weeks."

"Any way of telling how recently he had it in his mouth?"

"Not from the DNA specimen. But we can generalize from the condition of the tobacco. We're pretty sure the cigarette had only been out of the pack a day at most by the time we got it. Oh, and we did find a couple of Marlboros among the butts recovered from the balcony."

"Anything on the flying loafer?"

"My physics guy says it *was* further from the body than would be expected if it just slipped off as he fell. But remember what I said about if his legs had been flailing. The calculation may be slightly suggestive that it was tossed off the balcony after the victim went over, but I wouldn't take that to the bank."

"Got it. How about that loafer? Find any prints on it?"

"Nothing we could lift, just some smudges."

"Okay, thanks, Andy."

Fealder looked up at Berbieri. "So what have we got with this e-mail message? Was he being blackmailed? Or was he just some colleague whining about a proposal from Warburton to swap class times?"

"When we were looking over the faculty roster in Psychology I don't remember seeing anyone named Plaget."

"Good point. Well, in any case, we'll have to locate him and find out what that message was all about. See if you can set up an appointment for us to see him before dinner. While you're doing that, I'll call Westling."

They parted and Fealder put the call through to the Medical Examiner.

"Park, I really pushed the lab and I just got their report a few minutes ago. I had a hunch you'd be pestering me for the results before the day was over."

Fealder was tired and ignored the opportunity for a flippant rejoinder. "Thanks, Phil. Any drugs or poisons?"

"Nothing at all out of the ordinary. No drugs. We found a trace of alcohol, but probably just from a glass of wine with dinner. It was certainly not enough to suggest inebriation or poor balance. And the tissues all looked healthy. No tumors or unhealthy organs or occluded arteries. In short, everything was pretty normal for a late-middle-aged male."

"I see. Do you have any more detail on the abrasion on the leg?"

"Just that it was very fresh …within seconds or minutes, an hour at most - of his death if not sustained when he landed."

"That's helpful, Phil. I owe you one for speeding up the lab work. Thanks again."

Fealder considered Westling's opinion on the scrape. He reasoned that Warburton would be too fastidious to wear clothes that showed a stain, however faint. So, unless he severely barked his shin in his own office, it happened as he went over the balcony wall. More than ever, Fealder believed the man had not jumped of his own volition. Someone had violently propelled him off the balcony.

He looked across the room to see Berbieri approaching and holding two mugs.

"I needed some coffee and you looked like you might want some too. We're set to see Plaget in about half an hour at his home. Turns out he's a professor also. In Neurobiology. He sounded pretty nervous."

Fealder swallowed some coffee, strong from the heated urn near the end of the shift. "Thanks. I do get a little punchy this time of day. Tonight, I'm going to read that draft report we found on Warburton's desk, so we can make Plaget our last field work of the day. Show me his address and we can meet there."

8

Plaget had been at home only a few minutes when Berbieri called. It was his wife's day to cover the chemistry laboratory and she would not return until nearly six. Norman Plaget's face was dominated by his heavy black eyebrows and mustache. His receding hairline and the deep creases in his cheeks added to his intense mien. In the minutes since Berbieri's call, his hands had grown icy at the same time his face became moist with perspiration. He swallowed a valium tablet and mopped his face with his handkerchief. Plaget understood that the visit was related to Warburton's death. How had they known to contact him? He paced the floor of his home office, his agitation growing rather than receding. Had they found something in Warburton's records? Then he realized he had made the mistake of e-mailing the man last week when he could not reach him by phone. He prayed his wife would not get home while the detectives were there. He had to concentrate on what he would say to them. He had to regain the disciplined focus that marked his work in the lab. Several minutes later, the door chimes sounded. He mopped with his handkerchief again and edged toward the front door.

Fealder and Berbieri arrived within a minute of each other. Confirming the address, they saw a handsome, oversize English cottage set among the many gracious homes on Alameda Street in the Hollywood District of Northeast Portland. When the door was finally answered, they saw a man in his early forties in a crew-neck sweater, jeans, and sandals.

"Come in please. I'm Norm Plaget."

"Thanks for seeing us on short notice," said Fealder as they both offered their police badges.

Plaget showed them into a comfortable living room discretely decorated with what Fealder guessed were genuine English antiques. Beyond the living room, Berbieri saw a small sitting room with paned windows on two walls above built-in bookshelves. A cello leaned against a chair facing a music stand. Fealder made small talk to learn a little of Plaget's teaching assignments and observed the man's unease even discussing that benign subject. Plaget wanted to ask them why they had picked him out to question, but decided the better course was to hold back and see if they offered some explanation. Perhaps they were simply contacting everyone who had sent the man an e-mail message... just trolling for information. Fealder pulled his small tape recorder from his pocket and set it on the coffee table in front of him. "This just makes it easier to keep things straight. I assume it's OK with you?"

Plaget cleared his throat and looked warily at the device. "Well, I..."

"It's also for the protection of the person being interviewed. Most people like to have us use it," said Fealder as he activated the machine.

"Yeah. Well... yeah."

Fealder leaned forward to face Plaget across the table. "How long have you known Professor Warburton?"

"Well, I uh... not very long. Six months perhaps."

"You met socially? Professionally?"

"Professionally, Yes."

"So it was through your research?"

Plaget's deep-set eyes flickered beneath his course eyebrows in the second before he answered. "No, no. We, ah, met at an AAUP chapter meeting."

"AAUP?"

"The American Association of University Professors."

"So you've kept up the friendship since then?"

It wasn't a friendship really. We were just acquaintances."

"Have you seen each other recently?"

"No."

Berbieri asked, "Professor Plaget, We'd like to ask you about a recent e-mail you sent to Professor Warburton."

"Oh, that!" Before they arrived, he had found the e-mail in his computer's sent-messages folder and reviewed the exact words he had used. "There's an annual student-government fund-raiser coming up. It's kind of a street-fair type event. Sometimes in the past, faculty members have taken shifts at their dunk tank. Do you know what I mean?"

"One of those deals where they throw a baseball trying to hit a trigger that drops somebody into an open water tank?" asked Fealder.

"Exactly. Adam was trying to persuade me to volunteer for a shift. That's just not my kind of thing. I'm a pretty private person. I'm most comfortable in my laboratory. He'd bugged me about it a couple of times and I just wanted him to drop it. Besides, I'll have an experiment running that day and I didn't want to be out of the building."

"Your message talked about 'consequences'. What did you mean by that?"

"I'd earlier told him that I catch cold easily. I really didn't want to sit around for an hour or more in wet clothes on an autumn day."

"How was Warburton 'bugging' you about this? By e-mail?"

"No, in person. We bump into each other on campus fairly often."

"Why you? Why didn't he volunteer himself?"

"I think it very unlikely that he would've volunteered himself. I'm not sure why he asked me. He had a rather odd sense of humor. Perhaps it would have amused him to see others in that situation."

Fealder spoke up. "What exactly is your research field, Professor?"

"I work on neural development. That means the formation or regrowth of neural networks. I look for chemicals or natural substances that interfere with, or modulate, or stimulate the nervous systems of vertebrates."

Fealder took some seconds to write in his notebook. "Would that have any relation to Professor Warburton's work with depressed persons and their medication?"

"Not really. My work is at the pure research end of the spectrum. His work was in clinical psychology: working with peoples' anxieties and beliefs and attitudes. He's at the practical end of the spectrum, if you will."

"I see. And may I ask where you were last Friday evening?"

"You mean when Adam was killed? I was at home all evening."

"Are you married?"

"Yes. My wife teaches organic chemistry here at the university. But she was away at a conference if you mean could she verify my being home. She left Thursday night and did not return until Sunday evening."

"Do you have children?"

"We have a daughter, but she was doing a sleep-over at the home of a girlfriend so I was alone that night." The heavy brows squeezed into a frown. "You think I could've killed him? I didn't even know him very well!"

"We just need to nail down the whereabouts of everyone who interacted with him recently," said Fealder. "It's more or less a routine inquiry. Can you give us the name of the family in whose home your daughter overnighted?"

Plaget gave an audible sigh. "Yes. The Batemans. They live on Brazee."

Leaving, Fealder walked with Berbieri to her car and, leaving the door open, slid into the passenger seat. "What are your reactions?"

" 'More or less' routine?" she said with a slight grin.

"No point in letting him feel too comfortable."

"I agree. He was very uneasy talking to us. He's holding something back. Did you believe his story about the dunk tank?"

"No. A little too pat considering the language he used in that e-mail."

"Right. Strange guy. And no confirmable alibi."

"Tomorrow, will you check with the Department about his wife's out-of-town conference and ask around his lab on this experiment he couldn't even spend an hour away from? And verify the sleep-over with the Batemans. The overnight is probably true, but this guy's squirrelly so I want every detail checked out. If we find a chink somewhere, we'll sweat him good."

"For sure!."

" Did you notice that Plaget was the only one we've talked to who referred to Warburton's death as a 'killing'?"

"Now that you mention it, I do remember him saying that. You think it was a guilty slip?"

"Possibly. Or maybe it was just an assumption, given that two homicide detectives were interviewing him."

"Well, we'll dig into it some more tomorrow." He turned to face her more directly. "Have you always wanted to be a cop, Tami? Was it a family thing?"

"Hmm … that's a bit of a story, Park. It was a family thing, but not the way you might imagine. My dad was *not* a policeman. I had just received a Romance Languages degree from the University of Washington and I was living at home and getting ready to take the Foreign Service exam. That's when Stan proposed. He landed a job with a Portland realtor and I gave up my dream of a State Department job. But before we had even set a date, my older sister, Frannie, was raped and murdered."

"Oh, God! I didn't mean to pry," Fealder said, embarrassed.

"That's okay. You probably should know that about your partner. Anyway, the marriage date was on hold. Frannie and I were really tight. I was devastated and my parents were almost catatonic. I stayed in Seattle and became involved in the investigation. Frannie was working in a restaurant saving money so she could continue her graduate studies. She helped close that night and before she could get in her car – it was in the restaurant parking lot – they grabbed her. Her body was found two days later in Ravenna Park. The police questioned all the employees, but didn't turn up any persons of interest. I talked to everyone I could think of who knew or worked with Frannie. I could tell that one of her shift workers, a woman who tended bar, was scared. I spoke to the lead detective, Chuck Bailey, and told him I thought that lady knew a lot more than she had shared with the police. He actually listened to me and sent a female detective to talk to her again. This time, the woman said there had been two rather drunken men – muscular, buff guys -- at the bar who were ogling Frannie and joking about 'how nice she would be.' She was close enough to hear some of what they said and one of them grabbed her by her blouse and told her to mind her own business if she knew what was good for her. She told the detective that she had never seen them before or since, but she did manage to give her a passable description. Bailey got that bartender working with a sketch artist but, after that, she was even more frightened and wanted nothing more to do with the investigation."

"So it ended there? Unsolved?"

"Well, it seemed like a dead end and the homicide people had started to move on to other cases, but Bailey went through all the security camera footage and found two faces that were pretty close to what the sketch artist had produced. I told Bailey that Frannie had, until her money started getting tight, been a member of a health club in the same general part of town. I didn't ever know the name of the club, but Bailey – despite working several new cases – showed enlarged stills from what the videocams had captured to five different health clubs and fitness centers. At the fifth place, someone recognized one of the men as a member. Once they had a name, the police refocused their investigation. They got a DNA match and the guy finally cracked and gave up the second man as well. It turned out the first guy had been watching Frannie as she worked out. They eventually pled guilty to second-degree murder."

"What an awful way to get started!"

"Yes. Truly awful. But I really respected the way Chuck Bailey handled it. Six months later, Stan and I were married and I was living in Portland. I applied to be a police officer and made it through the academy. So now you know, Park, and here I am," she finished with a wry smile.

"I'm glad James made us partners, Tami. I'm betting you're going to have a great career at PPB!"

Fealder got out of the Explorer and walked back to his Corvette. Berbieri was starting to enjoy her new assignment in Homicide. Then she realized she had called him "Park" instead of "Fealder". Well, they were partners weren't they?

9

Fealder was preoccupied as he hurried through his dinner of warmed leftovers. Afterward, he settled into his favorite easy chair with a noggin of Glenmorangie on the rocks. He laid the report Warburton had been drafting on the walnut chairside table that he had crafted the year before. His fingers caressed the satiny smooth wood he had so painstakingly sanded and oiled. Like a perfectly executed double play or a grand-slam home run, a man could take great satisfaction from producing a decent piece of furniture. He squeezed the muscles at the back of his neck in an attempt to defeat the beginning of a fatigue headache. He sighed and reached for the first page of the report.

It was apparently an early version of what was to be the final report to Bradley Pharmaceuticals. The Executive Summary pages were blank. Fealder surmised those pages would have been easier to write after the body of the report was completed. He read through tedious descriptions of the experimental protocols dealing with everything from selecting participants, necessary disclosures and privacy safeguards, to benchmarking data and evaluation cycles. The protocol section was followed by a section on budget and expenditures. Fealder would ask one of the Bureau's specialists who worked on fraud and embezzlement cases to check the numbers more carefully, but everything looked in order to his layman's eyes. The next section was a detailed review of the statistical methodology they were using. Fealder could not fathom the mathematics. He could see that the section was well developed so far as it went, but was obviously unfinished. According to the Table of Contents, the last two sections would cover the actual experimental results and the "findings, conclusions, and caveats" of the investigators. Either Warburton had not yet written those sections or the other man, Townsend, was doing them. Fealder made a mental note to ask Townsend about that.

The first Appendix displayed, with numeric codes instead of names, certain characteristics of the experimental subjects, segregated by clinic and cross-sorted by age, gender, weight, previous treatment history, and work status. A second Appendix listed the academic credentials of the principal investigators and the qualifications of the professionally-licensed team members.

A third Appendix contained the initial review and approval certifications by the two schools' Protection of Human Subjects Committees. Fealder was fighting to stay attentive as he read through the pages of bureaucratic prose. It all looked like serious science and, although the subjects were not altogether happy people, he could not easily imagine anyone being or becoming so unbalanced as to want to kill either of the PIs. Still he and Berbieri should check to see if there had been any problems or complaints filed against the researchers or the clinical staff. He placed the draft back in his briefcase and, with a yawn, reached for the sports page of The Oregonian. There was time for a quick catch-up on the playoffs before he hit the sack.

By Tuesday morning, the television and radio news stations had dropped coverage of Warburton's death as they moved on to two lurid killings over the weekend elsewhere in the metropolitan area. The Oregonian had done one follow-up story in its "Metro" section suggesting a homicide and noting a lack of progress in identifying a murderer. A weekly "alternative" publication with a surprisingly large readership was still probing. Some faculty members had obviously spoken to that paper's self-proclaimed investigative reporter and had implied that Warburton's campus machinations had made him unpopular on certain fronts. Fealder could tell that the reporter had not learned anything of significance, but his stories offered appealing tidbits to those who constantly criticized what they perceived as the elitism and top-heavy administration of modern universities.

Lieutenant James, always sensitive to public relations, demanded a progress report before Fealder had even hung up his coat. As Fealder concluded, James commented sourly that Fealder's investigation was supposed to be converging on their prime suspect, but, instead was simply adding more candidates with every passing day. "You don't even *have* a prime suspect at this point, *do* you!"

"I still like Callison, the guy who was denied tenure, and maybe this new guy, Plaget," said Fealder trying to stay calm, "but, no, we don't have any hard evidence against anyone. Right now we're checking out everyone and trying to eliminate people."

"Well, try to step it up. That pissant of a reporter for The Portland Scene wants to turn the university into a soap opera, but he's making us look bad at the same time!"

Fealder left James' office and went to his cubicle to complete some neglected paperwork on a different murder case they had closed a week earlier. By mid-morning he was finished. He still smarted from James's demeaning attitude toward him and the unceasing pressure, sometimes overt sometimes subtle, that James applied to him. Fealder knew that James was a high school graduate who had worked his way up the ranks from patrolman. He thought James' martinet act toward the detectives under him was in part due to his resentment that most of them had the benefit of a college education. Fealder believed that James' bad attitude toward him in particular was traceable to the time, fifteen months ago, when James had a strong opinion as to how Fealder could smoke out a leading suspect. Fealder was convinced the evidence they had pointed to the wrong person. He quietly disregarded James's strategy and kept digging. Soon after, he uncovered the critical information that absolved the obvious suspect and led to the conviction of the real murderer. Fealder had thought he and James had nothing more than an honest difference of opinion in evaluating the evidence. But, early on, James had forcefully urged his strategy in a unit-wide meeting and must have felt that he had lost face through Fealder's independent course of action.

Fealder understood the politics of public service and knew that his aspirations as a homicide dick could suffer under James' smoldering resentment. He found James' pettiness repugnant, especially since the man's plan could have sidetracked the earlier investigation and possibly placed an innocent person in jeopardy. Fealder had lost his chance for the big leagues and he was damned if he was going to let James' harassment chase him out of this, his new career. For the time being, though, he had to bite his lip and ignore the barbs from above. He was making his name by successfully closing cases and he had a tough one on his hands at the moment. He needed to get back on task and stop feeling sorry for himself!

Fealder drove to the Eastmoreland district of south-east Portland. After his divorce, Warburton had lived in a smaller, but attractive house six blocks from the Reed College campus. The large, elegant homes near the college thinned out rapidly and this house was in the transition zone before all the dwellings to be seen were neat, but smaller, characterless, middle-class housing. Fealder rang the bell. He was met by the uniformed officer assigned to secure the premises during the earliest days of the investigation. Fealder identified himself and the officer let him inside. He saw that Warburton had an extensive library with a collection ranging from psychology through philosophy, religion, and modern history. The place had minimal furniture and the pieces were rather eclectic in style though of good quality. The medicine cabinet revealed no prescription drugs and the liquor supply was scanty. He did find several cases of what he guessed was rather good wine in the garage. The criminalists had already impounded Warburton's laptop computer and, when Feadler had looked at what was there, he saw nothing of interest. He spent over an hour examining the contents of a small file cabinet. He found nothing beyond investment records, bank statements, and some travel information. The travel file pertained to a tour in Europe arranged by the University Art Museum and scheduled for late spring. Fealder could see that Warburton had committed to go and had sent in a substantial down payment. The bank statements were from a local bank and revealed no mysterious deposits or withdrawals. Monthly accounts from Warburton's broker similarly showed no suspicious activity.

Fealder moved to the bedrooms. One bedroom with a nearly empty closet and empty drawers had to be the guest room. In Warburton's bedroom, the bureau held no surprises. The closet revealed a fairly extensive wardrobe including sport jackets and ties. There were, singularly, thought Fealder, no photographs of family on display anywhere in the house. He did find a photo album on a closet shelf, but – judging by the dates printed on the back sides of the prints – there had been no additions during the last three, post-divorce, years. On a bedside table, he found a well-annotated copy of Blume's "The Closing of the American Mind" and a somewhat newer book, Kahneman's "Thinking, Fast and Slow," with a bookmark at mid-volume. The writing table where they had found Warburton's laptop computer had only one central drawer. In it, Fealder found pens, pencils, a ruler, a stapler, and a few scraps of paper with scribbled notes. The only jotting he paused over was a cryptic "ask for police report on break in". It was clearly a reminder Warburton had written to himself, but Fealder could not even guess at its significance. Because it involved the police, Fealder placed it in an evidence envelope and put the envelope in his pocket. He was hungry and looked at his watch. It was nearly one. He said goodbye to the officer and walked out.

Berbieri reentered the thirteenth floor a little before two o'clock. She spotted Fealder at his desk and walked directly to him. He smiled as they made eye contact. "Partner!"

"Hello, Park." She pulled off her coat and plopped her notebook on his desk. "I turned up a tidbit or two."

"Lay 'em on me."

"First thing I did was check with student government. Their street fair is two weeks from Friday and yes, they are planning on having a dunk tank."

"With faculty dunkees?"

"Probably. They get plenty of volunteers, but of course they get the most paying throwers when there're faculty members on the seat, so they do encourage them to participate. And Plaget was right. Warburton had not signed up. But the really interesting thing was when I got to his lab. Plaget was out so I was able to talk to one of his graduate students. I asked if they were running an important experiment. He said yes, they had one running presently and would be starting another one in a couple of days. Both, he said, were fairly important. I asked if the experiments would still be running two weeks from Friday. He said the newest one would be for sure and maybe the other one as well. I asked if Professor Plaget would be in the lab pretty constantly while they were running. He said that a colleague named Murray was capable of overseeing them, but that Plaget usually checked in several times a day when he was on the campus."

Fealder raised an eyebrow, "And…?"

"Exactly! I asked whether Plaget would be there on that Friday. He said he thought that was the weekend Plaget would be attending a scientific conference in San Francisco. I asked him if he could check that schedule for me. He was uneasy about that, but said the departmental secretary handled all the travel and I should ask her."

"And she said…?" interrupted Fealder with mounting interest.

"She confirmed that Plaget would be leaving on Thursday afternoon for San Francisco and would not return until late Sunday."

"So our bushy-browed friend was giving us a line of bull about trying to beg off the dunk tank!"

"Seems so, though why didn't he just say he told Warburton he'd be out of town?"

"Because he realized he had to fit his explanation to the content and tone of his message." Fealder paused, reflecting for a moment. "But yes, he probably said too much by half. If he'd just left it as a simple begging off, we would probably never have been the wiser.

But he tried to embellish it with this experiment thing, either forgetting he'd be out of town, or else doubting we'd check a detail like that. Nice going, Tami!"

"Thanks. Oh, the slumber party for his daughter checked out and, yes, his wife was away at some academic meeting to the best of the Department's knowledge."

"We need to run a criminal history check on him and, in any case, see him again to confront him about the dunk tank story."

"Speaking of criminal histories, I got the records on Professor Callison, young Mayfield, and Gelbhorn. I found something of interest there, too. Callison and Mayfield are completely clean other than traffic stuff. But Mr.Gelbhorn has an arrest for assault. He pled it down to second-degree intimidation and got a suspended sentence and some mandatory time in an anger management course. That was eight years ago. It apparently arose out of his believing that the victim had made a move on his wife in a hotel cocktail lounge."

"Interesting! So the guy has some history of jealousy and rage. You've had a productive morning. Anything on the clinics? Complaints against Warburton?"

"We had already spoken with the University's Affirmative Action Office when we picked up the Burgoyne complaint so I only spoke to the AA office at the Medical School and the chairs of these 'Protection of Human Subjects' committees at both schools. There was nothing new anywhere. Other than Burgoyne in the classroom, no complaints were ever lodged against him by patients or by clinical staff."

"So that's a dead end."

"It looks that way. Did reading over Warburton's draft give you any ideas?"

"Not really. I'll have the business fraud guy look over the accounts to be sure, but the finances looked OK to me. The draft was incomplete so I need to ask Professor Townsend if he has the rest of it. Before we go back to Plaget, let's go to the conference room and just brainstorm this for a half hour or so."

They walked to a small room with a table seating eight and found it empty. Fealder closed the door and they sat at one end of the table, across from each other. "I keep wanting to go back to the keys," he said.

"I know. With keys, the perp could get into Bracknell Hall after dark and could leave the balcony. Without keys, there'd have to be an accomplice inside the building."

"We have three suspects who have keys: Callison, Lawson, and Susan Gelbhorn."

"And possibly William Mayfield and Kate Warburton, though Mayfield and Warburton's ex deny having a key to the balcony" added Berbieri.

"For that matter, Warburton himself could have let his murderer into the building. He most likely let him or her into his office and probably onto the balcony."

"But, if the murderer wasn't one of the three whose offices were in the building and who had a key, how did the perp leave the balcony? Surely, Warburton would not have handed his key over!"

"No. And remember the criminalists found all his keys in his pants pocket. Maybe the killer went down the balcony fire escape and dropped the last few feet."

"But," said Berbieri, "I thought the criminalists said the ground below was undisturbed."

"That's correct, they did. But I think a person who had the presence of mind to spend a few extra seconds while fleeing the scene could probably repair a depression in the soil and not leave much of a trace. The surface was just bark chips three inches deep over the dirt."

"So the keys are significant, but not determinative."

"Right. What do you make of that graduate student, Mayfield, being in the building at the very time Warburton was killed?"

"It certainly reinforces 'opportunity'," Berbieri responded. "But I still think he was too skinny to have dared trying to throw Warburton off a half-walled balcony."

"I'm less worried about the weight-strength issue. A determined person on an adrenaline high from anger or fear can perform amazing feats of strength. What bothers me more, is why would Warburton let a person he knew intensely disliked him into his office late at night? Let alone, then go with him to the balcony?"

"What if Mayfield was hiding in the hall, hoping that he could trap Warburton on the balcony if he went there for a smoke?"

"I wouldn't rule that out, but it would make for a pretty fragile murder plan. He'd have to hope Warburton would be in his office working late and that he'd feel the need for a cigarette. Meanwhile he, Mayfield, would have to avoid being seen skulking in the hall by a custodian."

"I suppose some of that reasoning applies to Callison as well."

"Yes, although courtesy to a colleague, even one who'd been angry with him, might have caused Warburton to let Callison into his office. It's probably a little different than with a young graduate student." He looked at his watch. "Let's see if we can find Plaget. It's time we get a straight story from him."

Plaget had attempted to forestall the requested meeting, claiming an important session with his laboratory staff beginning at three o'clock. Fealder, now distrustful of Plaget, wanted to keep him off balance and insisted that he postpone the session so the detectives could see him at three. Fealder and Berbieri parked in a "visitors" lot and walked past an older, stucco-surfaced building with courses of ivy climbing its walls between the windows. The detectives' arrival coincided with the break between classes. Students on foot and bicycles thronged the walkways inlaid in a quadrangle of lawn. Beyond the quadrangle, they saw the modern, four-story brick complex that housed the College of Science & Engineering. They took an elevator to the top floor of the complex where they found Plaget's office a few feet down the corridor from his laboratory. Plaget showed them inside and closed the door. Before Plaget had reached his desk, Fealder began.

"Professor Plaget, we want to revisit your message to Professor Warburton. This time we need you to tell us the truth."

"But I did! I..."

"Listen, Professor! This has become a murder investigation! We'd prefer to hear your explanation right here, right now. But if that doesn't happen, we'll continue this questioning downtown!"

"Detectives! What's this about? Why would I want to kill this man?"

"We're asking the questions, Professor!" said Berbieri. "And it's time for you to answer truthfully. We know perfectly well that you didn't intend to be hovering over your experiment on the day of the street fair. You will be in California at a conference. Your explanation of that message does not wash."

Fealder interjected, "It's time to drop the bullshit! Why did you send that message?"

Plaget, still standing, supported himself against the desk with his hands. Then he turned to face the window, his face a canvas of torment. Long seconds passed. He took a deep breath and turned back to face them. "What I say will be confidential?"

"There can be no ironclad assurances, but I can say this much:" replied Fealder. "If what you say turns out to be irrelevant to our investigation, it will remain out of the public eye. Of course, if it leads to evidence, you must understand that the proceedings of a criminal trial are public."

Plaget sat behind his desk and cradled his head in his hands, fingers covering his eyes. At last, he looked up and spoke. "Alright. One of Warburton's graduate students is Canadian. Given Warburton's interest in depression, she had chosen a dissertation topic that dealt with some issues in the pharmacological treatment of depression. This student was not a biochemist by any means, but she was very intelligent and thorough. Her research took her back to articles and reports some of which were almost fifteen years old. Because she is Canadian, she accessed some Canadian abstracts that are less often used by Americans."

Plaget stopped and gathered himself. "Those led her to a fairly obscure paper by a man named Hill that reported on his experiments with a molecule that was one of the precursors to a drug used quite successfully today. Her research also located a copy of my dissertation on the same subject which, though not widely published, exists in a few archives."

He stopped again and stared at the ceiling for a few seconds. "The experiment that was the centerpiece of my dissertation was different from, but on a parallel track to Hill's experiment. I was in the last year of the time allowed to complete my dissertation. My father had died of cancer a few months earlier. I was terribly distracted and my experiment was going poorly. Sometimes I wasn't capturing the necessary data. Other times my protocols became corrupted. I was getting desperate. In the meantime, I had stumbled onto Hill's work. It was insane, but I substituted his data for mine and used part of his most important chapter to convincingly describe the experiment I hadn't been able to pull off."

Berbieri's pen flew over her notepad and Fealder checked to be sure the tape recorder was running.

Plaget continued, "Warburton's student realized I had copied from Hill and essentially faked my experiment. She also must have known or discovered that I was here at this university, so she told Warburton. He was a terrible man! A self-righteous bully! He sought me out and told me that he had proof of my unethical behavior. Said I had not earned my Ph.D."

"So he was blackmailing you?"

"Yes and no. He didn't ask for money. He demanded that I confess to my Dean what had happened. He threatened to present the evidence himself if I did not reveal what had happened. You must understand! If those facts, this ancient history, became known, my career would be over! I'm tenured, but they would fire me 'for cause'. I'd be so disgraced, I could never again work at a university. I'm married to an academic. Our relationship has had some issues lately, but we've been in marriage counseling and things have definitely improved. But, if this came out, it could cost me my marriage!"

"So what did you tell him?" Fealder asked.

"I told him that a year later, I tried my experiment again with a little different equipment and a reworked protocol and that the data from the redone experiment *did* support my hypothesis and even improved upon Hill's findings. I told him that I had proven myself as a scholar and researcher since coming here. My subsequent work has appeared in respected, peer-reviewed journals. I've earned tenure. Two months ago I was even nominated for a teaching award!"

"What did Warburton say to that?"

"The bastard said how could anyone be sure that I hadn't also faked the data in my subsequent experiments! He would not relent. He gave me a deadline of the end of this month. I know what I did back then was wrong, but it's never happened again. I feel that I've redeemed myself! I just couldn't do what he was demanding. He was unreachable by phone, so I sent him that e-mail."

Fealder said, "We can see now why you did not want to tell us the truth about your message. Do you want to rethink your statement to us that you were at home all of last Friday evening and early Saturday?"

"No. No. Absolutely not! That's the truth! I *was* at home!"

As they drove away from the campus, Fealder thought that the part of Plaget's story about the plagiarism was very likely true. It made sense out of his message to Warburton and surely no one would fabricate such a damaging version of his own past. And, from what they knew of Warburton, the alleged demands made of Plaget were in character. So did that make Plaget a desperate victim? Desperate enough to kill the person threatening to disclose his secret? Was his visible anxiety caused by the terrible guilt of a person who had stepped out of his quiet, cerebral life to kill another human being? Or was the anxiety simply the product of stress and fear that his career and marriage could be ruined by a ruthless intermeddler? And what of the fact that this suspect had falsified parts of his dissertation and, more recently, lied to Fealder and Berbieri? Could anything he told them be believed? Had Plaget's latest lie been to protect his secret or to conceal a motive for murder?

10

Fealder and Berbieri sat in the Homicide Unit's conference room with their notes and the autopsy and criminalists' reports spread out on the table before them. Fealder tipped his straight-backed chair against the inner wall of the narrow room and gazed at the ceiling. Berbieri paced back and forth on the opposite side of the table. She looked at her partner and said, "We have a couple of people with motive *and* opportunity, but nothing to single out either of them!"

"You got that right," he answered. "We can be fairly sure Warburton was murdered, but there's no smoking gun. We need to dig deeper into the lives and backgrounds of our most likely suspects. If that gets us nowhere, we'll have to expand the in-depth effort. I'll ask James if we can have Tom Hokanson and Bennie Schultz to spend some time on the less likely ones. If

Tom and Bennie don't turn up anything new and relevant, that should help us cross a few persons off our list or at least back-burner them for the time being. Whom do you like for this homicide as of today?"

Berbieri reflected for a moment before answering.

"Howard Callison for one. And Norman Plaget."

"Yeah. I like them too. Mayfield certainly has a grudge, but I make him for a wimp when it comes to violence. Still, he's worth a little more probing. But I also like Professor Patty Lawson. She's tricky and deep and she's surely hiding something! She also has a key and we don't know where she was that night. And for that matter, there's Herb Gelbhorn, a cuckolded husband with a history of jealous anger."

"But he wouldn't have a key to the building or the balcony," objected Berbieri.

"True, but could have made a copy of his wife's key."

"Should we work the leading suspects together?"

"I don't think we have the time for that. You take Lawson and Gelbhorn. I'll cover Callison and maybe ask a couple of people about Mayfield. Then we'll get together and each of us can consider what the other learned."

Berbieri was glad that Fealder had enough confidence in her to let her dig into Lawson on her own. She also thought that each of them would be more objective evaluating the other's discoveries. "Did you see the two small plaques on the wall above Plaget's bookcase?" she asked.

"No. What kind of plaques?"

"They memorialized awards of a white belt and a brown belt in judo."

"I'll be damned. So the mild-mannered scientist had the skills to easily flip Warburton off that balcony!"

"The thought did occur to me," said Berbieri with a slight smile.

"But, again, how would he have been able to get inside the building?"

"Maybe Warburton himself let him in if Plaget had come to parley about the disclosure."

"Hmmm. I suppose that's a possibility. Anyway, I think we've done enough for today, Tami. Tomorrow we'll put these people under our microscopes."

Wednesday morning, Berbieri emerged from the elevator on the second floor of Bracknell Hall and strode toward the Human Resources office. She had made an appointment with the Director and a clerk led her through a large area filled with desks to a corner office. Her guide knocked on the door and announced her arrival. The Director greeted her, thanked the clerk and closed the door behind her. "I have the file on Professor Lawson, but I've already told you that I cannot share the file with you or tell you information contained in her faculty records, unless you have a subpoena. Even then, I would have to notify her first with sufficient time for her to try to defeat your subpoena if she chose to contest it."

Berbieri had hoped that her assurance that any information not germane to her investigation would be ignored and destroyed would have caused the Director to relent. It had not. "I understand." said Berbieri. "For now, I just need some generic information. Do you have any automatic insurance coverage for faculty?"

"Yes. Of course they have Blue Cross and there is also mandatory coverage under a group Accidental Death and Dismemberment policy."

"Who is the Accidental Death carrier?"

"For the last three years it's been National Life."

Berbieri asked a few more questions, then thanked the Director and departed. In her car, she used her cell phone to call the local National Life agent. Ten minutes later in the agent's office, she had convinced him to disclose to her the designated beneficiary on Lawson's accidental death policy. She was given the name, Ronald Talbourne. Leaving the agent's office, she pulled the campus phone directory from her briefcase. There was a Ronald Talbourne listed as an investigator in the university's Affirmative Action Office.

Berbieri had wondered if Lawson's reluctance to reveal her whereabouts on Friday evening was because she was protecting the identity of a lover. She rechecked the directory and saw that the Affirmative Action Office was also located on the second floor of Bracknell Hall. She turned her car back toward the campus. She was shown to a small office within the suite and introduced to a handsome younger man with a dark-brown, well-trimmed beard. He wore an aging tweed sportcoat over a white shirt, with chinos and sandals. She presented her credentials and asked Talbourne if he could excuse himself for a few minutes to talk. The man looked uneasy, but said he would take his morning coffee break. Berbieri led Talbourne to her parked Explorer and they settled into the front seats.

"I hope you'll forgive me if some of my questions seem blunt, but we need to move quickly and there are some things we need to clear up."

Talbourne swallowed visibly and frowned, but nodded his head.

"Do you have any kind of a special relationship with Professor Patricia Lawson?"

He looked out the window and then stared at Berbieri for a moment. "Yes. Why are you interested in us?"

"We're investigating the death of Adam Warburton. We need to verify where Professor Lawson was last Friday night."

Berbieri knew she was gambling, using the word "verify," but she hoped it would be enough to cause Talbourne to open up.

"She was... she was with me, at my place."

"All night?"

"Yes."

"So when did she leave you?"

"After breakfast. It must have been ten or ten-thirty."

Berbieri thought she saw fear in the young man's eyes.

"And your address?"

Talbourne reached for the door handle as if to get out and end the conversation.

"It will save time," said Berbieri softly.

"Yes…. Okay. I live at 1414 Southeast Harvey."

Berbieri thanked him for his cooperation and gave him a business card.

Ronald Talbourne closed his office door and punched in Lawson's campus phone number.

"Patty Lawson here"

"Patty, it's me. A detective was just here! She came about Professor Warburton's death. She asked me where you were Friday night!"

"Those prying assholes! What did you tell her?"

"I told her you were with me all evening…. I told her… about us."

"Alright. Calm down. Everything will be okay. Some snoop told them Warburton and I were fighting over that rule. I didn't tell them where I was that

night so they are just checking. Thank you for telling her that. We mustn't discuss this over the phone.
Come over this evening and we'll talk about it some
more."

🐚

Berbieri saw that the address Talbourne had given her
was an apartment complex. She pulled into a guest
parking slot and pushed the bell on the manager's
door. An older man with ruddy, unshaven cheeks answered the door. She flashed her badge and said, "I'm
just checking some details on one of your tenants, a
Ronald Talbourne."

"Oh, yeah. Number 213. He in some sort of trouble?"

"I just need to verify a couple of details, is all," said
Berbieri. "Does he have guests from time to time?"

"Well, I don't keep track of all the tenants, you know,
but yeah, I've seen a woman around here quite a bit in
the evening. Seen her some mornings, too."

"Could you describe her, this guest?"

He gave a fairly good description of Lawson.
Berbieri would have been willing to bet that this guy
kept damn good track of his tenants and their guests
and particularly the more outspoken guests like Patty
Lawson.

"Do you remember if this woman was visiting last
Friday night?"

"Oh, I couldn't remember specifics like … wait a minute. Did you say last Friday?

"Yes."

"Well no, there weren't no guests then. In fact, Mister Talbourne wasn't here either. You see, he'd been complaining about the paint in his apartment for months. I finally got around to painting it for him on Friday afternoon. The smell was pretty strong. He didn't want to stay in the apartment until it got better. I think he said he was going to his brother's for a day or so."

"Did he leave an address?"

"No, but I got the impression the brother's right here in town."

Berbieri asked him for a phone book and found the only other Talbourne in Portland was a Bruce Talbourne on Forty-first Southeast. Her call was answered by a woman who said she was Ms. Talbourne. Berbieri identified herself and asked for her husband, but did not explain the reason for her call.

"He's still at work. What's the matter? Why do you need to talk to Bruce?" the woman asked with alarm.

"It's nothing to be concerned about. Perhaps you can help, Ms. Talbourne. When was the last time you saw your brother-in-law?"

"Why would you want to know that?"

"We're just confirming some witness statements in an unrelated matter."

"Oh. Well, the last time we saw Ron was last Friday. He'd stayed with us overnight because they had painted his apartment. He left mid-morning on Saturday."

"When did he arrive at your house?"

"I think it was a few minutes before eight. I know we'd finished washing up in the kitchen after dinner."

"Did you have any other house guests?"

"Well, no. Oh, you mean was his friend, Patty, with him? No. Ron was alone."

Berbieri looked in the direction of Fealder's desk as she hung up the phone. He was out. When he returned, she would tell him they had uncovered another lie.

Joe Newton had been a custodian in Bracknell Hall for three years and was now a "lead person" for the Bracknell custodial crew. Fealder had asked the Physical Plant to have Newton call him in late afternoon Tuesday. Over the phone, Fealder arranged that they meet at six o'clock the next morning after Newton finished his shift. Fealder treated him to a pancake breakfast and showed him pictures of the various persons of interest enlarged from the driver's-license and university identification-card databases. Newton was a tall man, but he slumped with weariness over his plate. He ran a hand through his frizzled, graying hair and stared hard at the photos.

"So you're asking about Friday night?"

"Yes, or even the early minutes of Saturday morning. Did you see any of these people in your building that night?"

"Yeah, I think I did. I'm sure I saw this fellow," he said pointing at the picture of Mayfield. "He was in his office when I emptied his waste basket." Then he picked up the photo of Callison. "And it seems like I saw this man waiting for the elevator."

"What time would that've been?"

"Well, we work four ten-hour shifts. Besides kinda honchoing the whole crew, I cover three floors myself – five, six, and seven -- and I go back and forth. It was probably right away, around seven, when I started on the wastebaskets and the shredders and the garbage in the coffee pantry. Then I do everything on the request list. You know, 'screw that loose bulletin board back into the wall, replace that burned-out fluorescent in the faculty lounge', that sort of thing. Then, on Fridays, I make a pass dust-mopping and buffing the hallway floors. After buffing, I start on the lavatories. But it would be around two-thirty in the morning or later by then."

Fealder appreciated the detail, but he had a hunch where the man's explanation was leading. "So let's take them one at a time. Can you tell approximately when you saw this one?" He pointed at Callison's picture.

Newton again ran a hand through his hair. "I'm trying to remember what I was doing when I saw him by the elevator, but I just can't seem to recall. I'm pretty sure I wasn't buffing, but it could have been any of the other times and I don't even know which floor I saw him on."

Fealder lifted Mayfield's picture from the table. "And this man?"

"Well, like I said, I was doing the wastebaskets so it had to be after seven, maybe seven-thirty. I don't know the young man's name, but I know he's on the sixth floor. I've see him working late several times."

Fealder thanked the custodian and gave him his card. He was opening his car door when he heard the ring-tone of his cell phone.

"Fealder."

"Fealder, it's Matson. We just had a call from a guy named Scott Pradell. He wanted to talk to the detective on the Warburton case."

Matson gave him Pradell's home and office telephone numbers and hung up. Fealder called immediately hoping to catch the man still at home. On the third ring, Pradell answered. Fealder gave his name and explained he was the lead detective on the case and was returning the call.

"Well, I feel kind of strange doing this, but let me explain. I'm a professor in the Journalism School at the University. There's a group of eight of us that run together three times a week over the lunch hour. Howard Callison is also one of the group. Howard and I are not close friends, but we've both been running with the group for three years so we are, of course, pretty well acquainted. My wife and I have also run into Howard and his wife at women's volleyball games now and then. Yesterday, after we finished our run, I said something about last Friday's game. Howard immediately pulled me aside and told me he'd been there and had seen me, but was too far away to say hello. Then he told me the police were questioning him in connection with the Warburton death. He said the detectives didn't seem to believe that he'd been at the game."

The voice on the phone paused for several seconds. Fealder prompted with a "Yes?"

Pradell continued, "Like I said, I feel kind of weird about telling you this, but Howard asked me if I'd call you – I thought he said your name was Healder, but I'm sure he meant you – and tell you that I'd seen him at the game. I said 'well, gee, Howard, I'm sure you were there if you say you were, but I didn't actually see you.' Then he said something about how Ann Dyson played so well. That's true; she had a lot of kills. But I told him I just wasn't too comfortable with calling you."

"What'd he say to that?"

"He sort of pleaded with me for a few seconds. Said that I knew that he went to the games. Said his wife was away that evening and that he really needed someone to back up his presence at the game. He said it was ridiculous for the police to even think that he could've killed Warburton. Anyway, I declined. You can see why I'm uncomfortable. He seems like an okay guy, but obviously you're taking an interest in him for some reason. And I think he made a pretty unusual request of me."

"I agree. Thank you for calling us. You did the right thing."

Fealder asked Pradell for his address and said he would send someone by that evening or the next day to take a written statement from him. When he returned to the thirteenth floor, Fealder called The Oregonian's Sport's Editor.

"In last Saturday's or Sunday's paper, did you cover the women's volleyball game played at the university Friday night?"

"Yes, we did. No photos, but a short article."

"Did you print any kind of a box score? Player statistics?"

"No, although the reporter very likely described in the text of the article the performances of those who played well. And she might well have included a statistic or two."

"May I ask you to check your archives and read me the article?"

"I'm certainly curious what you're after, but hold on. I'll pull it up."

Fealder did not want to answer the newsman's implied question so he remained silent. After a few seconds, he heard keyboarding sounds. Then, the editor's voice: "Only one player singled out, Ann Dyson. Seems she had quite a game. She had a personal best for number of kills."

"Could you send me a copy of that article?"

The Editor readily agreed. Fealder good-naturedly scolded him for not having broader coverage of the baseball playoff games and ended the call. He made a few notes and leaned back in his chair. So far, he thought, things were not looking any better for Professor Callison.

After several minutes of meditating on Callison, Fealder switched gears and called David Mortinsen, the Head of the Psychology Department. He asked the names and phone numbers of the Graduate Teaching Fellows working under Warburton. Mortinsen gave him the information on a man and a woman. At the man's number, he got only an answering machine and left his cell-phone number. The second GTF, a woman named Norma Lassiter, was in her office and answered his call. Fealder introduced himself and came right to the matter at hand.

"We're simply looking into the background of persons who worked closely with Professor Warburton. How long have you worked for him?"

"Going on three years."

"How did you feel toward Warburton?"

"Oh, he was a little fussy about details, but I liked him well enough."

"Did you overlap at all with William Mayfield?"

"Will? Yes, but he taught sections in different classes than I, so I never really teamed with him."

"I see. We know he and Professor Warburton had some kind of a falling out. Can you shed any light on that?"

"The word around the Department was that it was over a scholarly article, though it may've also been over his teaching ethics."

"What do you mean by that?"

"Well, -- this is a little gossipy, I suppose – but there was an undergraduate woman who was in Will's section and she told a few people that he was sexually harassing her."

"Were you one of those people? What became of it?"

"Yes, she mentioned it to me, but she was not very explicit. Basically, he asked her out. They had a date and he came on pretty strongly to her. She was uncomfortable and decided not to go out with him again. He'd try to talk to her after class and even phoned several times to her house trying to get her to go out on another date."

"Isn't there some way she could have filed a complaint?"

"Yes, there are procedures for that through the Office of Affirmative Action. But Warburton found out about it and I think he assured her it would stop. So far as I know, she never filed anything. And, Professor Warburton did not assign Will to teach any of his sections the next term. It was about then that Will changed projects and advisors. Then, I believe he worked for a different professor."

"Can you remember the student's name?"

"I can, but I'd rather not tell you. She confided in me."

"How about this? You tell me and I'll contact her and just say we found a reference in Warburton's files that she had a complaint of some kind against Mayfield. We won't mention your name at all. And, unless she seems to have borne a grudge against the late professor, we won't even have to ask her for details. In other words, we'll be satisfied with just confirming that she had a gender-based complaint against her GTF."

Lassiter thought for a few seconds, then gave Fealder the student's name. He reached the student and found her reluctant to discuss the details, but she did allow that she felt wronged by Mayfield's continuing to try to date her. When he asked how she felt toward Professor Warburton, she described him as sympathetic and understanding and added that, whatever he said to Mayfield, it was enough that the GTF's behavior was never repeated.

Fealder made more entries in his notebook and then frowned as he remembered a detail he had forgotten to check. He leafed back to notes he took during his earlier interview with Mayfield. Satisfied that he had remembered the detail correctly, he called the

Psychology Department number and asked to speak to the Head's administrative assistant.

"I'm Detective Parkinson Fealder with the Homicide Unit of the Portland Police Bureau. As I'm sure you've heard, we're investigating Professor Warburton's death. I need to know if all the faculty and staff are issued keys to the building and to the balcony at the end of the hall."

"Yes, all faculty members have both keys. The staff has neither."

"Would the GTFs and Research Assistants be included with the faculty so far as having both keys?"

"Yes they would."

"Including William Mayfield?"

"I would think so. Let me check to be sure." A minute later she was back on the phone. "Yes. Mr. Mayfield has those keys."

"What if he didn't need the balcony key? Or had lost it? Would you know that?"

"Well, if a person wanted to turn a key back, he would have to go to Campus Security. He'd have to do the same thing if he lost it and wanted another. If he lost it and didn't need a replacement, he still would, sooner or later, have to account for it to Campus Security and pay a pretty stiff re- keying fee."

"Thanks, and please don't mention my inquiry to anyone."

Fealder called Campus Security and an officer there confirmed that Mayfield had been issued a balcony key and had neither turned it back nor reported it lost. So, Fealder mused, Mayfield had lied to him.

It was a nice day and, although Berbieri could have found the information on the internet, she put Herb Gelbhorn's driver's license photo in her purse and walked uptown a few blocks to the Public Library on Tenth Avenue. Entering the massive, block-long building, she climbed the graceful stairs to the reference section on the second floor. She found "Who's Who in America" and checked for the architect's name. She saw that he had a predictably flattering squib. Berbieri noted that he was a Syracuse graduate and had played varsity football there in the early nineties. The rest was professionally significant, but not helpful to her investigation. She remembered that Fealder had introduced Tom Hokanson as a Syracuse graduate and she knew Hokanson was about Gelbhorn's age. She made a mental note to ask Hokanson if he knew the man. It was good to get out of the office and Berbieri decided to walk the rest of the way to the campus.

She was not sure what she expected to learn, but she doubted that Gelbhorn's meeting with Warburton had been as short and simple as portrayed by the burly architect. She started knocking on the doors of the faculty offices closest to Warburton's. An older professor in the office next door remembered what he characterized as a "hub-bub" in Warburton's office on the day of Gelbhorn's visit. But he had not clearly seen the visitor and could not hear the voices well enough to know what was being said. The few others who responded to Berbieri's knock knew nothing of the incident and did not recognize the man in the picture. A young woman who said she was the "office assistant" came in to deliver a packet to one of the professors Berbieri was questioning and glanced at the picture.

"I think *I've* seen him," she said.

Berbieri smiled at her. "May I ask when and where?"

"I was coming back from taking something over to the University Press. It must have been nearly two weeks ago in mid-afternoon. Professor Warburton sometimes rode a motor scooter to work. I guess he was going somewhere because he had just unlocked his scooter and put on his helmet when this man passed in a car. The man slammed on his brakes, pulled over, got out and ran toward the professor. He yelled something at him. I wasn't quite close enough to understand him, but whatever he yelled, he sounded angry. Professor Warburton saw him coming and immediately started his scooter and drove away."

"And you're confident that this is the man you saw?" Berbieri asked, gesturing at the picture.

"Yes, I'm quite sure. You can understand that that little scene riveted my attention."

Berbieri got the office assistant's personal information and continued to knock on doors, but no one else with whom Berbieri spoke had any knowledge of the incident. Two persons did recognize the person in the photo as Susan Gelbhorn's husband, but neither had ever seen him in the building.

Berbieri saw Hokanson was on the phone when she returned to the thirteenth floor. She waited until his call ended and then approached his cubicle.

"Tom, I understand you're a Syracuse grad. Did you ever hear of a guy named Herb Gelbhorn? Class of '95?"

"Gelbhorn? Yeah, I think so. That was the class ahead of mine. Was he a football guy?"

"Yes. What do you remember about him?"

"Well, I barely knew him. But we had a couple of classes together and I ran into him at a couple of parties. The thing I remember the most was that there was some kind of a bar-room fight. Two or three football players beat up on a couple of locals they thought were insulting their girlfriends. Gelbhorn was one of the players. I think the three guys got suspended for a couple of games or something like that…. maybe had to do some community service. Probably the coaches smoothed it over somehow. Got something to do with your case?"

Berbieri kept a poker face and said, "Gelbhorn's a person of interest. And he seems to have a short fuse!"

Fealder had met Tandeen Ishwami as his opponent at a racquetball tournament last winter at the

Multnomah Athletic Club. Fealder had narrowly won, but they both enjoyed the game and ended up having lunch together during the mid-day break. He remembered Ishwami said he was a patent attorney. Fealder wondered if Plaget's science was as good as he claimed and as good as his athleticism on the judo mats. If Plaget had any inventions to his credit, he hoped Ishwami could do a patent search and turn them up. He called Ishwami and they arranged to meet for lunch at Giorgio's. At the restaurant, Fealder asked Ishwami if he would be willing to help. He emphasized the sensitivity of his investigation and the need to keep the inquiry confidential. Ishwami said it would be fairly easy and that he would be glad to do it. Fealder could not expense the wine – knowing James, he would probably even question the food bill – but he wanted to show his gratitude for Ishwami's help. So he went into his own pocket to make sure they shared a good King Estates Pinot Gris to go with Giorgio's "pompano en papillote".

Ishwami called Fealder forty minutes after they parted. He told Fealder that he had enjoyed their lunch and then reported what he had discovered. "Park, your man does have two patents. It looks as though both have been assigned to the university. To put it simply, one sounds like a process patent for isolating an enzyme. The other is a new ligand. That's like a peculiarly shaped molecule. His claim is that the ligand will block certain receptors in the brain. That, in turn, should suppress the secretion of an enzyme that is suspected to be one of the causes of depression."

"So the brain normally creates this nasty enzyme!"

"Not exactly. As I get it, the likelihood of depression seems to go up when the brain creates *too much* of the enzyme. So the hope for the ligand is that it will be able to dial back the secretion of the enzyme to the normal level. I was sort of interested in that second patent, so I checked a little further in some more arcane databases. I learned that the university licensed it to Bradley Pharmaceut..."

"To whom?"

"A company called Bradley Pharmaceuticals. It's trying to get established in the neurological area: stuff to combat or at least ameliorate multiple sclerosis, Lou Gehrig's disease, Parkinson's, depression, that sort of thing."

"What's the significance of licensing to Bradley?"

"Well, the license isn't part of the public record, but I'd guess that the company probably got an exclusive right to exploit the ligand. If they can find a way to commercialize it, they'll very likely have to pay royalties to the university based on some metric relating to their sales of the product or drug that incorporates it. I don't know what internal arrangements the university has with its faculty inventors, but I suspect it would share the royalty stream with Professor Plaget."

"Thanks, Tandeen! You've been very helpful. I and the PPB Homicide Unit are certainly appreciative!."

Fealder dug through the ever-thickening file to find the fax sent to him by the University's Director of Research. Yes! He *had* remembered correctly. Bradley Pharmaceuticals was the same company that had given Warburton and Townsend the contract to run clinical trials for their new anti-depression drug. So, Fealder chortled to himself, the 'pure researcher' and the 'practical clinician' never shall meet, huh?

11

The judge had issued subpoenas for the last week of Warburton's telephone traffic. Fealder had been too pressed to review the records of calls to and from Warburton's home and office. He sat down with sheaves of printouts from the University Telecommunications Office and Verizon as soon as he returned from his lunch with Ishwami. He found nothing of interest in the records for the six days preceding Warburton's death. The criminalists had highlighted one call to Warburton's home at eight-twenty-one in the evening of the murder, but the caller had hung up without speaking as soon as Warburton's answering machine engaged. Presumably a telemarketer, Fealder thought, but worthy of a notation in his case file. The records for Warburton's office phone showed a three-second incoming call at eight-twenty-two. Fealder found it difficult to imagine a conversation that lasted only three seconds. More likely, he concluded, that Warburton answered the ring and the caller immediately hung up. Were these two calls the killer's way of locating his target?

In mid-afternoon, Fealder looked up to see Berbieri approaching.

"Tami! What's new?"

"I found out that Patty Lawson has a boyfriend, Ron Talbourne. He's an investigator in the university's Affirmative Action Office. When I told him I needed information about Lawson's whereabouts on the night of the murder, Talbourne said Lawson spent the night at his place. I thought that was worth verifying, so did a little checking. I learned that Patty Lawson was *not* with her boyfriend the night of the murder! I haven't confronted Mister Talbourne yet, but both his apartment manager and his sister-in-law say he was staying at his brother's house that night and that Professor Lawson was not with him. I wanted you to decide how to play it with Lawson."

"We *knew* Lawson was hiding something. It seemed at first that it was just her relationship with a lover, who turns out to be this Talbourne guy, but now it must be much more significant. And it sounds like Talbourne knew enough about whatever Lawson was doing to feel the need to cover for her!"

"I agree, but I still can't see Lawson being so involved in her cause to have killed Warburton," said Berbieri.

"Yeah. She speaks with genuine anger toward Warburton, but it isn't easy to think she really had a motive to kill, based on what we know so far. Even so, I want to go back to Bracknell Hall and talk to some more people. I have a hunch she was in the building the night Warburton was killed."

"You were going to dig a little regarding Callison and Plaget. Turn up anything interesting?"

Fealder filled her in on what he called Callison's pathetic attempt to reinforce his alibi through Scott Pradell, and the fact that Callison had been in Bracknell hall the night of the murder. He also told Berbieri that he had, just moments earlier, learned about Plaget's opportunity to earn royalties from Bradford Pharmaceuticals. After they shared their findings about the character flaws of Mayfield and Gelbhorn, Fealder suggested they go to the campus to see if they could smoke out Lawson's whereabouts on Friday night.

Fealder had earlier e-mailed the Psychology faculty asking anyone who was in the building Friday night to contact him. One person had responded and she claimed to have been in her office on the sixth floor only from seven to eight-thirty. She said she had seen no one except the janitor while she was there, although she thought she had seen a light under the door of Mayfield's office when she left.

Fealder and Berbieri stopped first at the Campus Security office and asked to speak with the officer,

Dougherty, whose primary responsibilities included Bracknell Hall. He was called in early to meet with them.

"Hi, Officer Dougherty. We're back to check out a few more details on this Warburton business. Do you have any sort of a foot patrol through the building after hours?" he asked

Dougherty replied, "Sure, but only twice a night. The student patrolman you met does the outside grounds and I go through the buildings. My first pass at Bracknell is around nine-thirty, nine-forty-five and then my second pass would be about three-thirty or four in the morning. Of course, that particular night, we all met outside the building after Satino discovered the body."

"And did you see anyone in the building on your first round? Including persons whose offices were in the building?"

"No, I really didn't. I think I saw a few lights on under the doors … maybe two or three, but you know, on a Friday night not too many people work late. In any case, I don't remember whose offices were lit or even which floors they were on."

"Is there any other type of security in the building?"

"Well, there're security cameras on the first floor in front of the cashier's counter in the Registrar's Office and in the hallway outside of Financial Aid and Affirmative Action on the second floor. Human Resources is on three, but there is no camera there.

Above that, there are only faculty and departmental offices and, again, there are no cameras."

"Are these video or still cameras?"

"Video." Dougherty anticipated the next question. "The content goes to discs and we save the discs for two weeks, and then reuse them.

"We're going back to Bracknell and sort of wander around. Maybe we'll want to look at those discs. Will you please be sure the discs for Friday night and early Saturday morning are available for us?"

"Sure. I'll do that right now."

Dougherty led Fealder and Berbieri out through the rabbit warren of small offices, lockers, file rooms, a communications center, and the public counter that comprised Campus Security's office suite. The two detectives walked across the rolling lawns, past a residence hall and the library, and saw the high-rise that was Bracknell Hall. They entered the large lobby and moved toward the rather grand staircase rising in front of them. They saw a sign indicating that the cashiers' counter was down the corridor to the left and that the Admissions Office was to the right. There were three elevators to the right of the staircase.

Fealder turned to Berbieri and said, "The perp probably didn't want to risk meeting someone in the elevator. I'm guessing he or she took the stairs even if it meant climbing seven flights. Let's go that way."

They ascended the main staircase and could see that the wide stairs with the elegant balustrade stopped at the second floor. From there on, the stairs were concrete with steel railings and were enclosed in a vertical shaft. The stairs could only be accessed through fireproof doors on each landing. The access door on the second floor was across from the entrance to the Affirmative Action Office.

As they turned left at the top of the staircase, Fealder glanced up and pointed. "There's the security camera Dougherty mentioned. You know that would probably capture anyone entering the stairway on this level. I think we *should* check that footage."

Berbieri said, "This was the route I retraced to the seventh floor on the night of the murder. I'm embarrassed to say that I missed seeing that camera."

"All the more reason to revisit the scene," Fealder said with a grin.

They found nothing of interest during their climb on the stairs. Fealder called Dougherty on his cell phone to ask him to set up a monitor so they could view the second floor video disc. They hurried back to Campus Security. On the monitor, they saw a custodian buffing the hallway, but there was no other activity until ten-twenty-one when a short figure wearing a hooded sweatshirt could be seen using a key to enter the Affirmative Action Office.

"By God, that looks like Lawson!" exclaimed Fealder.

"It sure does," added Berbieri. "I wish the lighting were better so we could see the face more clearly. But the person has Lawson's build. You can't see hair, but that profile as she approaches the door certainly looks like her."

They reran the video several times, but could not be positive it was the Sociology professor. The time was imprinted on the disc at one-minute intervals. Twenty-four minutes later, the same figure emerged from the office. Her hands were empty and she had drawn the hood more closely around her face making a definitive identification impossible.

"It's time we talk to your Mister Talbourne, Tami."

"I agree. He seems like the weaker of the two. Let's see if he'll crack, before we confront Lawson."

They returned to Bracknell and discovered that the Affirmative Action Office closed at four. It was ten minutes before four so they retreated to the corridor until Talbourne emerged. Fealder tried to persuade him to follow them to the Student Union for a cup of coffee and some follow-up questions.

"Well, I really can't. I have a racquetball game start-ing in fifteen minutes. Sorry."

"Mister Talbourne, you're going to have to miss that game today. We'd like to have a friendly talk at the Student Union, but if you're not agreeable, we'll have to ask you to come downtown with us."

He looked angrily at Fealder. "You're saying I have no choice? Very well. The Union then."

They said little on the short walk to the Union. Talbourne used his phone to cancel the match. Once inside, Fealder bought them coffee and they sat in a booth in the nearly deserted cafeteria. "You told Detective Berbieri that Professor Lawson had spent all Friday evening and night with you at your apartment. Now we *know* that was a lie. We know where you were and we know that Professor Lawson was not with you. You need to tell us where she was."

Talbourne looked bitter and defeated. "All right, we weren't at my place, but we were together until the early hours of the morning. We…"

"Cut the crap!" interjected Berbieri leaning across the table toward him. "We know you were at your brother's from eight o'clock on. You're already guilty of impeding a homicide investigation. We have proof that your friend was in Bracknell Hall shortly before Warburton was killed. It's time for you to cooperate or you could find yourself an accomplice to murder."

Talbourne was himself an investigator and knew they were trying to panic him into blurting out more than he wanted to tell them. On the other hand, they had clearly caught him in a lie. He thought he knew why Patty had entered the building, but he did not know how long she had stayed or whether or not she had actually gone to Warburton's office. Patty was quite impetuous, but Talbourne thought that she had enough self-control not to have assaulted Warburton even if they had met and he had taunted her. But what if his assessment of Lawson was incorrect? What if Patty had started to carry out her plan and then had decided to confront Warburton then and there? And what if, at that point, something had gone terribly wrong? Then he thought, even if I tell them where I suspect Patty was, I'll lose my job and Patty won't be much better off. But what if I ….

His thoughts were interrupted by Fealder's taut voice. "We know she went into the Affirmative Action office and used a key to do so. We have it all on video from a surveillance camera. When we trace the key that she used to you, you're in this up to your neck! Think about it. Tell us what was going on!"

Fealder was bluffing about positively identifying Lawson and being able to trace the key, but he had a gut feeling that Talbourne had supplied the key and he wanted to press him hard.

Talbourne knew that Patty had not asked him to get any information from the AA office himself in order to protect him. Patty had not even asked him for the keys directly though he was sure that Patty knew which ones were his office keys. He had forgotten to take the keys with him to his brother's place on Friday evening and, when he returned from a fast-food dinner, he noticed they were missing from the wall peg in the kitchen where he normally left them. On Saturday, when he returned to his apartment, he discovered that those keys were back on the peg. He was sure that Patty had taken them. But now the police knew that Patty had been in the building and had entered the Affirmative Action office, so Talbourne decided that he could best protect Patty by telling them that that office was Patty's target rather than Warburton's office.

"Okay," he said in a quiet voice. "Patty was having this battle with Professor Warburton about the employment rule. She was convinced that Warburton was a sexist bigot. She knew he had been the Department Head for three years. I think she had this idea that if she could show that he biased the faculty hiring process during that time, she could force him to come around and stop fighting her stronger version of the rule. Warburton's headship was before my time in the office. I think she wanted to look at Affirmative Action's review of his hires to see if there was evidence to support her belief. There were also rumors of a grievance by a female student against Warburton. I'm guessing Patty wanted to see if there was such a grievance and whether it was predicated on gender discrimination or sexual harassment."

"But how could she have used this against Warburton?" interrupted Fealder. "That information is all highly confidential and she'd have to explain how she got access to it."

"That's true, but I guess she would have claimed to have talked to the complainant or to the persons who weren't hired. It would be risky, but I suppose she thought that if she found a smoking gun, it was worth the risk...that the end would justify the means. If she could get him to compromise a little on the rule, she probably figured she would never have to go public with anything. But she only wanted to look at the data in those files. She is *not* a killer! The fact that he died that same night is nothing more than a coincidence!"

"Did she remove anything from those files?"

"No. I checked two days later. All the records seemed to be intact. I looked at those files and I couldn't see anything that would've compromised Warburton in any way. I've heard he sometimes sounded insensitive and not politically correct, but his decisions and actions reflected in those files were always defensible and did not look discriminatory to me. The student grievance made a weak allegation of gender discrimination regarding the way he called on her in class, but the evidence was somewhat ambiguous and it ended up being resolved by mediation."

"Thank you for being truthful with us this time."

"Do you have to tell my Director about this?" asked Talbourne.

"Right now our interest is solely in finding out what else Professor Lawson may have done in Bracknell Hall that night. Once that's straightened out, we'll see," said Fealder.

They left Talbourne looking woefully into his coffee cup and walked through the cafeteria doors into the brisk air of late afternoon.

"The poor man doesn't know whether he's helped or hurt his lover by talking to us."

Fealder nodded. "True. He's had a tiger by the tail with this Lawson woman. He may love her, but he is also starting to realize that Lawson plays hardball and can be a hell of a liability. Now we'll have a little talk with our radfem professor."

Lawson had left her office early. She was at home trying to read a journal article, but her thoughts kept returning to Talbourne's call several hours earlier. She pressed her hands to her temples and thought: poor Ron. He always means well, but sometimes he does not think before he speaks. In his professional role, Ron was steady, meticulous and fair. But, strangely, away from the office, he was guileless and rather easily manipulated. Lawson could imagine that the detectives might have inferred that she claimed to have been with Talbourne on Friday night. Ron would have instinctively wanted to back that up. Lawson faulted herself for not telling Talbourne to keep his distance. She had worried that her rather high profile in connection with campus discrimination issues could lead to conflict-of-interest assertions against Ron. Because of that, they had kept their relationship a secret. And, she had taken pains to keep her lover out of the picture if her actions that night were ever discovered. Now, they would have to improvise. She would work something out when Ron came over after work. Her telephone rang and before she could answer it, the doorbell rang. Assuming it was Talbourne at her door,

Lawson went to let him in and let the phone call go to the answering machine.

She opened the door and the smile faded from her face as she saw Fealder and Berbieri. She was loathe for them to enter her home, but thought this was no time to be defensive. Lawson invited them into her foyer, but did not lead them to the living room or offer them chairs. She asked, "What do you want?"

Fealder thought it very likely that Talbourne had called Lawson after Berbieri's interview. He was less sure that he'd had time to call Lawson since the two of them had confronted him just minutes ago. He thought he might unnerve Lawson by skipping the now-demolished alibi and immediately challenging her about her presence in Bracknell Hall.

"We want to know what you were doing in Bracknell Friday night."

It took all the control Lawson could muster not to let her surprise show on her face. Had Ron suspected where she had been and told these people of his suspicion? Did they have some witness who had seen her? She needed to stall in order to determine what they actually knew. She would have to play the innocent for at least a while longer. "I was with a close friend. I told you that was none of your business. What makes you think I was in Bracknell?"

"You can drop that line, Professor!" said Fealder. "We have you on video inside the building."

So there was a surveillance camera and she had missed it! Lawson remembered her care in drawing the sweatshirt's hood around her face. "Well I wasn't there, detectives! The camera must have caught someone else."

"Cameras don't lie," said Berbieri.

"We know about Talbourne's keys," added Fealder. He would rather have not narrowed the focus to the Affirmative Action Office, but they had to move her past flat denial.

Ron had talked, Lawson thought with an inward sigh. Now she was in deep shit. She was comfortable with what she had done. Warburton was such a rigid bastard. He had to be dealt with and neutralized. She gave Fealder a flinty eye and said. "So what if I was on the second floor? I never saw Warburton, never went near his office!"

"Why should we believe that? You stonewall us about your whereabouts and we find you entering a secure area after hours. You were there because of your hatred of Warburton. You had better have a very convincing explanation."

"Alright. Yes. I was hoping to find evidence that Warburton was a self-righteous hypocrite. That he was in fact the very type of person a tougher rule would rein in. I thought there might be a smoking gun in the records. But even if there were such evidence, it makes no sense that I would murder the man. The very fact that I thought of taking some risks to exert social pressure on him shows I wasn't contemplating violence. Sure I had issues with him, but I'm not crazy! I wouldn't *kill* someone just because he was not a big booster of affirmative action!"

"Maybe, maybe not," said Fealder. "Another way of looking at it would be that if you couldn't find any way to blackmail him to do your bidding on the rule, you would escalate to physical violence. Maybe it was just a pushing and shoving match you had out there on that balcony and then you pushed too hard, he lost his balance…. you didn't intend that he go over."

"Get real, Detective! We're talking about an *administrative rule* for Christ's sake! I may have my values, my commitments, but a rule could not possibly be worth killing for!"

"You'd better hope there's nothing to put you on that balcony, Professor," said Berbieri.

"There won't be. I may've gotten carried away to go near the AA office, but I fully expected to see Warburton alive and well at our upcoming committee meeting. Why else would I have thought of examining those records?"

"We'll see," said Fealder, unwilling to let her completely off the hook at this stage of their investigation.

Lawson realized that Fealder had not been very specific about what the camera had seen, but the detectives seemed to know about Talbourne's keys. Lawson had spoken carefully, trying not to admit actually entering the Affirmative Action office, but she realized that the detectives had raised the ante by looking to implicate her in the homicide. It is time to cut my losses and protect Ron, she thought.

"I took those keys from Ron's apartment. He didn't have any part in planning or supporting my idea. If he said anything untrue, it was only because he was worried that I would be under suspicion for Warburton's death."

Fealder waited a few seconds before answering. "I hope for his sake that's true. We'll consider your explanation of his involvement carefully."

As they left, Fealder saw that Lawson's pugnaciousness and bravado had vanished. He saw, instead, a woman shaken and uneasy. They had done enough field work for the day. In the car, Fealder said. "She's hard as nails and she's sure as hell complicated our investigation, but I tend to believe her. The wording of a rule is simply not worth killing over."

"I'm not quite ready to take her completely off our list," said Berbieri, "but I, too, have trouble seeing her as the perp. What are you going to do about her entering the office?"

"If I was running a university, I sure wouldn't want a role model, a professor, sneaking into confidential files, compromising an employee, and invading people's privacy. I think when this is all over, we tell the AA Director or Campus Security."

"And Talbourne?"

"I don't know," he answered. "He either knew or suspected what his girlfriend was up to even if he didn't actively help her. That's certainly contrary to the trust placed in him to handle the sensitive issues of that office. On the other hand, I think he was just putty in the hands of Lawson. Maybe he's learned a lesson. Maybe we can just leave it that Lawson stole the keys from him. Anyway, that's not our priority at the moment."

"That's for sure," said Berbieri.

"I'm hungry and beat. You can just drop me off at my car."

Fealder settled into the seat of his Acura with weary sigh. Tomorrow they would have to sweat Professor Calison.

12

Fealder and Berbieri checked with the Departmental office on Thursday morning to ask when Callison's first class of the day was scheduled. The class started at 10:30. They knocked on Callison's office door at 9:30.

"Hello, Detectives," he said warily. "Look, I've got a class to teach in under an hour. I need to finish my preparation. Whatever it is, could we do it this afternoon?"

"This won't wait, I'm afraid," said Fealder stepping inside the office.

"Why? What do you want now?"

"We know you tried to talk one of the men in your running group into saying he'd seen you at the volleyball game, when he hadn't. What are you covering up, Professor?"

Callison shuddered and looked at the floor. "I see. That was a mistake. I shouldn't have asked him to do that. But can't you understand? I *was* at the game and I *did* see him there. He was just too far away to say 'hello' and – naturally – I didn't know at the time that I'd need to prove I was there."

"Listen, Professor!" retorted Fealder. "You ask *us* to understand, but your logic is lousy. You wanted this guy to invent a story that he saw you there and you expect us to say that was reasonable because you were there. But that's the very thing we don't know ... the very thing we're looking for proof of. And you tried to offer us a made-up story!"

"But Scott has seen my wife and me at other games! It isn't like I was asking him to fabricate it out of whole cloth."

Berbieri said, "Other games don't count. You need an alibi for last Friday night."

"You're right, of course," he said, suddenly abashed. "It was a stupid thing to have done. But you should put yourselves in the shoes of an innocent person. I had a grudge against Warburton, sure, but you were wondering if I had *murdered* him... well, I panicked. You may say that an innocent person should just be calm until the police find the real culprit, but I got rattled. I lost my head, I guess."

Fealder gave him a steely-eyed look and continued. "You say an innocent man panicked, but others could say a guilty man was trying to shore up a weak spot. We know you were in Bracknell Hall the night Warburton was killed. You told us you just went to the volleyball game. Isn't it time you gave us a straight story?"

Callison repositioned a paperweight on his desk, and then repositioned it again. He visibly swallowed and said, "That's true. I was there, but it was early in the evening. I told you I had finished grading those mid-term exams and decided to celebrate by going to the game. Parking my car next to Bracknell in my own reserved place was easier than hunting for a place near the fieldhouse. I brought the exams with me and dropped them off at my office, then walked over to the game. I couldn't have been inside Bracknell for more than three or four minutes."

"You never mentioned this to us before when we asked where you were that evening," said Fealder.

"Yes. I was afraid to admit I was in the building that had become a crime scene. I should have told you, but I thought no one had seen me and I knew it was irrelevant."

"We should be the judges of that!" exclaimed Fealder. "People who don't tell us the whole truth, who try to twist the evidence, get our close attention. Don't stack the odds against yourself worse than they already are."

"I'm sorry," said Callison quietly. "Like I said, I've been stupid. I've not had much luck lately and I won't monkey with the odds agai …. Wait! I just thought of something! I played bingo at the game."

"You what!" exclaimed Berbieri.

"They sell bingo cards as you come in and, during the breaks between games, they read off the numbers. I bought two cards. I didn't win, of course, but I think I stuffed the cards in my pants pocket."

Fealder looked skeptically at Callison who smiled weakly and said, "Probably a little anal on my part, but I don't like to litter even at a sporting event. So I normally take the cards with me or to a garbage can if I see one. I was wearing jeans that night and haven't worn them since. I'm hoping the cards are still there."

"But how would we know they were from last Friday night?"

"I'm not sure why they do it, but they date-stamp each card with colored ink. It seems like they use different colors for the stamps each game. Maybe it's something they do to prevent cheating. In any case, if I can find those cards, that would help you believe me wouldn't it?"

"Well, if you find them and if they're authentic, it would be presumptive that you were at the game at least for a while."

"Listen. You want authentic. I told you I didn't win, but I did punch out the numbers that they called that were on my cards. If I can find the cards, you can check the numbers I punched against the numbers they announced. That will not only show the cards are real, it will also show that I stayed through the breaks between the games. Please come with me to my house to see if I can find the cards. I'll tell the Department office to postpone my class."

Berbieri looked at Fealder who nodded. "OK, let's go," she said. "We can take my car."

Callison jumped out of the Explorer as soon as Berbieri pulled to the curb. The detectives followed him as he hurried to his front porch. He unlocked the door and rushed in, pausing only in the foyer to key in a code for his alarm system. "Follow me to our bedroom closet," he said.

Fealder held up his hand. "Hold on. This alarm system of yours looks pretty high-end."

Callison stopped and turned. "Yes. It's fairly new. My wife is very security conscious. This model is supposed to be very reliable and high tech."

"Do you always arm it when you leave the house?"

"Yes. Always."

"And are you connected to some security service?"

"Yes, we are. The alarm is connected to Three Rivers Security."

"Before we go looking for those bingo cards, I want to call Three Rivers," said Fealder.

Callison suddenly looked hopeful. "Are you thinking there might be a record of when I came home last Friday night?"

"It's a bit of a long-shot, but they might have a record with a sophisticated system like this."

They found Three Rivers' number on a decal on the keypad and made the call. Callison identified himself to the satisfaction of the woman who answered the phone and then introduced Fealder. "Professor Callison has your model UZ-twenty-one. Do you keep a record of every time the alarm is armed and disabled or just when there's an entry without a disablement?"

"Well, the Callisons have an up-graded service. Unless they instruct us otherwise, which they never have, we keep records that show the time of every arming and disablement as well as every entry without a disablement. However, we only keep those records for fourteen days."

"We need all entries for last Friday night through Saturday morning. Can you read them to me and then make a certified copy that we'll pick up later?"

"Yes, it will take me a few minutes. May I call you back?"

Fealder gave the woman Callison's number and hung up.

Five minutes later, she called back. "I have the record. From six PM on, I have an arming at seven-seventeen and a disablement at ten-twenty-four followed by a rearming at eleven-thirty-five. That's it until mid-morning on Saturday when someone inside coded themselves out and the system automatically rearmed itself."

Fealder thanked her and said he would send a patrolman over to pick up her printout. He turned to Callison. "We've already confirmed that your wife was away that night. Does anyone else know how to disable that alarm? Relatives? Cleaning person?"

"No. No one else."

"And the late night rearming?"

"I read until fairly late. Then put the cat out and armed the system as I went to bed."

"Of course, this doesn't conclusively prove that you were here between ten-twenty-four and eleven-thirty-five, but it does support what you told us about when you arrived home."

They followed a more relaxed Callison to the master bedroom. They watched while he located a pair of jeans hanging on a hook in the closet. Fealder lifted them off the hook and reached into the back right pocket with a pair of tweezers. He removed two folded bingo cards with last Friday's date stamped in magenta ink. He put them into a plastic evidence bag and looked at Callison.

"We'll check with the athletic department or the boosters or whoever runs this bingo operation. If these are the real McCoy, they'll go a good way toward establishing your presence at the game. Can you describe the person who sold you the cards?"

"Well, it was a woman. She was late-middle aged, darkish hair, glasses. About medium height for a woman, I think. She was wearing a green apron or bib with large patch pockets for the cards and the money. No name tag, so far as I can remember."

"Okay. We'd better get back now. Sorry to have interfered with your class."

"I'm actually glad you did. Something you said about 'odds' made me think of the bingo and I'm really glad you thought to check with the security company!"

They let Callison out at Bracknell Hall and drove back to the Justice Center. Fealder asked, "So is he a conniving sack of shit or is he just an anxious doofus?"

"Like you said, his alibi evidence isn't conclusive – he could've bought the bingo tickets and left before the final game or he could've left the house with the system unarmed – but it's starting to ring true. His asking Scott Pradell for an alibi is bothersome, but I think Callison's become more believable."

"Yeah," agreed Fealder, "I really don't think he knew about that recording feature of the alarm system and he didn't know we'd come to his house, so I don't think he planned that to set us off the trail. Even dropping off the exams, sounded pretty credible to me, especially since he had a reserved parking place and Newton could not remember exactly when he saw him. And, if he had bought those bingo cards just to show us, I think he would've done it before now."

Berbieri said, "I'll check with Campus Security about his parking slot, just to be sure. And I'll try to find out if the numbers he punched conform with the numbers that were actually called out. "

"Good idea."

"I also want to spend some time on Plaget today," said Berbieri. "Maybe call someone in Bradley's intellectual property office and find out more about that patent your friend turned up."

"Okay. While you're doing that, I'm going to get ready for our meeting with James'"

Berbieri got on the internet to find Bradley Pharmaceuticals' home page. From there, she learned that the company was a start-up, barely six years old, was not a public corporation, was headquartered in Hillsboro, Oregon, and had yet to earn a dollar through sales of its drugs. She saw that the company had a drug in early human trials. It was Zolane, the drug that Warburton and Townsend had been testing in their clinics. She noted the name of the company's General Counsel, Marian Ashton, then shut down her computer and touched Bradley Pharmaceutical's number into her phone. Ashton's secretary tried to have her leave a message, but Berbieri insisted on getting through to the attorney. She introduced herself and quickly came to the point.

"Ms. Ashton, Norman Plaget is a biochemist at a local university. The university has a patent – on a molecule isolated by Plaget -- that has been licensed to Bradley Pharmaceuticals. May I ask you a little about that?"

"Well Bradley has over a dozen patent licenses from scientists around the country. I'll have to check the particulars. Hold for a second."

Berbieri could hear the woman keyboarding. "All right, I have the information on my screen. Yes, we have such a license. What else do you want to know?"

"Does that patent bear on the drug your company currently has in human trials at the university?"

"You said you're in the Portland Police's Homicide Unit. What is the connection to this patent?"

"You probably know by now that Professor Adam Warburton, a co-investigator on your drug trial, died under suspicious circumstances. We are doing backgrounds on a number of persons who may or may not have had meaningful connections to the deceased. One thread we're following is whether this inventor had any scientific or technical connection to Warburton. It occurred to us that one way they could have become involved with each other was through your company and its drug trials."

"As a rule, we do not give out information about the promise of or applications for any patent we have the right to use. You can understand why, given the extreme competition in the pharmaceutical business."

"I can promise you that your information will never leave my file unless it somehow becomes relevant to our investigation or to a homicide prosecution."

"That's a huge 'unless'," responded Ashton. "Please don't take offense, but I'm going to hang up and immediately place a call to the Portland Police Bureau and ask for you. I do this out of an abundance of caution. We can't be too careful about discussions involving the company's intellectual property. I hope you will understand. I should be back talking to you very soon."

Two minutes later, the police switchboard rang Berbieri's extension and connected her to Marian Ashton's incoming call. "Sorry about that. I am more comfortable now that I know you are who you said you were. I've decided to cooperate because the answer is 'no'. The patented ligand certainly could turn out to have commercial applications, but it is no part of the compound we are testing in the trials."

"I appreciate your telling me that. I also need to ask if Professor Plaget has ever been to visit your headquarters or your labs or has become acquainted with any of your staff or, -- through your company -- with Professor Warburton."

" 'No' to your first question. I'll have to inquire of the scientists working on these projects to answer the second and third questions. May I get back to you later today?"

"You may. I have voice mail in case you miss getting me directly." Berbieri gave Ashton her office number and her cell phone number.

Fealder and Berbieri had been summoned to meet with Doug James at two o'clock. They knocked and entered his office. The chief of the Homicide Unit detectives looked up unsmilingly. "So have you cracked this guy, Plaget, yet?"

"Yes and no. We have got him to admit to a very powerful motive." Fealder explained Warburton's coercion to drive Plaget to admit the plagiarism in his dissertation. "Moreover, the man has no alibi for the night in question. And, he's a judo expert."

"He's your man! Do we have enough on him to get a warrant? To go over his house and office with a fine-tooth comb?"

"I don't think we do," said Fealder.

James scowled. Berbieri said, "I contacted the General Counsel at Bradley Pharmaceuticals. She told me confidentially that Plaget's patent is not involved with the drug, Zolane, that the university and the medical school are testing in their clinics. And she just called back a couple of minutes ago to say that Plaget has not visited their facilities and no one in the company knows him. She also said that they've never arranged or suggested a meeting between Plaget and either of the two professors, Warburton and Townsend, who were directing the trial. In fact, she implied such an arranged meeting might be unethical."

"Okay, so there's no connection through the company, but Plaget was still being blackmailed by Warburton. Don't let him off the hook!"

"No, Sir. We have no intention of forgetting about him."

"Damn right! Stay on him! So what's your next move?"

" I'm hoping you'll agree to assign a couple of the other detectives, perhaps Tom and Benny, to help us start cross-checking service club memberships, these curriculum vitae things, civil court proceedings, employment records if we can get consents, even property titles for all of our suspects to see if there is any overlap or connections we may've missed."

James stared at Fealder for a moment and finally said, "All right. You can have Tom and Bennie for the rest of today and tomorrow. But move fast. That crap newspaper is still trying to make us look bad."

Tom Hokanson and Benny Schultz, the taciturn and highly reliable veteran in the unit, were both on the thirteenth floor doing paper work when Fealder and Berbieri left the Lieutenant's office. In less than half an hour, they all had begun the grind of checking the documentary backgrounds of Fealder's suspects. They ordered take-out Chinese dinners from August Moon and worked into the evening. Berbieri had been focusing on Mayfield and she suddenly stood.

"Park, I may have a connection here!" The others gathered around Fealder's cubicle as she walked over to explain her find. "The Psychology Department posts the resumes of most of its faculty and GTFs on its web site. Mayfield's shows that last year, he worked eight months in the medical school. And guess where? He worked in the Depression Clinic under Professor Townsend!"

"I'll be damned!" said Fealder. "We probably should've checked that sooner. Anybody else see anything interesting? We need to share everything that presents a possibility so we can spot any convergence. Let's bring our notes into the conference room so we can all sit."

They discovered that Callison and Plaget were both members of the American Association of University Professors, a national support group with sizable local chapters on most campuses. Hokanson reported that Herbert Gelbhorn was a member of the local Rotary Club.

"Tom, why don't you run the same kind of background on Professor Townsend and start with the Rotary Club? Let's the rest of us read residence addresses and see if we get any matches or close neighbors. Bennie, why don't you start?"

Within minutes, they discovered the only overlap in residences was that for a few months eleven years ago, the Gelbhorns and the Plagets lived in the same eighty-unit apartment complex. They were considering the significance of this when Hokanson came back. "Townsend is also a member of Portland Downtown Rotary. They have a little over three hundred members so Townsend and Gelbhorn might or might not know each other from there."

Everyone was nearly through with their back-grounding work, so they went back to their desks to finish up. Fealder felt the collective effort well worth continuing, but he kept coming back to Berbieri's new information. He realized that they had not looked at Townsend with any particular suspicion. They had found no evidence of animosity between the research partners and Townsend had seemed calm and truth-ful when they spoke with him. He rebuked himself for letting their investigation focus too tightly on the persons with admitted hostility toward Warburton. Even now they had no reason to suspect the medical school psychologist, but the new-found connection to Mayfield meant they had to give Townsend some more attention. He asked the others to approach.

"I've been thinking on what Tami found about Mayfield working for Townsend. I think we've got to bear down more on Townsend and his clinic. I also should tell you, Tom and Bennie, that we found an unfinished draft of a research report on Warburton's desk. The report concerned this drug trial that Warburton and Townsend were running. Tomorrow, I'm going to personally learn more about that experi-ment. Meanwhile, I want everyone else to background Townsend. We'll keep at the computers for another half-hour or so, and then call it a night. I want us all to go full throttle tomorrow. Be discreet and stay away from Townsend himself, but get what you can from colleagues, neighbors, and credit-card companies. Call me on my cell if you turn up anything important."

At a quarter to eight, Fealder and Berbieri were the last to leave. They walked together out to their cars. He stole a look at his partner. He saw a tired detective, but one who was already proving her worth to the Unit..

"So how do you like your first days in Homicide?" he asked.

"It's everything I hoped it would be," she replied. "Homicides are ugly events and I guess even a university can have a dark underbelly. But the work is exciting and important. I'm really glad to be breaking in with you and I'm trying not to let you down."

Fealder smiled. "No problem on that score! You …"

Berbieri tripped on a small depression in the paving of the parking lot. Fealder instinctively held her against him as she regained her balance. The instant passed. Fealder said, "See you tomorrow, Tami. Let's hope something breaks this open for us!"

13

Fealder slept poorly and got out of bed even before first light. In his waking moments between fitful interludes of sleep, he kept replaying developments in the Warburton case. He was never quite alert enough to think clearly, yet he was overly stimulated by anxiety about their lack of progress. James' heavy-handed oversight did not help either. He needed to find his groove, to design a more insightful strategy, to anticipate his unidentified adversary's next move. He felt like a batter trying to shake off a bad hitting slump.

Fealder fixed his breakfast and read The Oregonian as he ate. He went to his woodshop and, in order to pass a little time and clear his head, he sanded some of the parts of the cradle he was making for a newborn niece. At seven-twenty-five, he called Berbieri and asked her to divide the backgrounding work on Townsend among Hokanson, Schultz, and herself while he delved into what was going on in the clinical trials. By eight-thirty, he was speaking with Ryan Plumley, the Director of Clinics at the Medical School. Plumley, a stout, jowly man in his early sixties wearing an expensive suit, said he was saddened to hear of Warburton's death and asked how he could help.

"We're trying to learn all we can about what Professor Warburton was doing and about the people with whom he had close associations. So I'd like to learn more about these joint drug trials and about Professor Townsend."

"Well, as you know, we do research and offer patient care as well as train doctors and nurses. Our hospital and our various clinics and labs provide us with vehicles to carry out all three of those missions. Students can rotate through those facilities, interns can be placed there, patients can be treated, and – in certain cases – empirical data can be generated for our research. Data from the wards and the clinics, naturally, is different than data from our laboratories. The clinical data and research is more at the applied end of the spectrum and ..."

Fealder did not have the time for a general public relations primer, so he interrupted. "I pretty much understand all that already. The kinds of things I really need to know are how far along were these trials? Who had responsibility for evaluating the outcomes? Where and how was the information maintained and secured? How well did Warburton and Professor Townsend work together?"

Ryan Plumley obviously was not used to being interrupted, but he recovered gracefully. "I see. The trials are nearly over. Bradley had pushed for the minimum duration that the FDA rules would allow. I believe they have about two weeks left to go, certainly less than a month. As far as responsibility for evaluation, the two men had joint responsibility for assessing the overall outcome. Of course, each man supervised his own clinic on a day-to-day basis. In terms of who was going to draft which parts of the report, I don't know, but you can be sure each had to sign off on the entire thing before it would be submitted. The two studies were identical in duration and protocol except for two things. Warburton's group of patients was smaller simply because he had fewer staff. And Townsend's group was given a slightly higher dosage of the drug than Warburton's."

"So wouldn't that lead to two separate reports?"

"It could have, but since the two men collaborated on the proposal to Bradley and were running parallel in every other way, Bradley asked for a single report. As I understand it, the numbers would be crunched in two subsets as well as on an overall basis."

"And how did the two men pull off their collaboration?" persisted Fealder.

"Quite comfortably, so far as I know," said Plumley. "They weren't, perhaps, the two easiest persons in the world to work with, but they both had a deep interest in depression, its causes and possible cures. That commonality seemed to overcome the differences in their personalities and lifestyles."

"And the security of the data?"

"The paper records were under lock and key until the attack, and the digitized backups weren't…"

"The attack?" Fealder asked with raised eyebrows.

"Oh, you don't know about that? Well the ARF people raided our building and…"

"Whoa! Who the devil are the ARF people?"

"Sorry. They're the Animal Rights Forever fanatics. You could almost say they are sort of urban terrorists united to protect animals from alleged suffering at the hands of biological researchers. Our primate research scientists have offices in the same wing of the building as Townsend's group. In fact the two different office suites are right next door to each other. It seems the ARF group broke in through a window in the dead of night about five weeks ago. They graffitied up a wall of the office, and then crow-barred a small, locked file cabinet and stole all the files. Only trouble was, they seemed to have missed their target by one office! They got into Townsend's suite instead of the primate researchers' suite. Anyway, your police colleagues haven't yet found exactly which ARF members are the culprits and Townsend's clinic lost the hard copies of their records. Luckily, the clinicians had backed everything up on a computer that we don't think the ARF people touched."

Fealder took notes and had a nagging sense that he had heard about this somewhere before, but he could not pin it down. "So how about Professor Townsend as a person? You implied he had a different personality and lifestyle from Warburton."

"Well, I didn't know Warburton very well, but even a quick interaction with the man would tell you he was quite formal and perhaps a little rigid ... conservative... everything by the book. Ralph, on the other hand, is somewhat ambitious, moves quickly on projects, and likes to live well. He even enjoys sojourns to Las Vegas every now and then from what I hear. Don't get me wrong. He's a good academic and pulls his weight in the department. He's a bit deep and hard to get to know, but really quite an acceptable colleague."

Fealder asked Plumley if he happened to have an organization chart for the depression clinic so he could acquaint himself with how the clinic operated and how the research data was handled. The Director made a copy of the chart for him, but told Fealder that he would have to ask Townsend for the particulars of how the data was recorded and managed.

"It would also be helpful if I could study a typical report for a clinical trial program," said Fealder. "I just need to get a feel for the format and the general content."

"Well you understand there is proprietary and confidential information in these reports. The actual outcome numbers and the names of the companies and the biochemicals involved would have to be expunged first. I'll find a representative one and have that done immediately. We can have a sanitized version delivered to you this afternoon."

"That would be great. That breaking and entering that you mentioned interests me. When I finish getting more background information, I'll certainly need to meet with Professor Townsend again, but I don't want to intrude on his work today. Could you possibly take the time to show me the outside of the building ... show me where the ARF people entered?"

The Director ostentatiously glanced at his wrist-watch, sighed and said, "Yes. Follow me, Detective."

From the outside, they could see that venetian blinds had been lowered and closed against the morning sun. Plumley pointed to the window in question and excused himself. Fealder thanked him and said goodbye. Alone, he walked across a stretch of recently mown lawn and studied the shrubs and soil in the eight-foot-wide band of landscaping between the lawn and the building. Then he stood next to the window, gauging the height of its sill above grade. Finally, he looked closely at the metal framing of the window. Satisfied, he walked to his car where he jotted a few notes before returning to the Justice Center.

Fealder was half-way back to the Justice Center when it occurred to him why the breaking and enter-ing at the Medical School had tickled his subconscious. It was the scrap of paper he had found in Warburton's desk. Scribbled on the scrap was a reminder to check the police report on "the break in." Fealder had meant to see if Warburton's home or office had been burglarized, but had not yet gotten around to it. He wondered if the note could have referred instead to the incident at the Medical School.

On the thirteenth floor, Fealder detoured to the far side of the detectives' area to visit the Property Crimes Unit. He checked the unit's log and saw that an acquaintance, Sean Burkhart, had been assigned to the Medical School case. He could see Burkhart silhouetted by the morning sun as he sat at his desk next to a window. Fealder waved silently to another acquaintance as he made his way across the room. Burkhart stood when he saw Fealder approaching.

"Hey, Sean, How goes?"

"Pretty good, Park. What brings you a slumming over to Property," Burkhart asked with a grin.

Fealder explained that he was working on a death at the university and was chasing down a possible connection to the burglary at the Medical School. "So I'm told they hauled off the contents of a small file cabinet. What can you tell me about the M.O.?"

"They apparently smashed the window near the latch, then got it open and crawled in that way. They and their booty left the same way, but not before they painted up a wall."

"What'd they write?"

"Oh, 'Save the Monkeys' and 'Justice for Lab Animals' and 'ARF v. Animal Torturers' … that sort of stuff."

"While I was out there, I had a look at the window. It opens by swinging outward around a horizontal axis. Even raised to the maximum angle, I'd guess it would be pretty tight for a person to get through and to get stuff back out."

"Yeah, we thought so too. Could be done, but had to be a slender person. They'd need an outside helper too: someone to hand the stuff to and carry it to their vehicle."

"It was on the first floor, but the window was rather high off the ground. Did you see any signs that they used a ladder or something to stand on?"

"No. They probably did have to use something like that, but we found no ladder and they left no impressions in the soil. It did seem to have been smoothed over, though."

"Any dirt or shrubbery twigs on the floor?"

"No. No traces on the floor."

"Any prints?"

"Nada. We've talked to people we know are involved in ARF, but of course they deny it. They *did* say that if their group had 'somehow come into possession' of records detailing the mistreatment – that's their standing assumption – of animals, we could bet they'd have leaked the records to the press by now."

"Yeah, I suppose so," said Fealder, "but if they got the wrong data, they'd have nothing to leak."

"You've got a point there, Park."

"Did you turn up any witnesses?"

"No. It was nighttime and in the office-building part of the campus. There was nobody around."

"So your case is still open?"

"Afraid so. The Medical School's lawyer checks in with us every so often. She's concerned about the human-subjects privacy issues. So we're still hoping for a break, maybe something from an informant or a more public-spirited acquaintance of the perps, but don't hold your breath! Funny thing is, like you said, the crazies broke into the wrong office and took the wrong stuff...amateur night!"

Fealder returned to the Homicide Unit's area, as he continued to consider the implications of Warburton possibly wanting to see the police report on the Medical School burglary.

Berbieri had made discreet inquiries of the bartender at the Charthouse restaurant, a little over a mile from Townsend's home, but the man had not recognized the picture of Townsend. She got the same result at the Vista Spring Café. On a lucky guess, she found that Townsend was a member of the Multnomah Athletic Club and she was able to learn the identities of the men whose lockers were on either side of Townsend's. She had been proceeding in the hope that people sometimes were more candid about their fears or aspirations or guilt feelings with bartenders or with semi-strangers whom they met at workouts in the gym. The two locker owners knew Townsend by sight, but rarely spoke with him and had nothing to offer. It was the same with the Club's bartenders.

Across the street from Townsend's house, Berbieri found a couple in their fifties, getting ready to leave for an extended weekend at the coast. She showed her credentials and told them she wanted to fill in some background details about Professor Townsend.

"Anything you've noticed about his personality, his friends, his lifestyle, hobbies, even his professional life if you know something in that area. This kind of background would help me."

"May we ask why the police are concerned?"

"I really can't say, except that we're looking into something across town and it doesn't in any way involve this neighborhood."

"We don't know Ralph real well," said the husband. "He seems like a fast-track kind of guy. He's a psychologist I think."

"I think he's a little strange," volunteered the wife.

"Like I said, 'he's a psychologist'," said the husband with a laugh. "He has a gardener and keeps his place up … drives a nice car. Oh, yeah. He goes to Vegas every so often. A couple of times he's told me about how he had a hot time at the crap tables. And he alluded to playing at the hundred-dollar blackjack tables."

Berbieri wrote in her notebook, nodding encouragingly. "That's helpful. Anything else you can tell me?"

The wife said, "He seems to be well off. Once we were talking about the initiative that got on the ballot about confiscatory land-use regulations and he mentioned he owned some acreage east of the mountains. That's all I can think of."

"*East* of the mountains?" her husband asked. "He told me he had a cabin near Zig Zag on the way to Mt. Hood."

"He didn't say anything about that to me," she replied. "Maybe he has properties in both places."

Berbieri found no other neighbors at home and when she called Fealder, he told her to meet him back at the Justice Center.

"Tami, did you find anyone who could shed any light on Townsend?" Fealder asked.

"Not a whole lot. But there was one family across the street. The wife thought he was 'a little strange' and the man said he seemed like a 'fast track' guy. Oh, and he said Townsend liked to gamble in Las Vegas."

"That's interesting. The Director of Clinics at the med school mentioned the same thing. Said he'd heard he liked his trips to Vegas. But even more interesting was the fact that there was a break-in at the med school clinic. The thieves took a bunch of the clinic's records, seemingly by mistake. What they got were all the hard copies of the drug-trial records."

"What do you mean 'by mistake'?"

Fealder told her about the primate researchers and how their offices were right next to the offices of the depression clinic and about the ARF graffiti.

"Do you remember when I came back from Warburton's house I mentioned I had found that little note about getting the police report on the break-in? I just checked and there were no break-ins reported at Bracknell or at Warburton's clinic or at his home. Now, I think what he wanted to see was the report on the med school break-in!"

"So you have some doubts it was done by this ARF group?"

"Well, the security where the animals are kept is very high, so it might make sense that these people would find the researchers' offices a softer target. And, from the outside, the windows for the two sets of offices are identical. On the other hand, getting in and out through that window would've been very tight. You know Sean Burkhart from Property. He's handling it and he has no leads at all. Somehow, it just seems a little too coincidental to me."

"So you think someone could have gone there to sabotage the experiment by taking their data?"

"Possibly. But I'm starting to wonder about Ralph Townsend. Suppose he had some reason to fake the break-in? Sean said they checked on the whereabouts of the clinic staff and, except for two persons, everyone is married and their spouses say they were with each other all night. Of the other two, one produced a plane ticket showing he was out of the state and the other is a sixty-two year old woman who is a long-time employee and who gives all the appearances of being totally happy in her job. But Sean said they never really probed the big guy, Townsend himself!"

"How about back-up records?" Berbieri asked.

"The Director of Clinics said they had the data on computers that the supposed ARF people didn't touch. That seems odd to me. They go to all the trouble to break in and haul away fifteen pounds of documents, but don't think to bring a magnet to run over the computer?"

Fealder did not want to go through Townsend, so he asked Plumley who provided the information technology service for Townsend's clinic. He was told to see Darby Lindahl, the medical school's Associate Vice President for Information Technology. A handsome, red-haired woman in her late-thirties answered his knock. Fealder saw three operational computer monitors and keyboards as he entered Lindahl's office. Cabling and several motherboards lay on a table near the widow.

"I must warn you, Detective, I have a meeting with an Associate Dean in just over half an hour from now, but I'll be glad to talk with you until I have to leave."

"That should be plenty of time. We're investigating a possible homicide and one detail I need to understand is how you handle security for the computers that are used in the Depression Clinic."

"May I ask why that interests you?"

"I can't really discuss that right now. But what you tell me could be important."

"Hmm. Well, we have firewalls on that little network and, of course, the medical school servers have their firewalls as well. Then the clinic's computers are pass-worded for access. Exactly who and how many have access, I don't know. One of my staff, Bill Collins, is the system manager. He could tell you. The operating systems on the PCs have the usual access logging capability. I think that clinic was also doing some kind of a study for a pharmaceutical company so that data was in a subdirectory. Even fewer people had access to that information. "

"Are the computers physically secured in the room in any way?"

"As a matter of fact, the machines in the clinic's network are secured. They are cabled to the desks. We have the keys to the locks. No computers in there have ever been stolen or moved to where they shouldn't be," Lindahl answered.

"Are the passwords changed from time to time?" Fealder asked.

"We've not been as good about that as I would like. I originally argued that they should be changed every six months, but our user group was against that. I'm afraid it's been nearly two years since we required new passwords from everyone."

"Do you back-up the researchers' data off their hard drives?"

"Only if they request it. For any automatic backing-up, I would have to do it through the medical school's computing center. The clinic people have not asked and we have not made those arrangements. Of course, any clinician with approved access could do an informal back-up on a thumb drive or a CD without having us do it."

"Do you know which PC has the drug trial data on it?"

"Not from memory, but Bill Collins' records would show that."

"You probably heard that there was a break in and many of the physical records of the trial were taken. Did the burglars do any damage to that PC?"

"Not that I'm aware of, at least not directly."

"What do you mean 'not directly'?"

"Well, after the break-in, Professor Townsend seemed convinced that some virus or a back door had been placed in a couple of their computers. He asked us to sterilize them back to zero and then reload everything including a new operating system."

"Did you find anything?"

"Well he was quite insistent, so we did what he asked and really didn't bother with trying to diagnose anything or with trouble-shooting."

"Was this the usual process?"

"No. I'd have to say it was somewhat unusual, but he seemed very concerned that someone might be trying to hack into those computers. He's a smart guy and he was really worried about patient privacy. And I don't think he was too confident about our young technicians just doing a check. It was easier to humor him and zap the entire hard drives, buffers, applications, OS, data, everything."

"You mentioned data. How did you preserve that?"

"We moved all the data to discs for him. He was a little nervous about the sterilization process, so he hung around and watched my tech do it. Once the machines were totally clean -- absolutely blank -- we installed a new operating system, the necessary software and, soon after that, he reinstalled the backed-up data."

"And nothing that was on there before remains?"

"We gave it multiple passes. There should not have been even fragments left. If there were, they wouldn't be addressable or retrievable."

"Thanks for squeezing me in before your meeting, Ms. Lindahl. I know hardly anything about computer security so I appreciate your tutoring."

"Glad to help." She glanced at her handsome interlocutor and added, "Come see me again if you have more questions."

Before he left the Information Technology suite, Fealder met with Bill Collins. "Can you tell me if a man named Will or William Mayfield had access to the drug trial data?" he asked.

Collins frowned and keyboarded a command into his computer. "The name is kind of familiar. Let's see." He stared at a listing displayed on his monitor. "Oh, yeah. He worked here until about four months ago. I think, at some point, he switched from being a counselor to doing some data entry for Professor Townsend. So he had at least partial access."

"Does he still have access?"

"He shouldn't." He keyboarded another command. "Wait a minute! I guess they never got around to revoking his access when he left. And it looks as though he used the computer just last Tuesday! Yes, late in the evening. That's strange. I wonder if I should report this to Professor Townsend?"

"I'm going to ask you to hold up on that for a few days. I'll take responsibility. I think our ongoing investigation will probably clear this up and I'd rather not complicate things just now."

Fealder walked out of the clinical building and turned toward the multi-story parking garage where he had left his car. Now he was thinking that the key to his case very likely lay in the database for the Bradley Pharmaceutical drug trial.

14

Will Mayfield nervously hummed a few bars from Gershwin's "Strike Up the Band" as he left one of the last remaining public phone booths in northeast Portland. He walked in the pale spill of a streetlight back to his car. He felt that his demands would be more effectively presented in person, so the phone call was merely to set up a meeting. Choosing his words, he obliquely referred to the grave importance of what he had to discuss without getting into specifics. He needed to play his cards carefully, but he could be about to hit the jackpot.

Mayfield knew he had taken a risk to reenter the medical school clinical building the previous night, but having a set of keys made it easy to get in. The keys were a windfall. For some reason that he had never understood, the Program Director had kept an extra set in an unlocked desk drawer. Mayfield had casually helped himself to that set months ago when he had misplaced his own keys. He had honestly forgotten to hand the extra keys back when he finally found his own and the Director had not noticed they were missing. When he left the job to concentrate on his dissertation, he was asked to, and did, surrender his own keys. He remembered the borrowed set at that point, but decided not to turn them in. He could not foresee specifically why they would have value for him at the time, but one never knew when he might gain some advantage by keeping them. The previous night they had proved their usefulness. Late in the evening there were few people around and no one had seen him.

He had read about the burglary in The Oregonian, but had not thought much about it at the time. In any case, he knew the records would be backed-up on the computer. He had left the light off and worked by the glow of the monitor. There was a chance that the manager of the tiny network of four computers had changed passwords or cancelled his access privileges, but he doubted it. He had keyed in the old system password and his personal identifier. They worked! He could only guess what he might find in the general file, but first he needed to check on the notes about Nancy. He had keyboarded a third password to reach an individualized directory, and then opened Nancy's file. He had found nothing there about her accusation: nothing about their brief affair; nothing about the fall-out when he had broken it off. More astoundingly, there was only one, cursory, dated paragraph pertaining to the drug trial: "Nancy Fallows voluntarily withdrew from and discontinued her participation in the Zolane trial." The date was *before* he had ended their affair. The last days of the affair were vivid in his memory: her demands were spiraling out of control. Her mood swings were becoming worse. She had become overly possessive and needy. He was greatly relieved to see there was no evidence of their assignations. The mysteriously truncated record had also gone some ways toward confirming his hunch.

He had returned to the more general file and found a status matrix. Then he had seen proof of what he had suspected. Five "Withdrawals" were listed in the matrix. Each person was listed only by number in the matrix, but he thought five was three too many. He then checked other entries in a column headed "Trial Outcomes" and saw benign descriptions with only modest variation. He had printed a copy of the matrix and then he hastily downloaded another copy onto a thumb drive. He had been inside for almost twenty minutes and did not want to push his luck. He shut down the computer and left the building. Arriving at his home, Mayfield had hidden the thumb drive behind a loose board in his garage.

The man he telephoned had agreed to meet, but said he was already in a chess game with a neighbor and could not get free for at least another forty-five minutes. He had given Mayfield directions to a small cabin close to the Salmon River and west of Mt. Hood. They were to meet there in two hours. Mayfield was uneasy about the venue. He would have greatly preferred to meet closer and sooner, but he understood that the delicate nature of their negotiation called for the utmost privacy.

Mayfield turned off Highway 26 onto a narrow, paved road. He could only see a dim suggestion of the moon behind clouds. He checked his watch. It was a little after nine. His headlights picked out numerous homes and cabins in the first half mile. He occasionally glimpsed an undulating whiteness to his right that he knew must be a rapid in the river. He drove on and the cabins quickly gave way to forest. He watched the odometer and shortly past the distance he had been given, he saw the graveled private road. After driving a hundred feet down that road, Mayfield saw a small cabin. It was fashioned of weathered logs with a stone chimney. A light showed through the curtained windows. A set of bleached antlers over the door told him he had found the right place. He notched up his determination and knocked on the sturdy door.

Fealder slept in until a little after eight and busied himself in his kitchen making a mushroom-and-ham omelet. Over his breakfast, his thoughts drifted to Mayfield. There was something about Mayfield's demeanor that Fealder mistrusted. He planned to go unannounced to Mayfield's office and lean on him. He would confront him with his lie about not having a balcony key. He knew that Mayfield might claim he had simply forgotten about a key that he never had the need to use, but it would be worthwhile just to keep him on edge. He knew that an unnerved suspect would sometimes let slip incriminating facts.

It was ten-thirty when Fealder knocked on Mayfield's office door in Bracknell Hall, but got no answer. He looked at a card on the bulletin board beside the door and saw that he had come at a time when Mayfield normally held office hours. Fealder went to the departmental office on the seventh floor and asked the secretary if she had seen Mayfield.

"No, I certainly haven't! He did not show up to teach his section this morning. We must have had two dozen students coming in to ask about it. If he had called in sick, I could've posted a notice. Professor Mortinsen is not at all pleased!"

"Well, thanks, I'll try him later."

Fealder called Mayfield's home number on his cell phone as he left the building. A woman, presumably Mayfield's live-in girlfriend, Deralyn, answered the phone. Fealder introduced himself and asked for Mayfield.

"Will isn't here! He didn't come home last night! I've called some friends and nobody has seen him. The school called earlier this morning and he hadn't made it to his section."

"Are you going to be home this morning?" Fealder asked.

"Yes. I work at Kell's Irish Pub, but today I have the late shift and I don't start until four o'clock."

"Please stay there. I'm coming right out to talk with you."

Fealder turned onto the Broadway Bridge and gunned the Corvette through a yellow light as he crossed Northeast Twenty-first. Eight minutes later, he pulled up in front of Mayfield's house. Deralyn shook Fealder's hand and introduced herself. "Deralyn Jones, Detective."

"Good morning, Deralyn. You probably know I'm investigating the death of Professor Adam Warburton, a faculty member in the Psychology Department. You may also know that your friend Will is a person of interest in our investigation. There is no warrant for his arrest and my only purpose this morning was to talk with him. Anything you can tell me will be helpful."

The young woman looked at him intently before answering. "Do you think he's run away? He can be kind of a jerk at times and we've only been together since July, but I'm crazy about him. I don't know whether I should talk to you."

"We haven't accused him of anything. I personally doubt that he is trying to escape from us. That doesn't mean we're through talking to him, but if you have any idea that he's in some kind of jeopardy, it wouldn't be ratting on him to share what you know."

She looked dubious, "It isn't like him not to come home. He works late sometimes, but he always comes home. I think he was going to do something last night that had him excited. Nervous, you know ... wound up. He was out late the night before too and same thing.... he was tense, on edge."

"Was he using?"

"No! Will didn't do drugs. Well, maybe he smoked a little hash occasionally, but no, it wasn't a drug thing."

"Did he talk to you about whatever he was doing those nights?"

"No. The first night when he left, I just thought he was going to his office. When he came back, I could sort of tell he'd been somewhere else. I was pretty sleepy, but I think I asked him and he just said he had run into an old friend."

"And last night?"

"I did ask him what was going on as he left the house. He just said he had to help a friend with a re-search project. I thought it was strange that he didn't name the friend since I know most of his friends." She hesitated. "He did say 'Relax, Deralyn, our ship is about to come in'."

"Did he explain that?"

"No, he just kind of said it as he went out the door."

"And he didn't say where he was going to help this friend?"

"No, he didn't say."

"May I look around the house? Try to see if he had any papers or anything that could help us figure out where he went?"

"I don't think I should let you do that. You don't have a search warrant. I don't believe Will had anything to do with Professor Warburton's death, but I'm not going to have you search our place without his permission."

Fealder's instinct told him a search might have turned up something helpful, but she was within her rights and he had no warrant. He thanked her for talking to him and started out the door, then turned back.

"He took his car?"

"Yes."

"Can you describe it? And give me the license number?"

"You really don't think he's running from the police?"

"Look, I can't know what's in his mind, but no, I don't think we've given him any cause to flee."

"Okay. I'm worried enough about him to tell you. It's a 2008 white Toyota Celica. YBT 499, I think, or maybe it's 449. I know it has a repeating number."

"We will work with you on this, Deralyn. In the meantime, here's my card. If you think of anything else that might indicate where he was headed, give me a call."

As soon as he left, Fealder called in an all-points bulletin on the Toyota with a description of Mayfield.

He instructed that if Mayfield was in or near the car, the officers were to notify Fealder immediately, but not try to apprehend the young man.

It was late morning when Fealder's phone trilled. It was Deralyn Jones.

"Detective Fealder, I'm sorry to call you so soon. I'm just very anxious. Do you know anything more about where Will could be?"

"No, Deralyn. Nothing so far, but, believe me, we're working on it."

"Thanks. I keep hoping he'll call me. This morning, you asked me about anything that seemed different about Will in the last few days. I did think of one other thing since we talked. Will asked to borrow my library card. He doesn't have one for the city library. I gave it to him and asked him what book he wanted. He wouldn't tell me, but the next day I dropped by his office and saw a book on his table that I could tell came from the city library."

"Could you see the title?"

"It was something like 'The Keys to Offshore Banking' or 'The Secrets of Offshore Banks'. He's never asked me for my card before. I know it may be nothing, but it was funny that he didn't want to tell me about it."

Fealder told her to keep thinking about things Mayfield said or did in the last few days and added that he appreciated her telling him about the book. He hung up and told Berbieri what Jones had said.

"Offshore banking! They're probably on food stamps! But he did make that remark about their 'ship coming in'."

"Do you suppose he was squeezing someone? Either he had something to sell or he might've been attempting blackmail. He used to work in the clinic, so he would know they backed up their data on the computer. If the records would be valuable to one of Bradley's competitors, there might be a market."

"And if he was going to blackmail someone, who? Plaget?"

"Maybe. Perhaps when he was in his office Friday night, he saw Plaget in the building. But what if it was Townsend he was going to blackmail? What if there was some dark secret in the clinic? Maybe they had to destroy some of the records, but Mayfield knew it from when he worked there?"

"Or maybe Mayfield killed Warburton at someone else's bidding and now he was going to get paid?" suggested Berbieri.

Fealder wadded up a sheet of paper and tossed it absently from hand to hand. "You know, I don't think our theory about selling data to a competitor plays out too well. If some rival company paid him to steal it, he would've been paid long before now. The burglary was almost six weeks ago. And if someone wanted to pay to have Warburton killed, they would use a contract killer and it likely would not have gone down in Bracknell Hall."

"Unless they wanted it to look like a jumper's suicide," reminded Berbieri.

"Yeah, possibly. In any case, I have an idea that that break-in and Mayfield's sudden interest in riches are somehow connected. And that makes it less likely Plaget was Mayfield's target unless Plaget is tied to that clinic in some way we haven't yet uncovered."

Fealder had an uneasy feeling that whatever adventure Mayfield had embarked on may have gone amiss.

15

Berbieri met with the head of the Vice Squad, Roscoe Verneau, as soon as he returned from lunch. She explained that they were interested in whether one of their persons of interest had run up debts in Las Vegas casinos and asked if he had contacts in that city. Verneau, a muscular, balding man in his forties, looked at Berbieri appraisingly.

"Police contacts I have, yes. But whether they can get you information from the money guys in the casinos ... that's a different story. You know they're tight-lipped about their credit lines and losses... stuff like that. And, if your guy was a high-roller, they protect their clients' privacy too."

"I appreciate that, Sir. Our problem is that we have more and more isolated facts pointing to this person, but so far we can't quite connect the dots. We've reason to believe he is a fairly frequent gambler. It could be very helpful to know if he's having a cash problem and if it had arisen out of his gambling."

"I'll call my friend in Las Vegas Vice. The casinos like to stay on the good side of Vice and maybe they'd be willing to talk to you if my friend in Vegas leans on 'em a little bit. I'll let you know later this afternoon what they can do for you."

It was five minutes before three when Berbieri's phone chirped. "This is Matt Abelson speaking. I head the Vice Squad for Las Vegas P.D. Roscoe called me and said it was important for you to get some gambling history on a person of interest in a homicide case."

"Yes, thanks for calling back. We'd be most grateful for whatever help you can give us to set up a talk with the financial people at the casinos."

"Roscoe assured me that no part of your case appears to trail back to Nevada," said Abelson. "I called some of the major facilities down here. Three of them weren't willing to be helpful; said the connection sounded too tenuous to jeopardize customer relations. But two of the places were at least willing to hear you out. Here're their numbers and the names of the people to ask for. Good luck!"

Berbieri nibbled on a Danish and called the first number Abelson had given her. She learned that Townsend had not gambled in that casino over the last three years. The credit manager to whom she was speaking did say he remembered Townsend's name on a high-risk list he had seen recently. He was not willing to elaborate on the source or distribution of the list.

Berbieri tried the second number and introduced herself. "We have a homicide and another person with ties to the first victim who is presently missing. Both of them had connections to a person of interest to us. We know this person makes several trips a year to gamble in Las Vegas. It is important to our investigation to know whether this person is having a gambling-debt problem; whether he has or, in the fairly recent past, has had a need for money. If you can give us any information about his credit standing and his activity at your casino, that could be very helpful to us."

"Can't you subpoena his tax returns? Or his bank statements?"

"Eventually, we may have to do just that, but right now we need to gather background information quickly. If what you can tell us is of no relevance to our investigation, the details won't even be entered in our case file. Even if it were of interest, it would remain confidential within our homicide unit and the district attorney's office."

There was a long silence. "Give me the name. Maybe, off the record, I can at least tell you some general stuff."

"Ralph Townsend. From here, Portland."

Berbieri could hear the man clear his throat. "Just a second. I'll bring the name up on my screen."

Berbieri waited for a full minute. "OK," he said. "Your Mr. Townsend has played here. He's been a good customer. He wins, he loses. We give him a nice line. But six months ago, he had a pretty bad streak. We were a little sloppy monitoring his losses. And now I remember hearing that he ran up a good tab at another place here in town, too. It was a rather large outstanding. It got a little tense, shall we say. Then, about seven, eight weeks later, he got current... all in one fell swoop. All paid off. He's had no action with us since."

"You said 'rather large'. Are we talking six figures?"

"Listen, Detective, I'm doing a favor for Matt down here. I'm giving you some information you say you need. It's completely off the record. You can make your own assumptions. That's all you're going to get."

"Okay, I understand," said Berbieri. "Thanks for your help."

As Berbieri ended the call, she saw Fealder enter the room. Hokanson saw him also and moved over to join him at his desk. Hokanson said a few words and then Fealder motioned to Berbieri to join them in the conference room.

Fealder began once they were seated. "Let's catch each other up. My talking with the computer security people at the med school turned up two new facts. First, Townsend ordered everything on the computer with the trial data deleted. And I mean deleted with a capital D. They were sterilized! He even wanted the operating systems scrubbed off the machines. They took the trial data off on a CD and he reloaded it later."

"That sounds kind of radical. What justification did he offer?" asked Hokanson.

"He told the techies he thought somebody – I guess the ARF people – put a back door into the system."

"Sounds pretty sophisticated if it's true," said Berbieri. "Did the techies find a back door?"

"No," said Fealder. "They didn't really look. Sounds like Townsend was sort of overbearing and it was easier for them just to purge the computer rather than attempt to verify that there really was a problem. The second fact was that our friend Mayfield used their computer to access the trial data on Tuesday night before he went missing on Wednesday night."

"Could someone else have used his password?" wondered Berbieri.

"Possibly, if they knew it, but, given what Deralyn Jones told us about his coming in so late Tuesday night, I'm guessing it was him."

"And that ties in well with your theory that he was blackmailing Townsend about something. Something that could have to do with the way the trials are going."

"That's what I'm thinking too," said Fealder. "Tami, did you find out anything about this gambling habit of his?"

"Yes. Not too definitive and we can't see records, but one casino told me that Townsend had run up a big debt about six months ago and then, eight or so weeks later, paid it off all at once."

"Do we know how big?"

"No, the casino wouldn't reveal that, but the way they referred to it made me think it was pretty substantial. They half-way admitted they let his losses get out of hand. And they thought that he'd run up a big debt at another casino in Vegas as well."

"So the man likes to live well, he gets in trouble gambling, and then suddenly he has enough cash to pay off the debt. Tom, did you learn anything?"

"For the most part, not anything that would deserve our attention," replied Hokanson. "He has an average credit rating. Sometimes gets a high balance on a credit card, but always brings it back down after a few months. Seems he inherited the house he lives in from his wife and some undeveloped acreage in eastern Oregon from his mother, but not much else according to probate records. He has an account at a brokerage house. They wouldn't reveal balances, but said he had 'modest' holdings, mostly in mutual funds. And there was no 'abnormal activity' in the account during the last year, whatever they mean by that."

"So is the acreage income property?" asked Fealder.

"Thought you'd never ask," laughed Hokanson. "The real estate angle was a little more interesting. Aside from his residence and a two-acre parcel with a small cabin near Zig Zag, I found nothing else at first. I kept wondering what happened to the eastern Oregon land. It took a while checking every county over there. I finally tried the grantor indexes going back two years and found a sale in Lake County. About four-and-a-half months ago, he sold a one-hundred acre parcel for $375,000."

"Four-and-a-half months ago," said Fealder thoughtfully. "That's just about when he paid off his gambling debt."

"That seems like a lot of money for acreage in eastern Oregon," said Berbieri.

"Yes, I suppose it does," said Fealder who had no idea of the price of raw land. "Tami, would you go down to Lake County and locate the parcel from the description in Tom's research?"

"Sure. Then what?"

"Then, get a professional appraisal. For now, it doesn't have to be forensically solid. Just get a ballpark. This sale seems a little too convenient! Tom, who was the buyer?"

"A privately-held company called Magnus Farming."

Fealder could not have explained it, but he chose to have them dig a little deeper. "Tom, find out who's behind this Magnus Farming. See if you can find out who the principal shareholders are or who the owner is if it turns out to be a sole proprietorship. And see which realtor handled it and how long it had been on the market."

They gathered their notes and the meeting broke up. Fealder decided it would soon be time to talk with Ralph Townsend again.

Berbieri spent the night in Bend, a fast-growing and prosperous town in the high-desert country east of the Cascade Mountains. The town offered many golf courses and was a magnet for retirees who relocated there to enjoy the dry climate and outdoor activities ranging from golf and skiing to hiking and fly fishing. She had called ahead to retain an appraiser, Neil Higgins. He specialized in ranch land in the high desert and told her the property description indicated the land was near Wagontire, off of Highway 395. They got an early start and drove to Burns, then turned back southwest on Highway 395. Berbieri saw mile after mile of sagebrush and rocky escarpments. She had not revealed to Higgins the sale price of the land, though she knew he would certainly check that were he to do a formal appraisal.

They cleared a summit driving through a pine forest, left Harney County and descended into Lake County. Soon thereafter, they turned onto a county road heading for Christmas Valley. When they reached the vicinity of the property, they inquired about survey benchmarks at a ranch house. With that information and Higgins' GPS, they were able to find a bumpy dirt road that led to the property. Berbieri put the Explorer in four-wheel drive. The land undulated in lazy swales and hillocks toward higher ground beyond. The ground had thin brown grass overlaid with sagebrush. Framed above by the gray of a high overcast, the property appeared drab and unappealing. They saw dry soil with occasional rock outcroppings. There were no improvements on the land and no fencing. There were no trees and no creek or stream coursed through the property.

"Pretty much wasteland," commented Higgins. "You could probably graze a few head of cattle here, but it clearly isn't economic for any serious cattle operation. There's no timber. You could maybe hunt chukar here. I'm guessing any wells would have to go pretty deep. If you could irrigate, you might try wheat, but the soils are poor and the wells and pumps would very likely be expensive to drill and operate."

"So what are you telling me? Can you give me a ballpark on value per acre?"

"Miss, you might move it -- if you were patient and could wait a while for an interested buyer -- for four-fifty to five hundred an acre. But that's about it."

"So for the whole hundred acres, maybe fifty thousand?"

"If someone were buying up lots of parcels to try to consolidate title for some reason, you might get a bit more, but I'd say you'd be doing real well to realize fifty thousand. I could do my full workup with more information: a percolation test, past sales of this parcel, comparable sales in the area, a little geology on the water table, investigation of mining claims, if any, and maybe some soil chemistry. But my estimate today wouldn't be far off."

"Thanks, but I think I have enough from what you've already told me. I think we can head back now."

As she drove north from Bend, Berbieri was tempted to spend an hour fishing the Metolius River. Her fly rod, waders and flies were in the back of the Explorer, but it was a long drive back to Portland and she knew every hour counted as the tempo of their investigation increased. She needed to use her wile to catch a bigger fish: a cold-blooded killer. She put in a CD of Pink Martini selections. As she listened to "Amado Mio", her thoughts returned to Park Fealder. She had to admit, he was an attractive guy. She could visualize him scooping up a ground ball to start a double play. What else could she visualize? She refocused as the CD advanced to the next track. She needed to concentrate on the Warburton case. Berbieri tried to tell herself that she needed a breather, perhaps even a long hiatus, from being involved with a man.

Fealder had asked Plumley for a list of all the staffers in the medical school's Depression Clinic. He divided the nine employees among Schultz, Hokanson, and himself. They were able to schedule weekend meetings with six of them and on Saturday morning they began interviewing. Fealder's first interview was with a graduate student. The young woman was curious to know why the police wanted to interview her. Fealder deflected her question and asked, "Do you remember a man named Will Mayfield?"

"Yes. I believe I kind of took his place as a counselor."

Fealder recalled the computer tech, Collins, saying something about Mayfield being switched to data-entry duties. "Do you have any idea why you were brought on to take his place?"

The woman flushed a little. "Well, only rumors. Nothing I really knew about."

"What were the rumors?" Fealder persisted.

Her hands began toying with the end of her scarf. "Ah, I think there was talk that he'd become too involved with one of our women clients."

"You mean just devoting too much time with the client or was it more personal ... romantic perhaps?"

"The talk was that it was definitely romantic."

"Did these 'rumors' reach the therapists? Or reach Professor Townsend?"

"I don't know for sure. I guess I'd assume they did and that was what led to the reassignment, but I'm uncomfortable making statements like that."

"Okay. Do you know anything about Mr. Mayfield's relationship with the co-PI, Professor Warburton at the University?"

"Oh," she said with a look of understanding, "The man who fell off the building?"

Fealder thought her choice of a verb was interesting. "Yes, that man."

"No. I never met him and I never heard that Will knew him."

"And how about Professor Townsend and Professor Warburton? Any sense of how they interacted? How they got along?"

"Well, we all knew that the two clinics were carrying out a drug trial and that the two clinical directors were working together. Other than that, I don't know anything about how the two men got along or interacted."

"Alright. You mentioned the drug trial. Can you tell me anything about that? Were the protocols adhered to? Was it progressing smoothly? Were there any difficulties or problems?"

"Please understand that I was just an intern counselor. I interacted and helped the clients directly, but wasn't involved in the research part of it. I did check with them to be sure they were taking their meds, but I didn't even dispense the meds."

"Okay, accepting that the research was beyond your direct responsibility, did you sense any problems or concerns?"

"Well, you may've heard the ARF people broke in and took the research data. That certainly caused a lot of consternation! I guess they had backed up the data, but between the proprietary information of the research sponsor and the privacy concerns for the clients, I know it was unsettling."

"Yes, we have heard about that incident. Everything else appear normal to you?"

"Sure. I guess so. I mean it was a real tough period for the clinic with the suicides and all, but you have to do your best with what you have to work with." She paused with a dismayed look. "I hope that didn't sound callous. What I meant was: the people here are very good at what they do, but we're all taught that you can't be omniscient. You can't blame yourself for unforeseeable developments, especially when your clients are, by definition, persons working through personal problems."

Fealder had stopped in his note taking, but let her finish her remarks. "You said 'the suicides'. What exactly were you referring to?"

"Well, three of our patients took their own lives. It was awful, and of course it was terribly discouraging for us on the staff."

"Were those persons in the drug trial?"

"Of the eighty-five or so patients the clinic can handle, I think all but four or five had agreed to be in the trial. So I think the answer is 'yes', but again, I wasn't involved in that aspect."

"You used the word 'unforeseeable' talking about those deaths. What did you mean by that?"

"We know that clinically depressed people have a slightly higher risk than the overall population of taking their own lives. But my understanding is that the differential in the risk is quite small. These persons are not, after all, psychotic. Well, I suppose we might discover that a very few *were* psychotic, but such people would usually be screened out and referred to a different clinic. So yes, that percentage of suicides was abnormally high. Surprisingly abnormal, I'd think."

"Did you counsel any of the persons who subsequently took their own lives?"

The young woman's lower lip quivered. "Yes. Two of them."

"You said earlier that one of your duties was to check that the patients were taking their meds even if you didn't know whether what they were getting was a placebo or the drug in the trial. Had the clinicians by any chance stopped the 'meds' for those two?"

"No, but sometimes a person took more than one pill. That would be because, regardless of the trial, they were ongoing patients that we were treating for depression."

"So you mean some of the patients might have continued taking medication that was not part of the trial?"

"Yes. Mostly we rely on non-drug therapy, but some people also require a pharmaceutical approach."

"But wouldn't doubling up on the drugs compromise the trial data?"

"I see your point. Such people might have been screened out from participating in the trial, but that's beyond my pay grade."

"Understood. Let's get back to the two suicides that you dealt with."

"I can't remember if those two kept taking the same number of pills or not, but I know they kept taking something."

The second employee that Fealder interviewed had joined the staff quite recently and did not know Mayfield or anything about him. He too was not directly involved in the drug research. He did not volunteer anything about the suicides, but when Fealder raised the subject, he acknowledged those incidents.

"So did it seem out of the ordinary to have several suicides?" Fealder questioned.

"Yes. I don't have a lot of experience working with the depressed, but it certainly did seem unusual to me."

"Do you know if the persons who committed suicide were taking the drug, Zolane, which was the subject of the trial?"

"No. I do not know if any of those patients were or were not in the group taking the drug. But I know I felt uncomfortable that the trial kept going after the second death."

"Did you voice that discomfort to anyone?"

The man frowned and looked down. "No," he said softly. "I mentioned it in a conversation with one of the therapists just a couple of weeks ago, but that was late in the day and the trial is almost finished by now. As I said, I've done relatively little work with depressed folks and I guess I was willing to follow the lead of those who had this specialized experience."

Fealder returned, energized, to the thirteenth floor as he ran through many of the possible scenarios in his mind. He saw that he had a voice-mail message from Berbieri. She told him of the relatively low price the appraiser had estimated for the land sold by Townsend. Fealder reflected on the additional facts they had learned in the last twenty-four hours. He felt sure Townsend had been aware of Mayfield's ethical lapse. And Mayfield had learned something from the database that probably caused him to blackmail Townsend. So, what if they each had the other in a dangerously compromising position? Would Townsend have felt threatened enough to kill Mayfield? He would, Fealder thought, if Mayfield could tie him to Warburton's murder. And what of the extraordinary number of suicides? Could that trail lead to Bradley Pharmaceuticals? And the seeming land fraud? Was Townsend bent in everything he did? Did the sale of acreage tie into the murder investigation? They weren't quite there yet, but Fealder felt that the pieces of their puzzle were starting to fall into place.

16

Tom Hokanson returned to the thirteenth floor shortly after noon and immediately joined Fealder in his cubicle.

"You look as though you have something, Tom."

"Park, I've called every realtor and escrow agent I could track down in Lake County and in Burns, Bend and Klamath Falls. *Nobody* has any record of handling this sale. The County Recorder thought she remembered that some lawyer handled the recording, but she can't find the man's name anywhere in the file."

"So maybe Magnus had an option on the property? Or it was sold to a friend who owns Magnus so Townsend didn't need to advertise? Were you able to find out who's behind Magnus Farming?"

"Yes. A man named James Kellogg. His address is in West Linn. I haven't had time to find out what he does."

"Nice work, Tom. Keep at it and we'll see where it goes."

Fealder treated himself to lunch at Veritable Quandary and, afterwards, took a walk along the river on the pedestrian path in the Tom McCall Waterfront Park. He had found that a solo walk or even time in his woodshop helped him see things more clearly when working on cases that seemed to have stalled. A breeze made him turn up the collar of his jacket, despite a clear sky and the late-September sunshine. The leaves of the trees in the greenbelt were already beginning to turn from green to bright orange. A man on roller blades swept by him on the left and an old lady sat on a bench feeding pigeons to his right.

Fealder decided to question Townsend at his home. He could bring him down to the Department's interrogation room, but that would probably lead to Townsend insisting that a lawyer be present. Townsend might refuse to talk further with Fealder or he could be away for the weekend, but it was time to put some hard questions to the suave clinician. Fealder was banking on the fact that Townsend may not have realized that the focus of their investigation had shifted to him and would still want to appear to be comfortable and cooperative. He also made a mental note to have Schultz talk to the police computer expert, Quigley, about "sterilizing" hard drives: when was that necessary and what were its implications? He wondered how they could get information on the poor souls who committed suicide. There were sure to be obstacles by way of record privacy laws and perhaps even privileged communications to the therapists. Nearing the end of his walk, Fealder concluded that it was time they met with someone from the District Attorney's office. He paused for a moment to look out over the Willamette River. He saw the Steel Bridge rising to allow a tall-masted yawl to pass underneath. Restored by his stroll and the peaceful routine of the waterfront, Fealder turned his steps toward the Justice Center.

Hokanson stood at his desk and beckoned to Fealder as he strode out of the elevator.

"Hey, Tom. Did you discover anything about this Kellogg guy?"

"That I did. You ready for this? He's the co-founder and Chief Financial Officer of Bradley Pharmaceuticals!"

"No shit!"

"The gospel truth, Park. *And* Magnus Farming was formed earlier this year, just weeks before it bought the land from Townsend. *And* it appears that its only asset was briefly cash and now its only asset is probably just the acreage. My contact at the bank was very reluctant to go beyond generalities without a subpoena for their records, so I don't have any precise figures on the cash in and out. In any case, the corporation looks like a front for whatever Kellogg and Townsend were up to."

Fealder's brain was racing. "Tom, Tami says Bradley is not a public company, but we need to know how many shares this Kellogg owns and if he has any stock options. Try my friend Mike Dobson at Evergreen Partners. They're a venture capital firm and, if we get lucky, they might be funding Bradley and could give us that kind of information. Even if they aren't backing Bradley, they may be able to tell you who is."

Fealder felt the same kind of elation he used to feel on the infield when he leaped to catch a hard line drive with one out and the runner on second most of the way down to third. He thought he had the makings for a nice double play.

"I'm on it!" said Hokanson with a grin as Fealder made his way to his own desk.

Fealder was making notes in preparation for their interview with Townsend when his phone sounded.

"Fealder."

"Detective Fealder, this is Deputy Rawlings with the Clackamas County Sheriff's Office. I just called in to OSP on the all-points bulletin on that Toyota Celica. They said it was your case and I should call you directly."

"You found the vehicle?" Fealder interrupted.

"Well, some guys scouting the terrain for deer season found it. They reported it to us. There are no plates on it, but the VIN's the same as the car you're looking for. Do you want it towed?"

"Where is it now?"

"It's still where these guys found it … just off an old logging road near Zig Zag."

"OK. Don't let anyone touch it. It's a possible crime scene. I'll send our criminalists out there ASAP. Did you get the names of the hunters who found it?"

The deputy gave his own cellphone number and read the hunter's names, phone numbers and addresses. He assured Fealder he would secure the site and coordinate with Fealder's forensic people as to the exact location. Fealder thanked him and immediately punched the number for Criminalistics. He told Delikoff of the latest development and gave him the Deputy's cell number.

"Andy, the deputy said there were no plates on the car. I figure they were taken off to make immediate identification a little more difficult. Either whoever drove the car there forgot about the VIN number or else he didn't have the equipment to grind it off. In any case, there's a chance he chucked the plates some-place very close. Could your guys do at least a quick search, say fifty feet around the car? And maybe even bring a metal detector in case he tried to bury them?

"You don't ask for much on a nice sunny weekend with the Beavers having a home football game, do you, Park," said Delikoff with a chuckle. "Sure, we'll make a pass and see if we can find 'em."

Hokanson had mentioned that Townsend owned a cabin near Zig Zag. Fealder now feared more than ever that Townsend had killed Mayfield. Fealder was still planning the Townsend interview when Schultz sat down across from him. Fealder looked into the dark eyes of the older man and reflected that he was fortunate to have a colleague like Schultz who rarely grumbled and was always willing to help.

"Park, I talked with Quigley about the computers. He said normally you wouldn't do this 'sterilization' thing unless you had taken the computer in a trade-in and were going to recondition it and resell it. Maybe also if it was so old and out-of-date or corrupted that it needed a new operating system."

"Did you mention this 'back door' thing that Townsend was ostensibly worried about?"

"I did. Quigley said any half-way good techie could find and eliminate cookies and spy-ware and back doors with the great diagnostic and scrubbing software they have now days. He didn't seem to think a modern PC with decent tech support would need sterilizing."

"So did Quigley have any ideas about why Townsend would want it done?"

"He thought the guy might've panicked at the thought that somebody could look at their data and just wanted the most drastic protection he, as a novice, could think of. But Quigley also said if a person wanted to wipe out the access log in the operating system and didn't know how to do it himself, he might want to have the machine sterilized."

"Thanks, Bennie. Later on, we may have to talk to Quigley again, but that gives me an interesting idea to chew on."

So why, Fealder wondered, would Townsend want to erase the access log? If Kellogg was paying him to jigger the trial outcome, he might have had to enter the database and improve some results or back out some results – like suicides – and he wouldn't have wanted to leave any "footprints". Damn, he wished Collins had looked for the alleged problem instead of just giving Townsend what he had asked for. Fealder ceased his musings when Hokanson approached.

"We got lucky, Park. Your friend Dobson said Evergreen Partners *was* involved with Bradley Pharmaceuticals. They did the mezzanine financing. He said, off the record, that Kellogg owns eleven percent of the outstanding shares. He owned an even higher percentage before the dilution when Evergreen bought in. Kellogg also has options for approximately one-hundred-and-forty-five-thousand more shares. "*And,*" Hokanson added with his typical relish, "if the drug trial goes well, Dobson said the company will very likely be bought out by a major pharmaceutical manufacturer. They've already entered into some preliminary discussions. He wouldn't name the company, but he said it was a serious player."

While Fealder was digesting the news from Hokanson's inquiry, Berbieri walked into the room. She nodded and smiled at him as she hung up her coat and laid her handbag and notebook on her desk. Fealder liked the smile, the eye contact. It seemed to him that there was something special about that look; that maybe it was meant just for him. She came to his cubicle and debriefed Fealder on her discussion with the appraiser and her own lay assessment of the property. Fealder brought her up to date on the suicides and the true identity of the buyer of Townsend's land. They reviewed Fealder's notes for the Townsend interview and agreed that dinner would have to wait. They were on their way to confront their prime suspect.

Fealder was reaching for his jacket when his phone rang. It was James, who told Fealder to come to his office right away. Surprised that James was in the office on a Saturday, Fealder said Berbieri was with him and asked if she should come as well. James said Berbieri would have to wait at her desk and that it would not take long. Fealder hurried through James' door and was reaching to pull up a chair when James spoke.

"Have you got enough on Plaget for the D.A. to go to a grand jury?"

Fealder suspected the question was rhetorical since James knew he would have reported progress of that magnitude. "No, we do not. We've had to concentrate on Warburton's co-researcher, Townsend. As a matter of fact, we turned up…"

"You're going in circles, Fealder! I called you in to tell you that you're running in slow motion on this one. I want an arrest. I'm even thinking of transferring the lead to Nabors. We have a killing in Northeast, probably a drug-based situation. Maybe I'll have you and Berbinni help out …"

"Sir, you can't do that. We *are* making progress! The new evidence we're seeing points strongly to

Townsend. We were on our way to talk to him when you called! Let me tell you what we've turned up yesterday and this morning."

James looked dubious and uneasy at the same time. "Fine. Fill me in."

Fealder reprised all they had learned and tried to convince James that the facts were pointing more and more unambiguously to Townsend.

"Look. You have no smoking gun against this guy Townsend. Maybe he, too, might have a strong motive, but you can't put him in the building the night Warburton was killed. You don't even know if this guy Mayfield is dead, let alone that he was offed by Townsend. Maybe Townsend made a killing on a land deal that won't pass the smell test, but that doesn't mean he was the doer in the Warburton case."

"But we're close, really close! We need to put the screws on Townsend! We need the time to do it right!"

Fealder was damned if he would outright beg James to let him keep the case, but he believed James was wrong about Plaget. Fealder wanted this case badly, almost desperately. It was not just to validate his good record in his second career. It was this man Townsend. In addition to probably being a murderer, he was a man who was so without a conscience that he had allowed the drug trial to continue after the first two deaths, risking the very lives of the other subjects. And there was Berbieri. His nascent personal feelings aside, she had done extremely well and deserved to be kept on the case. James' thick-headed vindictiveness and his decision to bring Nabors in, made him want to grab his lieutenant by the lapels and launch him into the nearest wall. But Fealder knew he could not lose his cool and succumb to that temptation. He leaned forward and locked his gaze on James as he awaited the man's response.

"Okay, Fealder. Here's how I'm going to do it. Nabors has gone to the coast this weekend and won't be back until mid-day Monday. Keep going and try to wrap this up. Next week, I'll see how it's going. If you're getting somewhere, I'll have Nabors help with the narcotics killing."

Fealder stood and turned to go. "We'll keep you informed, Lieutenant." He thought it typical of James' indifference toward the detectives under him that the man had not even managed to learn how to pronounce the name of the newest member of his squad.

Fealder and Berbieri used an unmarked police sedan and, as they drove, Fealder told her what had transpired in James' office.

"So he gave us less than a week to wrap up the entire case. What a butt-head!"

"So true, Tami. Let's nail Townsend down good and tight. Pull out the stops!"

Fealder parked the sedan at the curb, two doors down from Townsend's house. He rang the doorbell and they waited. There was no answer, so Fealder rang again. They heard footsteps as they stepped off the porch and turned back to face the door. Townsend's expression tensed as he recognized them, but he immediately recovered his composure.

"Good afternoon, Detectives. You're on the job, weekend and all. How can I help you?"

"May we come in?" asked Berbieri.

"Yes, of course," he said, opening the door wider and gesturing toward the living room.

They sat and Fealder placed his recorder prominently on the coffee table as he began. "Professor Townsend, we want to start by asking you about Will Mayfield."

Townsend removed his glasses and studied his visitors as he polished the lenses. "Ah, Will. Yes, he worked for a while as a counselor for us."

"Did you know that Adam Warburton used to chair Mayfield's dissertation committee?"

"I think Adam mentioned something once about a falling out they'd had. I believe he said Will had asked for a new committee. He also said the man seemed to be extremely bitter and vindictive toward him."

"And yet you hired him to work in your clinic?"

"Mayfield was already working for us by the time Adam brought it up. That kind of information doesn't show up on an employment application. Perhaps I should've inquired if Adam knew the young man, but it's a good-sized department over there and it didn't

occur to me that Adam could've been on his dissertation committee or that he had been doing research
under Adam. Besides, it sounded quite personal to
me … limited to the two of them. It certainly wasn't a
positive thing to hear, but I doubt it would have caused
us to not hire him – or, in this case, to fire him."

"Why did you remove Mayfield from his position as
a counselor?"

"I'm sure that is part of his confidential employment record, Detective, but let's say he committed
an indiscretion and I no longer wanted him in that
position."

"But you did not terminate him for this 'indiscretion'?"

"He was young and was going to need a job when
he graduated. Everyone makes a mistake or two over a
lifetime. I didn't want to jeopardize his entire career. If
someone in the future contacted me as a reference for
Will to gain a *clinician's* job, that would've been different. In such a case, I would offer details."

"Have you seen or heard from Mr. Mayfield in the
last week?"

"No, I have not. He left his employment with us at
least two months ago. Said he needed to concentrate
on finishing his dissertation."

Fealder pressed on, loading his questions with a
few more facts than he could actually prove. "Tell us
about the subjects in your clinical trials who committed suicide."

Townsend visibly straightened with astonishment. "Detective! You know I can't talk about the medical status of our patients!"

Fealder guessed that the psychologist-client privilege might still apply, but he decided to try to bluff Townsend. "But those former patients are no longer alive! Their interest in privacy has ended."

"Well, in any case, what could that possibly have to do with Adam's death?"

"I'm afraid we have to be the judge of what is relevant to Warburton's murder," said Fealder.

"Do I need a lawyer here? Are you questioning how we ran the clinic?"

Fealder did not want Townsend "lawyered up".

"You've been cooperative with us," he said. "We'd like it to stay that way. With nothing to fear, whatever you can tell us could help identify your colleague's killer."

Berbieri could see a fine sheen of perspiration on Townsend's forehead. Townsend paused with a calculating expression on his face.

"I'd have to check with the school's lawyer on that privileged information question," he replied. "It's true that, tragically, we weren't able to see, in time, the depth of the depression or the psychosis of a few of the clinic's patients. They were all among a group of persons who had voluntarily withdrawn from the trials months before their deaths. They seemed a little less social and more nervous than the rest. In any case, they were no longer willing to participate. Anyone is free to withdraw and, in any given trial, a few do drop out. My staff felt very badly when those persons took their own lives, of course. I personally reviewed the case files on each patient, but could find nothing that caused me to second-guess my staff. Suicide is never a normal event, but in the work we do, you have to accept some failures."

"So how many folks are we talking about here?"

Townsend hesitated a second or two. "There were three."

"Were there any suicides in Professor Warburton's clinic?" asked Berbieri.

"I don't believe so. Not in this trial."

"Getting back to your clinic," she continued, "and granting that suicide is not a 'normal' event, are three suicides in a group the size of yours statistically unusual? Even very rare?"

"Three is more than one would ordinarily expect. But we work in the real world, Detective. We're not talking about a classroom exercise or a demonstration in a statistics laboratory! Even if this is an aberrational group, it is the group we have in our clinic. The group we were and are trying to help."

"Your human trial for Bradley Pharmaceuticals was primarily to establish the safety of their drug, you told us," stated Fealder. "Why didn't you determine that this 'aberrational' number of suicides was related to these people using the Bradley drug?"

"As I said, Detective, these people withdrew from the study months before they took their own lives. They remained with us in the clinic, but were no longer in the experimental group. The drug would have metabolized out of their systems well before they killed themselves. Besides, I'm not even sure they all started in the half of the group that was taking the drug. Some might well have been in the control group taking a placebo."

"We'll have to look at those records," said Fealder and added, "with a subpoena if need be."

"Certainly, but as I said, I'll have to check…"

"Sure, 'with the school's lawyer'. Please do that today. We need to see those records no later than tomorrow. And we need to know who was writing the portion of your report to Bradley Pharmaceuticals covering the results of the experiment and your conclusions," said Fealder.

"I had offered to draft the 'results' section, and we were going to write the 'conclusions' section together. Of course, we each would read the other's drafts and then would agree on the final language. Is that all, Detectives? I have a dinner engage…"

"We're not quite finished, Professor," Fealder said sharply. "Tell us about your sale of acreage to James Kellogg."

"Wha… What business could that be of yours?"

"We are examining the activities and transactions of many people in the course of this investigation," said

Fealder matter-of-factly. "Tell us why you were able to sell high-desert wasteland for over seven times its actual value to a top executive at Bradley Pharmaceuticals."

"I don't know why he wanted the land so badly … maybe to develop it. Maybe he thinks there's a reservoir of oil underneath the land. Even if I knew, I don't have to let you trample on my private life. I'm not going to let you harass me! I'm asking you both to leave now."

"Tell us again where you were on the evening of a week ago Friday?" Fealder asked without making the slightest effort to stand up.

"So I'm a suspect now, is that it?" demanded Townsend.

"As I explained, we have asked many people that question," said Fealder evenly.

"I went to a movie, as I told you." He gave them the name of a new release.

"What time did you get to the theater?"

"I'm not sure. Nine-forty-five? Ten? It was the late show. It got out around quarter after midnight."

"Did you go alone?"

"Well, yes. I'm a bachelor…. Ah! You want to know if I can confirm that I was there?"

"That would be helpful," said Berbieri.

"Well, since I was alone, I can't very well …. Oh, perhaps the ticket taker would remember me. I got bumped from behind and spilled my tub of popcorn right in front of him. He was nice about it. Told the concession counter to give me a new one and he cleaned it up. It was a little embarrassing."

"So you could write out a narrative of the film for us?" Berbieri asked.

"Why on earth…" began Townsend with obvious annoyance. "Oh. So you know I really watched the movie. Alright. I'll do that."

He produced a sheet of paper from a writing desk. In under ten minutes, he had filled the page with many of the characters' names and an outline of the plot.

"There, take it!" he said handing the paper to Berbieri. "I meant it about this harassment you've put me through. I know you think you're just doing your jobs, but if this continues, you'll be dealing with my attorney!"

Townsend marched them to the front door. Fealder guided the sedan along the curving streets that led down the hill to the city center and glanced across at Berbieri. "You think there was any truth in the things he told us?"

"Very little, I'd guess. His comments on the suicides were filled with carefully chosen words: more-or-less plausible explanations and non-committal statements. These 'withdrawals' sound suspicious to me."

"They do. And they are certainly convenient for Bradley and its drug, too. Also, Townsend wouldn't give us squat about the land deal. 'Oil under the land'!" Fealder harrumphed.

"His explanation about protecting Mayfield's career sounded contrived to me," added Berbieri. "If the rumors you heard are true, Mayfield could just as well prey on female undergraduates in academia as on female patients in clinics!"

"Good point. Let's go to the theater and check out that movie schedule and the popcorn story."

"I'm with you. The spill could've been deliberate to make sure he was remembered."

"Same thought I had!" said Fealder. "And did you notice that even after clamming up towards the end of our questioning, how he was more than willing to give us that movie narrative? He seems to know the plot all right, but he could've walked out Friday night and seen the end of the movie on a later day in a different theater."

They detoured to the Justice Center to extract a digitized photo of Townsend from the Department of Motor Vehicles' drivers-license database. At the theater, Fealder told the manager they needed to speak to the male employee who was taking tickets a week ago Friday for the late-evening showings. The manager said they were in luck. The man they wanted would be showing up for his shift if they could wait another ten minutes. Soon afterwards, the manager escorted a young man to where they stood looking at movie posters mounted on the lobby wall. Fealder made introductions while Berbieri produced the photo from her purse.

"Have you seen this person recently?" she asked and handed him the picture.

"Hmm. He looks sort of familiar, but I couldn't really say."

"Think back to when you were taking tickets about a week ago." Fealder suggested.

"Uh, a week ago? Oh! That's the guy who spilled the popcorn! Yeah. I *do* remember him now. Either he was a real klutz or else he got bumped by the person behind him. Anyway, he was quite embarrassed … lost most of his tub."

"Do you remember which day it was?"

"It was a Friday night. I know that because there was a high-school football game I was interested in and as I was cleaning up this guy's mess, I heard another customer talking about the game."

"What time of day was it?"

"I'm quite sure it was the late showings. There weren't a lot of people there at the time and we always have a big crowd for the first showings after dinner on Fridays."

"So the time would've been …?" prompted Berbieri.

"There were a couple of films that started around nine-fifty, but I think all the others started at ten or a little after. So it was definitely close to ten."

They thanked the young man and returned to speak with the manager. Playing a wild card, Fealder asked, "Did anything unusual happen during the late show screenings a week ago Friday? A projector break-down or a power failure or a fight in the audience? Anything like that?"

"No. It was an uneventful night. There was nothing unusual at all."

"Can a person get out through the 'exit' door while the movie is running or would he have to use the door to the inside hallway?"

"A person could certainly get out the 'exit' door. It's a fire regulation. A person has to be able to open it from the inside while we're showing films."

"Can you tell us," Berbieri asked, "when the late shows got out?"

"Let's see," he answered, reflecting for a moment. "All of the films were over two hours that night so even the earliest ones would've run until just a few minutes before midnight."

The two homicide detectives left the theater to find the day had turned blustery and cold. In the car, Fealder told Berbieri he had prevailed upon the District Attorney to grant him an appointment late that afternoon to report on their progress and to discuss the possibility of getting subpoenas and search warrants. She laid her hand on his arm and wished him luck. Before they reached the Justice Center, Fealder and Berbieri agreed that tomorrow was the time to turn the spotlight on James Kellogg.

17

District Attorney Clayton, "Clay", Osborne was serving his third term as Multnomah county's chief prosecutor. His office had a good record of getting convictions, but he was a realist about how far his staff could push judges for search warrants and subpoenas. He was well aware that an investigation was under way regarding the Warburton death, but he had not yet assigned one of his assistant D.A.s to oversee the investigation.

"I understand you found that quite a few persons had motives to at least disadvantage the professor, if not kill him. Has anyone emerged as a prime suspect?"

Fealder summarized the reason suicide was unlikely, including the fact that Warburton had booked a European tour for the following summer. Then he quickly reviewed what they had learned about the various initial suspects. He gave a more detailed review of

Plaget's situation and then recounted what they had learned in the last forty-eight hours. "So, at this point, we're focusing heavily on this Ralph Townsend. There's a definite convergence with Warburton, Mayfield, and Townsend. The med school clinic seems to have been the scene of several strange occurrences and Townsend could be behind or connected to all of them. Then we turned up the sale of land as a device for passing money from a Bradley executive to Townsend who appears to have needed the money to pay off a king-size gambling debt. Finally, Mayfield, who was very likely trying to blackmail Townsend about the suicides and/or Warburton's murder, has disappeared. His car was found in the forest less than four miles from Townsend's cabin. If Townsend's a killer, Mayfield may be another victim."

"I can see why he's your prime suspect," said Osborne. "What are you planning to do next?"

"We'd like to search Townsend's city house and his wilderness cabin. We want to search the computer files of the drug trials and look at Kellogg's financial records. If Mayfield's significant other won't consent, we'd like a search warrant for Mayfield's house. If the university won't cooperate, we will also need a warrant to search Mayfield's office. And we'd like to start immediately, if you agree and if a judge will cooperate."

"That's quite a wish list," said Osborne. "I'll approve our attempting to get a search warrant for the computer records, but I'm not too confident we'll be successful. Besides, the med school probably has various confidentiality agreements with Bradley and that may well lead it to resist. I'm not willing to go to the mat on searching Townsend's places, just yet. Mayfield at this point sounds like a possible missing person as much as a murder suspect. And Kellogg may well be involved in some fraud involving the drug trial, but how does that get us a warrant in a homicide case?"

Fealder leaned into the District Attorney's mahogany desk and said, "How about this? By Kellogg conniving with Townsend to continue the trials and ignore or back-out evidence of the first suicide, more deaths were caused. In fact, the trials haven't quite ended and there are patients still taking the drug. There could even be further deaths!"

"I like that thinking, but we need to see what those computer files tell us first."

"But, if our theory is correct, Townsend has reconstituted those records and had the changed records reloaded onto the clinic's computer. So the records we find now will probably back up Townsend's version!"

"Townsend can't be running this large clinic by himself," responded Osborne. "How about interviewing his staff to see if they know whether the suicides had withdrawn from the study?"

"I have a couple of colleagues who are already doing that and will probably be wrapping up that process tomorrow. But – because of the experimental controls, the secrecy of who had the drug and who had the placebo – it's looking like no one besides Townsend would be able to find out which patient was getting what. And, given that it was what they call a double-blind experiment, even he is not supposed to know until the trial period is over. As we understand it, the patients continued to receive therapy – perhaps even other medication -- from the clinic regardless of whether they had withdrawn from the drug trial."

"I see. But, still, it's worthwhile finishing your interviewing of the staff."

"Absolutely," agreed Fealder. "As I said, we intend to complete that process even if we can't see the computer records. Right now, two of the staffers are out of town, but we'll contact them as soon as they return. We do know this much: one of the intern counselors told us that she worked with two of the suicides and they were still taking some kind of pills right up to the end."

Osborne checked his watch and rose from behind his desk. "I'll assign Beth Saunders to your case. Beth's very capable and I'll tell her to contact a judge tonight or tomorrow morning. That won't be real popular, but we'll try our best to get that search warrant for the computers. I'll brief Beth, but from now on you and she should be in direct contact with each other. You have a fine record, Park. Don't get impatient on this one. If he's your killer, we want to nail it down tight."

They shook hands and Fealder left grateful that the prosecutors were limbering up, but disappointed that Osborne would not step up to the plate to ask for all of the search warrants he wanted. He had not mentioned to Osborne that part of the reason for his urgency was that James was threatening to turn the investigative lead over to Nabors. He called Schultz and Hokanson on his cell phone and requested that they continue interviewing the clinic employees on Sunday. Fealder emphasized the need for them to ask questions about the suicides and to see if anyone knew whether those patients had been taking Zolane and whether they had "withdrawn" from the experimental aspect of their treatment.

James Kellogg had won a Bausch & Lomb science award as a senior in high school. He became a biology major at Duquesne University where he excelled in most of the courses. Graduate school was a different matter. Like a distance runner "hitting the wall", he suddenly found the courses much more difficult and the research requirements a lot tougher. After Kellogg struggled for three years, his advisor suggested that he take a terminal masters degree instead of continuing to try for a Ph.D. Kellogg accepted the man's advice, but promptly applied to the Business School. Two years later, he had a M.S. in molecular biology plus Masters in Business Administration.

Kellogg worked in the finance divisions of three different biotechnology companies over the years and ended up as an entrepreneur. He and a scientist-turned-business-executive, Gerry Bradley, founded Bradley Pharmaceuticals and Kellogg became the company's Chief Financial Officer. The company had careened along from cash-flow crisis to cash-flow crisis for five years. When the founders' money was nearly exhausted, they sought venture capital infusions. Evergreen Partners liked their business plan and the commercial potential of their prototype drug. Evergreen came to their rescue. Bradley Pharmaceuticals had licensed the Plaget patent from the university, but had developed the Zolane molecule internally. The potential for the Plaget patent was far from clear, but the prospects for Zolane seemed considerably better. They had been able to formulate the Zolane molecule into an ingestible medicine. Tests on mice and pigs had shown no deleterious side-effects, though tests on animals regarding its performance as an anti-depressive were nearly impossible to administer and evaluate.

If Zolane showed positive results in all three phases of human trials and received approval from the Federal Drug Administration, it could be a huge success in the market. But the years of development and the stresses of keeping the company afloat had taken a toll on Kellogg. He was eagerly looking forward to retirement. He thought of his training and career path as one long, exhausting prelude to the financial reward of owning a profitable company. Though he would never admit it to himself, he had long ago stopped thinking like a scientist. He knew he did not have the stamina or perseverance to stay in his CFO position for another decade while the company labored to gain more interim financing, to discover further new drugs, to satisfy FDA requirements, and to market what drugs they did manage to perfect. As he saw it, his only chance for wealth and an earlier retirement was for the company to be acquired by a larger corporation. He could exercise his remaining stock options and the new shares, together with his original holdings, would make him rich when the company was sold.

Almost as soon as the trials had begun, a major pharmaceutical company had made an overture to Bradley. The venture capitalists were ready to sell and his fellow founder, now the president, was confident that he could negotiate a place in the executive suite of the acquiring company. But there was one critically important obstacle to surmount. The company's only promising drug had to pass the trials and gain approval.

Kellogg had met Townsend quite by accident one weekend three years ago in Las Vegas. The two had taken a liking to each other and spent a long evening drinking single-malt Scotch and talking about applied pharmacology. Back in Portland, the two would get together for a social lunch once or twice a year. Kellog had told Townsend of his hopes for the company and how he was looking forward to a lucrative early retirement if the company were acquired. When the university and the medical school submitted their proposal to run the clinical trials for Zolane, the science staff at Bradley gave approval. Kellogg did not see the need to mention to the Board of Directors that he was a casual acquaintance of one of the Principal Investigators. The protocols were approved and the trial began at both clinics. Then, some four months ago, Townsend called Kellogg at home to tell him that one of the clinic's patients in the trial had committed suicide.

Kellogg had spent a sleepless night worrying about the implications of what Townsend had told him. He did not want to believe that the drug Bradley's scientists had worked so hard to develop and refine could be the cause of the patient's death, but he knew if that could in any way be proven, the chances of the drug's acceptance by the FDA were very slim. He anguished over that possibility for two weeks. Then Townsend suggested they meet for lunch at Higgins.

They were shown to a table in the back corner on the lower level. The wood paneling and white linens seemed to envelop them in an ambiance of warmth and gastronomic pleasure. They both ordered the special of the day. Over servings of glazed pork loin, Townsend lamented that he had suffered a terrible run of luck at the casinos and was under considerable pressure to pay off his markers. Minutes later, he casually mentioned that he could discreetly "rearrange" the data so that the death could "disappear" from the final statistics. For the right consideration, he suggested, both his and Kellogg's problems could be solved. Kellogg immediately understood that there was a way to protect the takeover deal and secure his retirement to the good life. Townsend said it would simply be a matter of disregarding an "outlier" in the sample and should not stand in the way of the development of a new drug with tremendous potential.

Their arrangement had seemed so straight-forward, so expedient at the time. They had settled on an amount and a payment mechanism. They agreed to communicate further, if necessary, by both exercising in the fitness room at the Multnomah Athletic Club at seven in the morning on Tuesdays.

Three weeks later on a Tuesday morning at the club, Townsend informed him of a second suicide. Townsend's remark that they were "in for a dime, in for a dollar" had caused Kellogg to run from the fitness room and vomit in the lavatory. Kellogg was too troubled to sleep that night and told his wife he had indigestion to explain his restlessness. One more subject in the medical school trial killed himself in the weeks that followed.

Kellogg's guilt and torment steadily increased so as to virtually incapacitate him at work. His ulcer flared up and he snapped at subordinates for no apparent reason. Sitting at home after dinner pretending to read his financial newspaper, he asked himself over and over how he could have been so greedy, so callous, to have been convinced to go along with such an evil scheme. He knew then that he could not enjoy his eventual retirement even if the bogus data resulted in the drug's approval and they sold the company. He would sometimes begin to sweat profusely as if his guilty mind were changing the metabolism of his body. A week later, at home on a Saturday evening, he saw Townsend standing in front of his house. Kellogg told his wife he felt like some fresh air and was going to take a short walk.

"Why are you here!" he asked Townsend anxiously as they walked down the road.

"I had to tell you that two homicide detectives questioned me this afternoon at my home. They know about the suicides. They know about the land in eastern Oregon. They know you're behind Magnus Farming. They will probably want to question you, too."

"Why detectives from homicide?" asked Kellogg.

"I don't know. Maybe they have to investigate suicides," answered Townsend lamely.

Kellogg swallowed three Tums from the bottle he carried in his jacket pocket. The pain in his gut crescendoed as he listened to Townsend. "What should I do? What did you tell them?" he blurted out.

"I told them just what our records will show. That those patients had all earlier withdrawn from the trial and, even if they had been in the half taking the drug, it would no longer be having any effect on them when they took their own lives."

"Did that convince them everything was all right in the conduct of the experiment?"

"Not entirely," said Townsend. "They asked if that many suicides would be extremely rare. I said the number was unusual, but with a group of depressed persons, one never knew what to expect. As for the land deal, I told them it was none of their business, but that for some reason, you really wanted that land."

"We had those aerial photos taken. I'll show them the photos and tell them I wanted the land to develop a high-desert resort and was willing to pay top dollar to acquire your parcel. I wish now that I'd hired a planner to do a rough layout of a resort development."

"A planner would have needed more than some photos. He'd at least want a topographic survey. But the detectives probably won't know that. Just be relaxed and sound enthusiastic about your hopes and it will seem convincing. But what if they ask your wife about it? Is that the sort of thing you would've planned without telling her about your hopes?"

"No, I suppose not. God! I hope they don't ask her. This is not good! Our meeting each other and getting acquainted was innocent enough. If they ask how I knew about the land, I'll just say I'd met you casually and you'd mentioned that you had raw land in the same area that interested me and one thing led to another. I wanted to follow my dream of developing a resort and you just happened to have the land I needed to get the project started."

"I suppose you can't deny that you knew I was the person administering the trial, but at least don't say we ever talked about how it was going."

"Of course not! I have to get back. I just told Nora that I was going to get a breath of air."

Kellogg tossed and turned and could not fall asleep that night. He apologized to his wife and said he would move into the guest bedroom. He took a sleeping pill and drank some hot chocolate. The next morning his wife, as was her custom, went to church without him. Kellogg sat at the computer in his den and keyboarded a short note. He kept a Smith & Wesson thirty-two caliber pistol on a small tray suspended under their bed. He climbed the stairs to their bedroom and retrieved the gun. He entered the guest bathroom and placed the barrel of the gun in his mouth. It was to be a different end to his career than he had previously imagined.

18

Pierre Richard was a French-Canadian who had emigrated to the United States and, eventually, had become a citizen. Soon after he had entered the States, he discovered baseball. Although he had been aware of the Montreal Expos as a young man in Canada, it was a stint working in St. Louis that saw him become a devoted fan of the Cardinals. He had lived in Portland for the last six years and worked as a forensic scientist for the Portland Police Bureau. Two years ago he had worked on a case handled by Parkinson Fealder. The two men got along well and they learned of each other's passion for baseball. Richard had told Fealder that he would give anything to watch the Cardinals play in the upcoming World Series. Fealder had called an old friend from his playing days who then worked in the Commissioner of Major League Baseball's office. Was there any chance they could find a decent ticket for at least one of the games in St. Louis, he had asked the friend. The friend had come through and Richard was able to buy a seat behind first base for two of the games.

The friendship between Fealder and Richard, cemented by their common interest, made it possible for Fealder to ask a favor. Fealder knew that Delikoff had put Richard in charge of the work on the Warburton case. On Saturday afternoon Fealder had asked Richard if he would work the rest of the weekend to analyze everything they found in Mayfield's car. Richard had obliged, and he joined Fealder at his desk early Sunday morning.

"Park, I've finished going over the missing man's car. It's a good-news, bad-news story."

"Thanks for getting that done on your days off, Pierre. Give me the bad news first."

"Okay. The car and most everything in it had been wiped of prints. Found some prints on the owner's manual in the glove box, but they will probably match this guy Mayfield or his girlfriend. The tires showed nothing but dirt and mud from the logging road. We got some dandruff from the headrest that might be worthwhile, but no other trace evidence. But here's the good news. I was unloading stuff from the glove box and the side pockets and putting it all aside for finger printing later. Then I saw something protruding a little from inside a folded road map. It was a scrap of paper with directions to a cabin with deer antlers over the door somewhere in the Zig Zag area. I went to the United States Geological Survey web site and printed out one of their large-scale maps for the area around Zig Zag. Then I brought up Google Earth. I wanted to see if I could trace the route. Between the directions, the USGS map, and the aerial view, I hoped to zero in on the exact location."

"Fantastic!" Fealder praised. "Did it work?"

"Yes, it did," laughed Richard. "There is a cabin there. I couldn't tell about the antlers, but it gives you something to go on. I also pulled up the County Assessor's database to see if I could get an approximate match that would show us who owned the cabin. It's not easy to relate the Assessor's parcel maps to the USGS map, but I got it down to two possible lots. And one of them is owned by this guy Townsend who's one of your persons of interest."

"Bingo! So Mayfield was heading for Townsend's cabin. Any prints on the scrap of paper?"

"Yes, we got two partials. Here are the directions," Richard said as he pushed the scrap of paper, protected inside a transparent envelope, across Fealder's desk.

"Anything else on the good-news side?"

"Possibly. Also folded up and tucked inside the map, we found a printout of a matrix of some sort. It looked like it summarized or tracked data for some kind of a human-subjects experiment in the health field. It didn't make a whole lot of sense to us. You can have it."

"Can you hang around your lab a little longer? I think I can have some prints of Will Mayfield to you in under an hour. If we can get the prints, I'll ask Tami Berbieri to bring them to you."

"No problem. I'll be here."

Fealder motioned to Berbieri to come to his desk. "Can you get hold of Deralyn Jones? If she's home, head out there and look for anything you can think of that would uniquely have Mayfield's prints on it. Just be sure she doesn't go around the house touching such things before you get there."

"I'm on my way. Should I tell her they found Mayfield's car?"

"You might as well tell her. I'm sorry that the inferences aren't good, but that should make her more willing to help us. If you two turn up something that would have his prints on it, take it to Pierre Richard on the twelfth floor. He'll be waiting for you. And Tami, one other thing: just in case we might need them, see if Deralyn has any samples of Mayfield's handwriting."

An hour later, Fealder punched in the number the District Attorney, Osborne, had given him for Beth Saunders. She had planned to go with her family to the eleven o'clock church service, but agreed to meet Fealder right away. She joined Fealder in the conference room at ten minutes before nine. Fealder had met her twice before, but had never worked directly with her on a case. She was a slender woman in her mid-thirties and was still wearing the tailored beige suit she would have worn to church. After a few minutes of polite conversation, they addressed the Warburton case.

"Clay told me you wanted to move on the search warrant for the med school computer right away. I'm afraid the judge will be reluctant to issue a warrant because of the medical-records privacy issues, but I'll give it my best shot."

"I'd settle for having the names blocked out for everyone except those who committed suicide. There shouldn't be any great privacy concerns for deceased persons and it could be helpful if we could talk to their families. But, if the judge won't go that far, the really important thing is to see if the deceased folks were taking the drug or the placebo and when, if ever, they 'withdrew' from the study."

"Those concessions will help. I'm going to try Judge Usher if he's available today. He's usually pretty reasonable with law enforcement."

"I know Clay only approved seeking a warrant for the computer records, but we've just learned something that gives us new leverage for a warrant to search Ralph Townsend's cabin up near the mountain."

"How so?"

"Another person of interest, William Mayfield, has been missing since Friday night. As Clay probably told you, we have reason to believe that Mayfield was blackmailing Townsend; most likely over the way Townsend's clinic was running the trial, but possibly over Warburton's murder as well. We had a BOLO out on Mayfield's vehicle and it was found, abandoned, off an old logging road just a few miles from Townsend's cabin. When a criminalist went over the car last night, he found a piece of paper with directions to Townsend's cabin. I immediately asked my colleague, Tom Hokanson, to drive out and confirm the location. The directions mentioned a log cabin with antlers on the outside over the front door. Tom just called in a few minutes ago. He found the place and the description matched. He had a GPS device with him so we know it's the parcel owned by Townsend."

"You're thinking Townsend may've murdered Mayfield?"

"We think it's a very real possibility."

"I can understand your theory, but the judge may have trouble accepting your logic. We start out with Professor Warburton's murder and now we sort of switch to a missing person who may've been blackmailing Townsend about something else."

"No, it's not a logical disconnect at all. The murdered man was the co-investigator with Townsend on this drug trial. Mayfield knew both men and was in his office in Bracknell Hall on the floor below Warburton's office the night Warburton was killed. Mayfield's live-in girlfriend has not heard hide nor hair of him since the night he left their house, presumably to meet Townsend."

"Could the directions have been for an earlier meeting? Say, to a picnic six months ago?"

"Right now, we couldn't prove otherwise. But, as Mayfield left, he told his girlfriend that their 'ship was about to come in'. We figure he thought he was meeting Townsend at his cabin to collect money he had demanded."

"Alright," said Saunders putting her note pad into her briefcase. "It looks as though I'll have to cancel my church plans. I'll add Townsend's cabin to our …"

Fealder's cell chirped before Saunders had finished. "Fealder," he said while keeping eye contact with Saunders. .

It was Berbieri. "I'm at Pierre Richard's desk downstairs. I found an electric toothbrush and an electric razor in the bathroom and a little daily planner on Mayfield's desk. Pierre says the prints on the directions match the prints on the stuff I brought him. And I gave him a note that Mayfield had written to Deralyn. But, listen, the real reason I called was that, on my car radio coming back from Mayfield's house, I heard the local news doing a breaking story on the suicide of a local biotech company executive. James Kellogg killed himself at his home this morning!"

"Christ on a crutch! The dominoes are starting to fall! I've got Beth Saunders here beside me. I'll fill her in. Don't even bother coming up here. Get out to Kellogg's house and size things up. If it was a suicide, see if he left a note. I'll get the criminalists over there too and we'll ask the West Linn police to declare it a crime scene, it if hasn't already been too mucked up by the family."

He turned to Beth Saunders. "My partner just heard on the news that the Bradley Pharmaceuticals executive who not long ago essentially 'gave' Townsend a very large amount of money has killed himself. His name is James Kellogg. Can you try to also get warrants for Kellogg's personal finances, his share ownership in Bradley, and his phone records at the office and at home? He's in on this somehow and we need the details!"

Saunders said, "You're thinking there was some fraud in the drug trials engineered by Kellogg and Townsend?"

"We think there's a good chance of that. We even think the 'break in' may have been Townsend's doing to get rid of the hard copies of the original records."

"If we get to the conspiracy to defraud issue, it will be a federal matter. I'll give someone at the FDA a heads up. Well, Parkinson, I'm off to see Judge Usher and a Clackamas County judge if I can snag one on a Sunday"

"Thanks, Beth!"

Berbieri took Macadam Avenue south to Lake Oswego, quiet on an Autumn Sunday. Past Lake Oswego, she turned southwest into the West Linn hills in the direction of the Oregon Golf Club. Here, "estates" enclosed with gleaming white fences on five-acre lots dotted the rolling hills. Some homes were surrounded with expansive lawns while others had green pastures where one or more horses grazed. She turned into the lengthy entrance road to the Kellogg house and saw the Medical Examiner's van in front of the brick colonial home. Stopping beside the van, she got out and walked toward one of the technicians and produced her badge.

"Is the body already loaded?"

"Yes. It's inside the van. You're Portland Homicide?"

"Right. We'll ask you for a full work-up on Mr. Kellogg. Any reason to believe it is not a suicide?"

"If Homicide's here, you must think maybe not. But for my money, it was a suicide. The powder burns and type of wound strongly suggest he stuck a pistol in his mouth. It isn't pretty. Not likely some other person could've made him do that without signs of a fight."

"Who discovered him?"

"The wife. She came home from early church. Couldn't find him downstairs, so she looked around upstairs. Found him in a guest bathroom."

"Is she inside?"

"Yes. It turns out a 'next-door' neighbor is a good friend and she's with her."

Berbieri rang the bell. The neighbor answered and Berbieri introduced herself. The woman told her that Mrs. Kellogg was too distraught to speak to anyone.

"I will respect that for the moment, though we have a forensic team on their way. But what I need to know right now is whether Mr. Kellogg left any kind of a message…. a note perhaps?"

"I don't know the answer to that. Can't this wait?"

"We are investigating at least one murder and others' lives may still be at risk. It's very important that we quickly learn everything we can about Mr. Kellogg's death to make sure it was not connected … to make sure he did, in fact, take his own life."

Berbieri knew she could be stretching the facts in view of what the technician had told her at the van, but she needed the widow's cooperation. The neighbor's eyes widened. She bit her lip as she considered what Berbieri had said.

"Wait here, please. I'll see if Nora will allow you to look around. But, as I said, she's very upset. I don't know how she'll react."

The neighbor returned looking apologetic. "There was no note. And Mrs. Kellogg is very distressed that this team of yours is coming today. She asked if they could wait a few days. You have to understand what a shock she's had. She was the one who found him and his head…. I'm sure it was terrible …"

"I'm sorry to have to say this, but the lead detective wants a forensic team here. They'll be here soon. These specialists have to at least inspect the room where … where it happened and the firearm he used and probably his home office. I'm afraid they'll have to do it right away. You'll have to tell Mrs. Kellogg that we're asking that this be declared a crime scene."

The neighbor looked stunned. She said she would tell Mrs. Kellogg and closed the door.

Berbieri used her cell phone to call Fealder before she started the engine of her car. "The Medical Examiner's man said it almost certainly was a suicide. Naturally, the wife is upset and she doesn't want anyone else inside the house. I could only talk with a friend of hers who's there to comfort her. I asked if he left a note and the wife passed word through the friend that there was no note."

"Damn! That must be especially hard on the wife, not to even know why he did it."

"Maybe he was trying to avoid anguish and scandal for his family and decided no explanation was best."

"Hmm. Scandal. I wonder if he could've left a note, but she found it and doesn't want it to see the light of day."

"That's a pretty cynical speculation, Park."

"Yeah, I suppose it is. This case is bringing out the cynic in me."

"In any case, I warned them that the criminalists were on their way."

Fealder told Berbieri that he had obtained the co-operation of the West Linn police and asked that she call the Medical Examiner and press for an immediate autopsy. Hanging up the telephone, he continued his examination of the matrix found in Mayfield's car. He believed he had deduced the meaning of the abbreviated remarks in each cell of the matrix, but, to be sure, he called Ryan Plumley. The Director agreed to meet Fealder at his office in the clinical building.

"What I think is displayed here," Fealder began, pointing to the left column, "is a code number identifying each patient.The next column has one of two numbers and probably relates to who was in the control group and who took the drug. The wide column in the middle seems to be reserved for comments on changes in presentation or physical symptoms and the dates they were observed. Then, over here," he pointed to the right half of the matrix, "it seems to show dates of therapy sessions or meetings with a counselor and then this wide column seems to be for comments on improvement or regression. And these last two columns, with only a few entries, show who dropped out and when."

"That's basically it," agreed the Director. "As I said, this is a double-blind experiment so, until the data analysis begins, the clinicians as well as the patients don't know who was taking the drug. The key to that code is held securely and, in the end, it will reveal who was taking what."

"Does this look like a matrix that Professor Townsend would have used?"

"It's a pretty standard format, so it certainly could have been. But you should ask him. I can't say for sure because I never saw their computer records or spreadsheets."

"And these five entries in the right-most columns? They would represent patients who withdrew?"

"Five? Yes, that's what's indicated. That seems a bit more than normal for a study of this size... a Phase One study."

"We know there were three suicides among the group that started the experiment. Professor Townsend told us that they all had withdrawn earlier in the study, considerably before they took their own lives. Can you give me the names of those suicides and confirm that their identity numbers match up with three of the numbers shown here as 'withdrawn'?"

"I don't think I can give you the names without a court order, but I can tell you whether the suicides – whoever they were -- are shown as withdrawn on this matrix. I'll contact Townsend or his assistant and get back to you later today. Now I have a question for you. How did you get a copy of this matrix?"

Fealder considered what he could tell Plumley. "You've been cooperative with us and I'd like to answer that question for you sometime. Right now, all I can say is that no one in law enforcement invaded the clinic or hacked into its computer system to get it."

The message light on Fealder's phone was blinking when he returned to his desk at the Justice Center. He listened to his voice mail and realized that he had narrowly missed the call. He heard Saunders telling him that she had obtained warrants for searching Townsend's property at Zig Zag, for the computer records at the clinic with names blocked out, and for Kellogg's financial information. She said they had just served the warrant on Townsend at his Portland home and that it did not appear he would attempt to have it quashed.

Fealder walked over to tell Berbieri the good news about the warrants. He used her phone to call Andy Delikoff's cell phone number. "Andy, this is Park Fealder. Sorry to mess up your Sunday, but we urgently need another forensics team to get out to a property near Zig Zag. We just got a search warrant. Can you round up a team?"

"It won't be too popular, but I'll contact Pierre and have him get a team up there."

Fealder thanked him and gave him directions. He called the Clackamas County Sheriff's Office and explained to them why he believed there may have been a homicide in the county's jurisdiction. He notified them of the impending search at the cabin near Zig Zag and suggested that they have someone present. Finally, he asked if they could bring a cadaver dog. While they were still standing at Berbieri's desk, her phone trilled. She answered and heard a woman who announced herself as Mrs. James Kellogg.

"Detective Berbieri, I'm very ashamed of myself. I'm sorry I did not allow you to come in earlier today. I really *wasn't* in a condition to see anyone at that moment, but I did hear most of what you said to my friend. I did not tell you the truth. Jim *did* leave a note. It was a terrible message and I panicked. I guess I was afraid of the embarrassment, afraid of what he'd done getting out to the media, even afraid of ruinous lawsuits against his estate…. just self-centered thinking on my part. But, since you left, I've been thinking about what you said… that there'd been a homicide … that others could still be in danger. Can you come back out here? I don't even want to trust it to a FAX machine. I'll give you the note. Even if I can somehow get my emotions straightened out after all this, I'm sure I will not want to see that message ever again!"

Berbieri had listened patiently as the woman unburdened herself. She placed her hand over the mouthpiece and whispered to Fealder that there *had* been a suicide note. Berbieri was exasperated that the woman had not told her about the note originally and would not read it over the phone or fax it. But she knew they had to obtain this new piece of evidence.

"I'll come as quickly as I can. Things are moving fast here, but I'll be there within the hour. Thank you, Mrs. Kellogg. You did the right thing."

Fealder had almost reached Zig Zag when he heard the ring tone of his cell phone. "Fealder."

"Park, it's Tami. I have the note. He did it on a word processor … probably used the computer and printer in his den."

"I'm still driving. Can you read it to me?"

"Sure. Here's what it says: 'I have let my greed cause me to do something terribly wrong. I collaborated with a co-investigator in the Zolane Phase 1 trial, Ralph Townsend, to destroy evidence that the drug may have caused some of the patients to kill themselves. No one in Bradley Pharmaceuticals but I knew of this omission. I am overwhelmed with guilt and I cannot face the humiliation of my actions being made public. My life has become a living hell. I offer my profound apologies to the families of those who died, to my partner, and most of all, to you, Nora, my loving wife.' And he signed it. Mrs. Kellogg assured me that it is his signature."

"My God. Just what we suspected. If that note is admissible, it will certainly convict Townsend of some kind of fraud and perhaps even negligent homicide. But I still want him for murder. Leave the note in our evidence safe, Tami. I have to go to the search site at Zig Zag. Would you please show James the note? Tell him that this looks like some serious research fraud and that the FDA will be in the loop. Then go home and get some rest. Keep your cell phone on, though. We'll be back at it as soon as this search is completed."

19

Fealder found three deputy sheriffs and one cadaver dog and her handler awaiting him at the cabin. He noted that Townsend had not put in an appearance. Richard and two Portland Police criminalists arrived ten minutes later. They all parked their vehicles on the county road so as not to disturb possible tire prints on the property. The simple cabin was set off by an unirrigated lawn that was only then returning to green with the first autumn showers. Behind the cabin, the ground was cleared for another twenty-five feet and covered with a carpet of fir and pine needles. At the edge of the cleared area, Fealder saw a rustic shed with cobwebs draping its window.

One of the deputies picked the lock to the cabin and the team entered. The dog was fitted with paper booties and trotted through the three rooms of the cabin, but displayed no excitement. Two criminalists, also wearing booties, gloves, and impervious, hooded suits began the careful process of collecting potential evidence. The handler led the dog back outside where Richard was making casts of several tire prints. A deputy opened the lock on the shed and the dog was led inside. She seemed slightly agitated, but Fealder saw there was nothing other than some garden tools, a chain saw, and a light-weight log splitter inside the shed.

As the dog went back outside, she moved to where fireplace wood was stacked three rows deep and three feet high against one wall of the shed. The men caught the fragrance of the split pine logs, but the dog caught something else. She immediately began to bark and paw at the wood. Her handler said, "She's found something in this woodpile."

Fealder took a picture of the shed and the stacked wood with a digital camera. "Let's start unstacking it," he said. They spread a tarpaulin on the ground so they could throw the wood on it without unduly contaminating the scene. The three deputies joined Fealder in the work. After fifteen minutes, the stacks had been reduced almost to ground level. The men were disappointed, but the dog continued to bark and seemed even more determined in her signaling.

"I think whatever she smells must be under the ground right where the stacks sat," said the handler.

"Can she smell through the earth?" Fealder asked.

"Yes and no. She probably couldn't smell something six feet down, but she can tell if a body has been dragged over the earth and she probably could find a shallow grave."

They removed the last of the wood. Fealder looked in the shed and found two shovels. Richard dusted the shovels for prints, but found none. He handed the shovels back to Fealder, who said, "Let's dig."

The criminalists had found nothing of evidential value in their search of the house. Outside, they found two tire prints that were matches for the type of tires on Mayfield's car. They loaded their equipment into the van as the men who were digging reached a depth of eighteen inches. The diggers worked in teams of two and traded off using the shovels to keep a steady pace. The soil was softer and less compacted than would be expected in undisturbed earth. That fact and the dog's excitement had kept them digging.

Suddenly one of the deputies shouted, "I've hit something!"

They all knelt down to see what the deputy had uncovered.

"It looks like woven wool, maybe a sweater. Let's dig some more, but be careful with the shovel point."

The criminalists heard the deputy's shout and hurried back to the grave site. The diggers gradually uncovered more and more of the body. The handler led the dog back to his SUV, her mission accomplished. Fealder and the deputies tugged Mayfield's body out of the grave. Fealder, on his knees, could see something sticky around the dead man's mouth. The body had already begun to decompose and he thought perhaps the sticky material was nothing more than microbes doing their work. One of the deputies called for an investigator from the Clackamas County Medical Examiner's staff and gave directions to help her find the cabin.

Fealder had a hunch that the sticky substance could have been the residue of duct tape, but he would have to ask the criminalists and the Medical Examiner to be sure. He walked into the shed and hunted for a roll of duct tape. Finding nothing, he returned to the cabin and looked through cupboards and closets. He had given up and was walking out when his eye fell on the copper wood-basket beside the fireplace. A silvery-grey surface was visible behind the top-most chunk of wood. He gingerly picked up the roll of duct tape and placed it in a sealed evidence bag. He noted the time and place of its collection on the label, and signed his name. The criminalists were screening the dirt that had covered the body and had recovered a nine-inch strip of duct tape. They told Fealder they would check it for prints.

"I'll bet the murderer wore gloves, but it's worth a try. But look what I found inside the cabin." He showed them the roll inside the transparent bag. "Have a close look at the tear boundary. I'll bet the piece you found will match up."

Fealder had intended to stay on the scene until the M.E.'s investigator arrived, but his cell phone again sounded its ring tone. It was a Federal Bureau of Investigation agent, Mark Holloway. He told Fealder he would be handling the initial investigation of possible fraud in the drug testing on behalf of the FDA and asked if they could meet as soon as possible. Fealder was determined to make preparations for the arrest of Townsend, but said he could spare Holloway fifteen minutes and would leave immediately to return to his office. Minutes later, he called Berbieri and told her what they had found. He asked her to meet them at the Justice Center.

Holloway was wearing the classic FBI dark suit and Fealder guessed him to be in his late forties. Fealder told him what little he knew about the suicides in the clinic and showed him Kellogg's suicide note. He also explained that they had a search warrant to examine the clinic's computer files and were planning to do so tomorrow.

"I'm sure the FDA will issue an immediate hold order to stop the trial," said Holloway. "And I'll be going over all the records on Zolane at Bradley Pharmaceuticals, starting in the morning."

"What can you prosecute Townsend for?" asked Fealder.

"Well, normally, these shoddy investigation cases are devilishly hard to prove. And the case law in this Circuit is not favorable either. But, in this situation, if he actually removed data on the suicides from the files or fabricated a different set of data, we should have little trouble. Bradley has lots of oversight and reporting responsibilities which it has not fulfilled due to this conspiracy. Since one of the conspirators was an officer of Bradley, we could probably fine the corporation under section 333 of Title 21 of the U.S. Code. And this Townsend guy, under the FDA regs, he's obliged to 'prepare and keep' case histories of everything pertinent to each subject in the trial."

Fealder's eyes were starting to glaze over, but Holloway, who knew his material, kept talking. "He also was supposed to immediately report to Bradley any 'alarming adverse effect' that was probably caused by the drug. And then Bradley was supposed to report to the FDA any 'adverse experience associated with the drug that is both serious and unexpected.' I suppose their lawyer will fight us over whether the suicides were 'probably caused by the drug,' but we'll add those allegations to any charges we file."

"So this section 333 is how you'll get Townsend, too?"

"We'll try it, certainly, but we're probably on more solid ground to use one of the false-statements statutes in the criminal code. That law can reach anyone who knowingly and willfully falsifies or conceals a material fact or creates a false document within the jurisdiction of a federal agency such as the FDA. He can do up to five years in the pen if we can convict him."

"Maybe so, but I hope you'll let our state courts convict and sentence him for a couple of murders first."

Fealder saw Berbieri enter the room and introduced Holloway. "Now, if you'll excuse us, we need to put the collar on one Professor Ralph Townsend. You're welcome to come with us, so long as we get first bite."

"Two murders, huh? Well, I guess we can afford to let you make the arrest. Just don't let your D.A. – Mr. Osborne isn't it? – make any plea bargains without the feds at the table."

"Thanks, I can't speak for the District Attorney – actually one of his assistants, Beth Saunders is handling it -- though I imagine they'll be willing to cooperate."

Fealder called Saunders to tell her they had found Mayfield's body at the cabin and to alert her to Holloway's appearance. She approved of their plan to arrest Townsend and said she would come along with them and confer with Holloway then. Fealder's second call was to James. He tried his level best to detail developments in a neutral, objective way, with no gloating that his strategy had worked. James listened without interruption.

"Looks as though you pulled a rabbit out of your hat, Fealder. The Chief will be glad to see an arrest. Sounds like you got him in a pretty tight box on the Mayfield death. How about the Warburton killing?"

Fealder almost chuckled audibly at the man's determination not to pay him an unqualified compliment. "Nothing new on that, though the circumstantial evidence will seem even stronger now that we can prove Townsend's a killer."

"Well, stay on it. We need that one wrapped up too. And don't forget…."

"Yes. I know. 'Don't forget Norman Plaget'."

"Exactly!"

Fealder was holding the receiver a little away from his head so Berbieri could also hear. She was rolling her eyes in disbelief when her cell phone sounded its ring tone.

"Yes? This is Detective Berbieri."

"Ms. Berbieri, this is Tony Warburton, Adam's brother."

"Oh, yes. We spoke last week."

"Right. Listen, I discovered something odd this afternoon. I don't know, but I think it could have significance for your investigation."

"Thank you for calling back. What did you discover?"

"Well, I have two cell phones. One I have just for work and I use that one constantly. I have another we keep around the house. But neither my wife nor I use it very often so we leave it turned off unless we're on a trip or something. Anyway, we had to use that phone this afternoon and the display said we had a voice-mail message. When I listened to it, it was Adam and it came into our voice mailbox late on the night he died."

Berbieri put her phone on "speaker" so Fealder could also listen. "What did he say?"

"That's just it. It didn't make any sense. He said, 'Tony, It's Adam. I'm sorry I can't make that drink with you tonight. I've got a colleague here and we're going to have to work late. We just fell behind and need to keep going. Hope you get the picture. We'll have that drink next week.'"

"But you weren't up here, were you?" asked Berbieri.

"That's exactly my point. And Adam perfectly well knew that. Then I noticed that my cell phone also displayed a prompt to receive a picture."

"Were you able to see the picture?"

"Yes. I think when Adam said 'hope you get the picture,' he wasn't being figurative. I think he was referring to this photo! It's a picture of a man. I don't recognize him, but I can see that the picture was taken in Adam's office."

"Can you describe the man?"

"He was wearing a crew neck sweater. He has graying black hair, a trim beard, and rimless glasses. He looks to be in his fifties."

"Townsend!" exclaimed Fealder. "Would you please forward the call and the image to us."

Berbieri told Tony Warburton that they now were sure that his brother had been murdered and there was good reason to believe Adam had used his camera phone to photograph his killer. She promised to get back to him and gave him Fealder's cell phone number. A minute later, Fealder opened the mixed-media attachment to the voice message forwarded by Tony Warburton.

"I'll be damned!" said Fealder. "No question, that's Townsend's picture. Somehow, he got into the building

– maybe with some coerced help from Mayfield – and probably surprised Warburton by announcing himself outside Warburton's office door. Warburton let him in, but was nervous about seeing him. Remember, he was working on the draft report for the drug trial. He may have already stumbled onto Townsend's fraud. Perhaps he had already confronted him. It would be just like Warburton to take the high ground and try to get Townsend to go back to using the correct data. Or, maybe Warburton only suspected, but had hinted to Townsend that he had questions about the data. In any case, he was moxie enough to stage the phone call, snap a picture of his possibly threatening late-night visitor, and distract Townsend long enough to transmit the photo. And his murderer never knew he'd been photographed!"

"Can we link the photo to the time of the murder?" asked Berbieri.

"We should be able to," Feadler said and fetched Warburton's cell phone from the evidence locker. Back at his desk, he checked the list of outgoing messages. "See? He transmitted the photo at 11:20 PM!"

"So much for watching a movie!" said Berbieri.

"Damn right. Tony Warburton and his late brother have just busted Townsend's alibi wide open!"

They looked over at Holloway who was standing off to one side with a bemused expression. Fealder said, "You never heard any of this. You must have been off getting a cup of coffee."

"Understood," said the FBI agent with a smile.

Fealder reflected for a moment on the late Professor Warburton. He may have been inflexible and overly righteous and even a bit of a bully. And he apparently was outspoken in questioning how broadly affirmative action was to be interpreted and applied. But in this case, by God, he had stood up for integrity and transparency in the course of testing a proposed new drug and paid for it with his life!

Fealder called James' home again, but this time got no answer. He tried James' cell phone and heard a recording telling him to leave a message. Fealder was loathe to go into detail on the carrier's voice-mail system, so he simply said there had been a further development tying their man to Warburton and that he would explain later.

Fealder looked at his watch and saw it was already five o'clock. "Right! Now let's get a tactical detail set up to make this arrest."

20

Ralph Townsend had almost always managed to get what he wanted in life. At age ten, he got his revenge for a beating from the neighborhood bully by poisoning the boy's dog. It really had not been hard. He had used some pesticide from his parents' gardening cupboard and, in the darkness of early evening, climbed a fence into the other boy's backyard. He found the dog's food dish on the backporch steps. He was back inside his own house in minutes. At twelve, he stole a baseball glove he coveted from a player on a visiting Little League team who had carelessly left it unattended for a few minutes following the game. By his middle teens, he was dating. When a rival stole the affections of a girl on whom Townsend had a crush, he planted some marijuana in the boy's locker and sent an anonymous tip to the high school principal. Townsend reveled in the boy's month-long suspension from school though he never won back the favor of the girl.

Townsend was very bright and had no trouble getting into a good university. When a dalliance with a fellow student resulted in her pregnancy, Townsend sent her packing to an abortion clinic and never looked back. He cut many classes in a required course from a professor he disdained. Unwilling to catch up at examination time, Townsend stole a copy of the multiple-choice answer key and passed the course. Greater competition and more mature personalities in graduate school made getting what he wanted more complex, but scarcely impeded Townsend. His manipulations became more subtle, but he always managed to get his desired advisor or the plum of the clinical internships. Other graduate students found him reasonably amiable so long as their goals did not conflict with his. But, if Townsend perceived someone as opposing him in any way, he bore grudges and, sooner or later, caused that person trouble.

Townsend occasionally considered why he, who cared very little for anyone else and who followed no moral code, had chosen clinical work. In more honest moments with himself, he would admit that he was quite indifferent whether his patients improved and worked out their problems or lost their abilities to cope and spiraled into ever-deeper inadequacies and personal anguish. He stayed in the field because peering into people's minds, even if they were troubled minds, and understanding how the patients succeeded or failed, triumphed or despaired, followed authority or resisted control was fascinating to him. If his intervention helped them, he certainly did not begrudge their improvement. But if he could not help, there was no empathy or remorse: he simply viewed the interaction as adding to his knowledge of human frailty and vulnerability.

Townsend's wife had died of breast cancer after they had been married for seven years. She was a child psychologist. They had met in middle age. They pursued their careers with ambition and had agreed not to raise a family. Their marriage was largely a marriage of convenience: socially comfortable and a nice accoutrement to their professional lives, but not a union that committed either partner on a deep emotional level. Their nice house on the hill overlooking downtown Portland had been in her family and, after his wife died, Townsend inherited it.

At one point, after starting his academic career, Townsend had administered the Minnesota Multi-Phasic Personality Assessment to himself. As he scored it out, he was not surprised to see high values on the sociopathic axis and indications of a risk-taking personality. He was well-schooled enough to have had suspicions of these dangerous shortcomings, but he also knew that his intelligence and self-control allowed him to function acceptably in the everyday world.

Of course, he reflected, that was before the risk-taking part led him to excesses in the Las Vegas casinos and to accepting Kellogg's money to fudge the trials. He rather liked that verb, "fudge". There was a nice, innocuous ring to it. So what, if the stronger dosage of Zolane had pushed some of those people over their psychic edge? It was certainly not the first time there had been bad side-effects from some investigational new drug. He had simply performed a little service to corporate America. The lower dosages in Warburton's clinic had looked to be quite safe. It would all be adjusted and stabilized in time, he told himself.

His thoughts stayed with Warburton. The stuffy fool had enough contact with the staffers in the medical school clinic to have heard about the suicides. Warburton had pressed him to reveal whether those patients were involved in the trial. As the number of deaths mounted and it grew closer to the time to analyze the data and prepare their report, Warburton had begun to hound him. He had tried to placate Warburton by showing him the substitute records, but the man was increasingly suspicious. Warburton insisted on at least identifying and explicitly discussing the deaths in their report, rather than simply footnoting the withdrawals without further explanation. Warburton had also been pestering him about the alleged break-in where the hard copies of the records had disappeared. He had originally thought he could succeed in his deception because Warburton would not be deeply interested in the details of what was happening at the medical school clinic. In this, he now realized, he had underestimated the man's obsessive attention to detail and his inclination to poke his nose into another person's business. He had attempted to dissuade Warburton from discussing the suicides in their report. His efforts had only made Warburton more suspicious and determined to learn why three of Townsend's patients, withdrawn from the study or not, had so unpredictably killed themselves.

A little over a week ago, he had decided to take drastic measures. He had known that if his last effort at persuasion was unsuccessful, he would have to eliminate Adam Warburton. He smiled as he reflected how carefully he had planned it. He had remembered that Warburton, since his divorce, had fallen into the habit of working late on Friday nights so as to free the rest of the weekend from academic work. He had carefully planned the incident of spilling popcorn at the theater to solidify his alibi. He had known that he could use his hold over Mayfield to get a key to enter the building. Both he and Warburton smoked and Townsend had seen that as an opportunity to get Warburton out on the balcony. He was enough stronger that he had been confident that he could surprise his victim and propel him over the balcony wall.

As he continued to think back on that night, he shuddered as he remembered the two flaws in his plan. The door to Warburton's office had automatically locked when Warburton closed it behind him as they left for their smoke break. Townsend had had no way to get back inside to retrieve the draft report and turn off the radio and the light. The balcony door, too, had presented a problem. As they left Warburton's office and approached the balcony, he realized that that door had a hydraulic closer and would probably be self-locking. He had not told Mayfield his intentions, thus the man had never mentioned anything about needing a key for the balcony door. He had not been keen on dropping to the ground from the lowest balcony and he did not want to lower the fire escape, which would negate any chance the death would be seen as a suicide. This meant that he had to leave by the balcony door to the hallway. Once inside, he could run down the stairs and exit the building before Warburton's body was discovered.

Townsend had known that he could not get Warburton's balcony key away from him and still take him by surprise. He had improvised. He had a matchbook in his pocket. As the door was closing behind them, he had unobtrusively held the matchbook against the jam, preventing the door from closing completely and locking. When he catapulted Warburton off the balcony, the man's shoe must have come off. He had noticed the shoe just before he left and he had to lift it with a ball point pen as he flung it over the balcony wall.

And then there was that brazen fool, Mayfield. Townsend's thoughts reprised their last meeting, with every detail of that fateful night etched indelibly in his mind. He had stalled Mayfield with his story of a chess game to give himself time to get to the cabin first.

When he opened the door, Mayfield had called him, for the first time, Ralph instead of Professor Townsend. At that instant, he knew his instinct was right. Mayfield was trying to get out from under his dominance, perhaps even thinking of blackmailing him. He had been willing to see how Mayfield played it, but he was determined to carry out his plan, regardless. Mayfield had become a definite liability.

With a drink in his hand, he had gestured to Mayfield to take a seat on the couch in front of the fireplace where a snapping fire was burning. "Drink?" he asked.

Mayfield frowned and seemed ready to refuse until his eye found a bottle of Glen Fiddich on the side table. "Alright. Scotch on the rocks."

He had pretended to fuss over the ice as he poured the drink. He came around from the table behind the couch and handed the drink to Mayfield. "So what is it that we suddenly have to talk about, Will? What is it that is so pressing we had to meet tonight?"

"Well, Ralph," Mayfield had said, "I got to thinking about why you wanted to use my key. Why you wanted it specifically on Friday night. Interesting too, that poor Adam fell off that balcony on the same night."

"Will, please stand up. I want to see if you're wearing a wire."

"Fuck off, Ralph!"

"Keep a civil tongue in your head! If we're going to have this talk you seem to want so badly, you can't blame me for wanting to be sure it's only you I'm talking to. Now stand up!"

Almost reflexively, Mayfield had started to stand at the imperative, then caught himself and hesitated, half-way up. Then he affected a bored sigh and straightened up. Townsend remembered somewhat clumsily, but effectively, patting down his visitor. Satisfied, he told Mayfield to sit down. "Your assertion that I asked you for the key is easily deniable. At worst, it would be your word against mine. Besides you have no idea whether the key was ever picked up or used."

"Oh, so you asked me to tie it, along with some coins, in a white handkerchief and drop it out my window after dark because you were doing some Newtonian experiment about the law of gravity?"

He had ignored the sarcasm. "You let yourself into the building the next morning so, if you did happen to drop your key out the window, you must have found it down below."

Seeing that Townsend was trying to stalemate him, Mayfield had taken a new tack. "I've looked at the data base and the status matrix for the trial. You've altered the records. The entry for Nancy Fallows said she withdrew, Ralph. And the records say the other suicides, both of them, I'd guess, in the group taking the medication we were testing, 'withdrew' from the experiment long before their deaths. I read about that break-in and the stolen records. At the time, I thought it was really bad luck. Now, I don't think luck had mush to do with it."

"That's a lot of wild conjecture, Will" he had answered with almost patronizing calmness.

"Con … conjecshur or not, it explains Warburton's death and it's going to be the bazzish of a neish financial arr …aransement between us." Townsend could see a look of puzzlement cross Mayfield's face as he realized he was slurring his words. With an obvious effort, Mayfield continued. "I can forget all about these little dishcovries, Ralph." Now Mayfield was visibly unsteady and a sense of alarm flashed in the young man's eyes. Townsend had merely gazed at Mayfield as he labored to shout, "You fucking put shumthing in my drin-n-n-k!" Mayfield's eyes closed and he fell forward off the couch.

Townsend had pulled on a pair of latex painting gloves, then reached into the wood basket and pulled out a roll of duct tape. With great effort Mayfield had opened his eyes, but could only have seen a strip of silver-gray tape moving toward his face. Townsend had forced the tape over Mayfield's mouth as the graduate student drifted back to unconsciousness. Then he knelt beside the prostrate man and pinched his nostrils shut.

When he was sure Mayfield was dead, he had lifted the body into a fireman's-carry position and lugged it out the door. He remembered staggering slightly under the weight, as he walked to the shed. He had dropped the body and walked over to his own car and turned on the lights to illuminate the work he had to do. Returning to the shed, he began, methodically, to unstack the cord-and-a-half of wood that had been so neatly stored alongside. The cabin sat on a two-acre parcel away from the river and the adjacent parcels were undeveloped and densely forested so he did not worry about neighbors noticing his arrival or the shoveling he would soon begin.

Two hours later, he had finished digging a grave where the woodpile had stood. He tugged Mayfield's body into the trench and shoveled the dirt back over it. Even in the crisp night air, he was soaked with perspiration. He made the site as natural looking as possible and then began restacking the fireplace wood.

Townsend smiled as he remembered how easy it had been to get Mayfield to drop his key out the window at Bracknell Hall. The unfortunate Miss Fallows had been insistent on talking with Townsend directly instead of to her assigned therapist. She had described how Mayfield had been assisting the therapist and how she and Mayfield had become attracted to each other …how they had "fallen in love" and had an affair. She had told him Mayfield had thrown her over and how devastated she was. He had known immediately that he, as clinic Director, was facing a ruinous set of circumstances. He had assured her that Mayfield would never again be allowed to interact with the patients in his clinic and that he would help her get past this unfortunate happening. He did remove Mayfield from further patient contact, but he never mentioned the incident between Fallows and Mayfield to anyone else and he never included any reference to it in his case notes. His assurances had seemed to pacify Fallows, but a few weeks later she took her own life.

He had marveled at Mayfield's lusty stupidity in taking advantage of a patient under care in the clinic. Ordinarily, a mistake like that would have ended the man's chances of getting a Ph.D. or ever becoming a practicing therapist. But Townsend himself was playing for high stakes and his own ethics had already been bought and paid for. Besides, he had thought it could be useful to have someone who would, without question, do his bidding. Do his bidding yes, but then the ungrateful prick had been ready to blackmail him!

He had returned the shovel to its place in the shed and walked back to the cabin. He carefully washed and dried both glasses and returned them to the cupboard. Then he wiped the door handles. He emptied what remained in the small vial of chloral hydrate that he had used to subdue Mayfield and put the vial in his own car. It was fortunate for his plan that he had had some chloral hydrate left over from experiments he had been doing that involved hypnosis. He checked his watch and saw that it was twelve-forty in the morning.

He had taken Mayfield's car keys from the body before carrying it from the cabin. He had spread some polyethylene on the driver's seat of the GTF's car and keyed the ignition. He drove the car toward Zig Zag and across Highway 26 onto a paved county road. A half-mile further, he turned off onto a logging road. He knew of a spur that joined the logging road not far from its beginning. He turned onto that spur. The logging roads had been abandoned five years ago. The road bed had reverted to deeply-rutted, packed earth and the underbrush was already encroaching on the roadway in places. Townsend drove slowly, the headlights arcing erratically across the foliage as the car lurched forward. Shortly, he maneuvered the car into a stub turnoff. He forced the car forty feet into the underbrush and saplings beyond the end of the turnoff and turned off the lights and engine. He had removed the license plates at the cabin. He carried the plates a few yards further, kicked a shallow trench, and buried them. He retrieved the polyethylene from the car seat and, using a flashlight, started hiking.

He remembered being near exhaustion from his digging and his three-mile hike when he reached the cabin. He got into his own car and drove west, stopping only once to dispose of the vial, the latex gloves, and the polyethylene in a rubbish barrel behind a hardware store. It had been four in the morning as he entered the city. He turned north onto Interstate 205, an eastside beltway nearly deserted of vehicles at that time of night, then took a connecting ramp to travel west on Interstate 84. He took the Thirty-ninth Avenue exit and quickly turned west again on East Broadway. He approached the Broadway Bridge and crossed over the dark Willamette River, its east bank sparkling with the lights of piers and grain elevators. He pulled to the curb near the center of town. Lifting Mayfield's car keys off the seat by thrusting a pencil through the loop of the keychain, he dropped them down a storm drain. Ten minutes later, he was home.

As he concluded his reliving of those events, he shuddered and arose. It had been an unpleasant matter, but it had to be done and he had carried it off extremely well. But now this cop, Fealder, had jeopardized everything! Their first meeting had gone smoothly and Townsend had felt in full control of the situation. The second time Fealder and the woman, Berbieri, had interviewed him, it had been hostile. They clearly had suspicions and were trying to provoke him into making a mistake. But equally clearly, they had no real proof to connect him to Warburton's death.

This Sunday afternoon, everything had changed for the worse. First, the police had served him with the search warrant for the cabin and he worried they would find Mayfield's body. Even if they did not, they must have some evidence tying him to Mayfield's disappearance. Then, he heard a television newscast announce that Kellogg had taken his own life. Kellog had seemed fragile and guilt-obsessed. Townsend feared that Kellogg might have left a note confessing what they had done. He debated holding his ground and hiring a criminal defense attorney to attempt to quash the warrant, but concluded that his time was better spent in making his escape.

Townsend hated to be stifled in getting his way. He hated to lose. For some reason, Fealder and his partner had shifted their focus to him. Grudgingly, he decided to cut his losses. When Townsend had first contemplated killing Warburton, he knew that he had to have an exit strategy. If the authorities were not convinced that Warburton had jumped from the balcony, there would surely be an investigation and, sooner or later, he would come under their scrutiny. If his story stood up, well and good. If it started to crumble, he had to have a plan.

One of Townsend's patients in the clinic had been an ex-felon who had bragged about his contacts in the shadowy network of fences, counterfeiters, and muscle men that serviced the underworld. He had used the former patient to find a person who would sell him a counterfeit passport and a drivers' license with a Washington address. Digital manipulation on the counterfeiter's computer removed his beard. By wearing a gray wig and taking off his glasses, his appearance in the passport and drivers license photos looked quite different from his usual visage Later, he had traveled to Salem where he bought contact lenses that changed the appearance of his irises from brown to grey. On Sunday afternoon, after he was served with the search warrant, he shaved off his beard and dyed his hair gray.

He poured himself a Glen Fiddich on the rocks and considered his odds. With a new identity and a changed appearance, he calculated his chances of getting on a plane to Atlanta were fairly good. A red-eye flight could get him there the next morning. Paying cash for the ticket might draw attention, but, if the clerk at the airline counter looked dubious, he would claim his credit card had been stolen or that he had won money in a poker game. From Atlanta, he could book a flight to Sao Paolo. Brazil did not have an extradition treaty with the United States and he would have to start a new life there. After paying off his gambling debts, he still had a little over one hundred and thirty thousand dollars of Kellogg's money left. He had transferred that money in a series of smaller amounts to a Cayman Islands account months ago. He had withdrawn nearly all of the balance of his checking account, almost two thousand dollars in cash, and would carry that with him in a money belt. He had not had time to acquire professional credentials under his new identity, so the hundred and thirty thousand would have to support him while he learned to live by his wits. If he could get out of the United States, he was confident that he could survive and be comfortable in Brazil. He felt that learning Portuguese would present only a minor problem as he was already reasonably fluent in Spanish. And he could buy a new, Brazilian, identity once down there.

Townsend knew his biggest problem would be getting to an airport and actually boarding the plane. If he were treated as a fugitive, he felt sure Portland

International Airport was one of the places that the police would alert, and possibly watch. He thought his odds of safely boarding a plane in Seattle were much better. He was reluctant to use his own car in case they did find Mayfield's body and would send out an alert on his license plate. He had driven slowly down the hill on quiet streets the day before to scout a suitable place to meet a taxi. He had chosen an apartment complex on Harrison Street. It was close enough to reach on foot, yet far enough from his own address to confuse anyone checking taxi dispatches.

His plan was to take a cab across the river to Vancouver, Washington. From there, he would take AMTRAK's Cascades train to Tukwila, followed by another taxi to the Seattle-Tacoma International Airport. The timing would be close but, with luck, he could catch the Atlanta plane scheduled for a 12:10 A.M. departure. Leaving by plane was a high-risk, high-reward gamble. But, unless he intended hiding out in Oregon by renting some run-down, backwoods house – which he most certainly did not -- he would have to leave the country. The time to leave was upon him. He phoned for a taxi, picked up his carefully packed shoulder bag, locked his back door behind him, and walked casually down the street in the dusk of late afternoon. He carried a cane hooked into the inside sleeve hole of his overcoat.

Townsend timed his walk well, arriving at the Harrison Street address a few minutes before the taxi braked to a stop in front of the apartment building. The driver was pleased to have a long drive with a good fare. Townsend mentally classified cab drivers as introverted or garrulous. He felt unfortunate to have drawn the latter. He was not altogether successful in discouraging the man's questions and general conversational gambits. He told the man he had been in Portland to visit an elderly aunt who had taken ill and that his car was at the mechanic's necessitating his use of taxis. Townsend gave the driver an address that was seven blocks from the train station in Vancouver. He paid the driver, the taxi departed, and he walked to the station.

21

Fealder and Berbieri drove their own cars to Townsend's home and two uniformed police officers followed in a squad car. Fealder asked one of the officers to position herself on Spring Street below the property to guard against any attempt to escape by climbing fences and cutting through back yards. The other officer parked the squad car across the driveway, effectively blocking Townsend's use of his car. These precautions in place, the three of them rang the door bell. There was no answer. They pounded on the door and still got no response. The couple to whom Berbieri had spoken on Friday, came out on their front lawn, suddenly needing to study their rose bushes. Fealder had an arrest warrant along with the search warrant in his pocket and wasted no time with the locked door. He used a speed-key. As he opened the door, Fealder called Townsend's name and shouted their own identities. They heard no answer, so they drew their weapons and, covering each other, cleared the rooms on the first floor. A similar procedure downstairs revealed the entire house was empty. Fealder checked the garage and saw the Lexus was still inside. The police officer checked a painted-aluminum garden shed in the corner of the back yard and announced that it, too, was empty. Saunders and Holloway arrived in an FBI car and entered the house.

Fealder flipped a light switch and saw that the power was on. He wondered if Townsend had made a last-minute escape or was simply taking a late-Sunday-afternoon stroll around the neighborhood. Surely the man would have been on full alert knowing the authorities were searching the very property where he had buried Mayfield's body. Fealder's instincts told him Townsend had become a fugitive. Berbieri went across the street to ask the couple in front of the rose bed if they had seen Townsend recently. She returned saying the neighbors had not seen the professor since the preceding day, though they had noticed a policeman on his doorstep earlier on Sunday.

Fealder left the others starting with an open-view search of the premises and sat on the living room couch. He needed to put himself inside Townsend's mind. How would an intelligent man like Townsend, with available funds, try to escape? There were many small, obscure communities in Oregon where he might try to lay low. But very small communities had their drawbacks from a fugitive's standpoint. A stranger would stand out prominently and questions would be asked, especially of a person with Townsend's erudite and urbane veneer. No, Fealder did not see a man of Townsend's tastes and habits choosing that means of avoiding capture. Without a car, Townsend had to have either rented a car or used public transportation. Unless the man had managed to obtain an entire new identity including a credit card, renting a car would be fairly risky and difficult. He faulted himself for not having already sent alerts accompanied by faxed photos to all the car rental agencies in the city.

Berbieri, Saunders, Holloway, and the police officer returned from their walk-through and reported they saw nothing of interest. Fealder told the officers to stay in the house in case Townsend returned. He asked Berbieri to handle the alert to the rental agencies and to do the same with all the check-in counters at the Portland airport, the train station, and the bus depot. She was to include in the alerts a faxed photo with a warning that Townsend might have altered his appearance, might use a different name, and might use cash to buy his ticket or rent a car. Berbieri and Holloway left: she to organize the alert and establish a communications net and he to notify other federal agents about the fugitive.

Fealder then called all the Portland taxi companies to see if any had made pickups at Townsend's address or nearby in the last four hours. It took twenty minutes to contact the twelve companies plus Uber. No company had dispatched a cab or a car to Townsend's address. Only two companies had made pickups within eight blocks. Fealder called back and asked the dispatcher of the first of those companies to patch him through to the driver. The driver said the fare he picked up was a woman in her early thirties. Fealder repeated this process with the second company. He identified himself to the driver and asked for his help.

"I understand you picked up a fare about an hour ago on Harrison Street. Can you describe the person you picked up?"

"Well, sort of, yeah. He was an older guy, gray-haired."

"Did he have any luggage?"

"No. Just a good-sized shoulder bag."

"Can you estimate his height and weight? Was he wearing glasses?"

"Well, he wasn't wearing glasses. Sort of medium weight, I suppose. Maybe one-eighty... somewhere in there. Under six feet, I think."

"Did he have a beard?"

"No. No beard."

Fealder wondered how much Townsend could have changed his appearance. The height and weight seemed about right. "Do you remember what your fare was wearing?"

"Not exactly: a dark overcoat, maybe dark blue and I think I saw a sweater, also dark, underneath the coat."

"That's helpful. Where'd you take him?"

"Across the river to Vancouver."

"Did he say anything about where he was going?"

"No. Not really. He just said he'd come to Portland to see an elderly relative who'd taken sick."

"That's a bit of a cab ride. Did he not have a car?"

"Yeah, I wondered about that too. I asked him and he said his car was at the mechanic's for repairs."

"What was the address where you dropped him?"

" I'll have it in my driver's log if you can wait a minute while I pull over."

Fealder waited until the cabbie continued. "Here it is." He read it out. "That's right at the corner of West Thirteenth and Ingalls"

Fealder thanked the cabbie and sat back on the couch. He again tried to place himself in Townsend's mind. Unless the man had an accomplice totally unknown to them, he would be on his own. He probably had enough money to purchase an entirely new identity, but would he have had enough time? And would he have known whom to contact for the necessary documentation? Assuming Townsend had secured some new ID, he could risk flying and Fealder thought he would try to leave the country. He would probably head for a developed country, one where extradition would be impossible or at least not obligatory by international treaty. An Islamic country was not likely, given Townsend's lifestyle. That left a few countries in Central and South America. That, in turn, most likely meant a southward flight from one of the gateway cities in the south: Atlanta, Miami, New Orleans, Houston, Dallas-Ft. Worth, Los Angeles, or San Diego. A fleeing Townsend would expect the Portland airport to be closely watched. Fealder knew that his quarry would have to get to those gateway cities by plane, bus or train. By plane meant somehow first getting to San Francisco or Seattle. Trains all the way to the southern cities would be too slow. The same would be true for buses. Something in this line of thought triggered a flash across Fealder's consciousness, but he could not capture it at first. He stopped and reviewed the logic he had just considered. Seattle! That was it! He remembered from the background information Bennie Schultz had dredged up that Townsend's undergraduate and graduate degrees were from the University of Washington. But how was that relevant, he asked himself. An accomplice known from student days seemed very unlikely. A relative in Seattle? That was conceivable, he thought, but it probably would be impossible to track down such a person tonight. Townsend's familiarity with the city would be helpful to him, but Seattle was too close to Portland for Townsend to go to ground there. If the man needed to reach a southern gateway city in a hurry and could not risk using the Portland airport, he might attempt to reach another city's major airport. By going north to Seattle instead of directly south, Townsend might think he could make a plane connection with the added element of misdirection to confuse his pursuers.

But how, Fealder puzzled, would Townsend *get* to Seattle? By train? Fealder vaguely remembered that one of the AMTRAK trains, perhaps The Cascades, went north in the evening. Would Townsend risk the train station given that it too would likely be watched? Fealder doubted it. Unless…. unless he caught the train *north* of Portland. The old man in the taxi! The taxi had taken him to Vancouver just across the Columbia River from Portland. Fealder ran into Townsend's home office and sat at the computer. Townsend had a broadband connection to the internet and Fealder did not have to cope with passwords. He made a guess at the website address of AMTRAK and the railroad service's home page immediately appeared. He keyboarded in a trip leaving Vancouver, Washington with Seattle as a destination and checked the schedule. There it was! The Cascades stopped in Vancouver after leaving Portland and then left for Seattle at 6:33 P.M. Then he pulled up a street map of Vancouver. The intersection the cabbie had given him was not all that far from the train station.

He turned off the computer and tried to call James, but got no answer. He left a message saying he was going to Vancouver to check a lead. He reached Hokanson at home and asked him to go to the apartment complex on Harrison and question all the tenants to see if they or anyone they knew had called a taxi. Hokanson, as always, ready to help, said he would get right on it and report his findings to Fealder by cell phone. Before he left the house, Fealder went into the bathroom next to the master bedroom. He found a drinking glass on the counter beside the basin. He held the tumbler at the very bottom and slid it into an evidence bag in case they needed a set of Townsend's prints. Fealder pulled the front door shut behind him and ran to his car.

Once the taxi left him in Vancouver, Townsend extracted the cane from his overcoat sleeve and used it openly as he approached the train station. The station-master had posted the train as "on time", but it had not entered the station at the time shown on the schedule. Townsend purchased his ticket, then stood on the platform beyond the area illuminated by the lights and stole glances at his watch. There were only three other people on the platform. At last, he heard the rumble and growl of the locomotive and the soft squeal of the wheels on the tracks as the train rolled into the station. It had seemed to Townsend that the train was greatly delayed. In fact, it was only eight minutes late.

Townsend boarded the train and limped to his seat. As soon as the conductor checked his ticket, he left for the dining car where he chose an unoccupied table. He ordered a glass of rosé wine with an entrée of glazed ham and pineapple and cheesecake for dessert. Returning to his seat after his meal, he noted with relief that there were no more than a dozen persons in the car and no one else in his quartet of seats. He found a Time magazine abandoned on a seat and, to keep himself occupied, began to read it.

Fealder pulled the Corvette into the parking lot next to the Vancouver AMTRAK station. He found one person at the only ticket window and politely, but firmly, asked him to step aside while he conducted police business with the clerk. He produced a photo of Townsend.

"Excuse me," he said to the clerk, "but this is very urgent. Have you seen this person this evening? Perhaps sold him a ticket?"

"No, I haven't. We haven't had much business this evening. Kind of surprising too, being it's Sunday."

"Has anyone bought a ticket for Seattle on the six-thirty-three?"

"Yes. I think I sold three tickets for Seattle. The Cascades has left, you know. About … " he paused to pull out a pocket watch, "… thirty-nine minutes ago."

"Can you describe the customers, please?"

"Well, let's see. There were two women, one of them young… in her twenties; the other was a little older. And I sold a ticket to an old man. That's all the tickets that I sold here at the window. There was another person in the waiting room. He was young soldier. He already had his ticket."

"Tell me about the old man. Did he use a credit card?"

"I don't think so. Let me check." The clerk riffled through paperwork in his drawer. "No, he paid cash."

"Please look at this picture again. The person in the photo may have tried to change his appearance. Perhaps he'd taken off his glasses or dyed his hair? Could it be the same person as the customer you called the 'old man'?"

The clerk deliberated over the photo for several moments. "Yes, it *could* be the same person, but the man who bought the ticket sure seemed older. He didn't have a beard and he limped and used a cane."

"What kind of luggage did he have?" Fealder asked.

"Sorry. I didn't notice."

"When does the train arrive in Seattle?"

"A little before ten. Nine-forty-five if it holds schedule, but it left here almost ten minutes late."

Fealder wrote the clerk's name and phone number in his notebook, thanked him for his cooperation and trotted out to the Corvette. He drove to the Vancouver police headquarters and introduced himself to the night Sergeant. He asked for a professional courtesy: that he be allowed to use a computer and a telephone. He also asked the location of the helipad they used. He found the website for Seattle-Tacoma International Airport and ran a search for all flights leaving after eleven in the evening for any of the southern gateway cities. The search produced three flights: a Continental-United flight to Los Angeles at 11:15 P.M., a Delta flight to Atlanta at 12:10 A.M, and a Continental- United flight to Dallas-Ft.Worth at 12:30 A.M. There were no international flights listed for late-evening or early-morning departures. He printed out the information and laid it on the desk in front of him. Fealder was tiring. The fast-breaking developments in his day had taken their toll on him. He put his elbows on the desktop and cradled his head with his hands.

He knew he could be chasing a will of the wisp. The passenger on the train headed for Seattle might simply be an older man making a trip to see his grandchildren. Meanwhile, Townsend might be driving south on I-5 in a borrowed or rented car. Or he might be apprehended at the Portland airport, while he, Fealder, was tracking down a phantom traveler with a hypothetical plane connection. He had a choice to make; a choice that Doug James would be second-guessing for the next five years if his hunch was wrong. Fealder believed his hunches usually paid off, whether he was calling for a pitchout because he sensed the runner on first would attempt to steal on the next pitch or was predicting the future actions of a murder suspect. He chose to follow the man on the train.

He called Berbieri's cell number. She answered and he told her to order a police helicopter and to come with it and meet him at the helipad the Vancouver police used. He told her they would fly from there toward Seattle. She confirmed that she had issued all the alerts he had requested and said she would try to have the helicopter there inside half an hour.

Fealder considered how they could best intercept the man on the AMTRAK train. Because he could not be sure that Townsend would head straight for the airport when he disembarked, Fealder favored trying to capture him on the train. Even with a helicopter, he calculated they would be too late to board the train until it reached Tacoma. If they could get aboard there, they should have a good forty minutes before arrival in Seattle to scrutinize the passengers and find their man. He thought they could always use the airport as their back up if, God forbid, Townsend somehow eluded them on the train.

Fealder used the communication center at the police station to contact AMTRAK security and the Tacoma police to work out the details of their boarding. The Tacoma police told Fealder to land the helicopter in the parking lot of the Tacoma Dome which was not in use that evening. They told him they would provide surface transportation to the train station that was less than a mile away. Tacoma would have a team of three officers to make the arrest if Townsend was, in fact, on the train. Finally Fealder called James again on his cell phone. This time, James answered.

"It's Park Fealder. I'm still in Vancouver."

"What's this about 'following a lead', Fealder?"

"First, let me tell you we've broken Townsend's alibi for the night of the Warburton murder. Better than that, we can put him in Warburton's campus office minutes before Warburton went off that balcony!"

"That's good work!" said James, almost in spite of himself. "What'd you turn up?"

Fealder told him about the photo taken with Warburton's cell phone and sent to his brother in California.

"I'll be damned!" said James. "Warburton must have suspected there was trouble ahead. Now we have motive, means *and* opportunity. Plus, he lied to us about being there. But what are you doing in Vancouver?"

"When we went to arrest him, he'd flown the coop, but his car was still in the garage. I figured that meant he took a cab. We checked and learned that none were dispatched to his house, so I checked on cabs sent to anyplace inside an eight-block radius from his house. Only one picked up a man. The cabbie said it was an old man with gray hair, no beard, and no glasses, but the height and weight sounded about right. He took the fare to Vancouver."

"That sounds pretty speculative! Have you alerted the airport, the buses, public transportation terminals?"

Fealder inwardly winced. If James thought his driving across the state line was speculative, he was sure to be critical of his subsequent decisions. "Yes we have all those places alerted. I figured Townsend was looking to get on a train to Seattle, where he used to live, and that he didn't dare use the Portland station. I checked the Vancouver station and found that an 'old' man with a somewhat similar description, except that he limped and used a cane, had bought a ticket for Seattle with cash and had boarded the train about forty minutes earlier. I've checked the airlines out of Seattle and there are three flights to southern cities' international airports he could theoretically make a connection with tonight after the train arrives."

"Wait a minute, Fealder! You want to alert law enforcement all across western Washington about a gimpy old man who you have this 'hunch' *might* be our fugitive?"

"Yes, it is a hunch, but think about how it all adds up. I believe it's exactly the sort of escape Townsend would try. Unless he turns up at a Portland terminal, it's the best strategy we have!"

"So, have you contacted the authorities in Seattle?"

"Yes. Airport Security at Sea-Tac International for the airport part and the Tacoma police are going to assist us in boarding the train."

"Boarding the train! Come on, Fealder! How are you going to catch the train in Tacoma?"

"Well... Berbieri's meeting me in Vancouver with our chopper."

"Our chopper! Goddammit, Fealder. You go chasing all over creation on this *hunch* of yours and we'll be the laughing stock of the Seattle and Tacoma police departments! Why don't you just go to Reno and take your chances at the roulette tables?"

Fealder's phone indicated there was a call waiting. He did not want to further annoy James, but it might be Hokanson, he thought. "Can you give me a few seconds? I have an incoming call waiting."

James grunted assent and Fealder switched over to hear Hokanson's voice. "Park, I checked that apartment complex. There were sixteen units and thirteen of the occupants were at home when I came by. No one had called a cab or had any guest that called a cab. And I didn't come across any elderly woman who was ill, either."

Fealder cut back to James. "That was Hokanson. I asked him to see if anyone in that apartment building had called for that cab. He couldn't reach three occupants, but he said no one in the other thirteen units had made the call. That makes my suspicions even stronger. I want to get up there and settle this train idea. If it holds up, we'll have our man. If not, I'll be back in Portland in the morning."

"Go ahead, Fealder, but you're hanging out there all on your own on this one. And don't forget, I still may turn this over to Nabors on Tuesday."

"Thanks for the green light. At least we know who the murderer is. We'll get him if he's on that train."

Fealder checked his watch. He asked the Vancouver watch officer for permission to leave his car at the police helipad. He had just pulled up when he heard the whump-whump-whump of the approaching helicopter. With a blinding landing light and a terrific roar, the craft landed and the passenger-side door swung open. Fealder saw Berbieri wave and he ran to climb aboard.

22

Fealder fastened his seat belt and adjusted the headphones on his ears. The whine of the engine in the Robinson R44 rose in a mighty crescendo. They were aloft seconds later, hurtling through the darkness with the lights of Vancouver growing ever smaller beneath them. Berbieri looked questioningly at Fealder.

"Want to fill me in?"

Fealder told her about the grey-haired man and his cab ride to Vancouver. He said he thought the same man – probably Townsend in a simple disguise – had boarded the train for Seattle. He explained that he had checked plane schedules and discovered some possible flights to southern cities.

"Have you told James?" she asked.

"Yeah. He was glad we've broken Townsend's movie alibi, but gave me hell for choosing to track down this guy on the train. He thinks I'm on a wild goose chase. And now I've roped you into it as well."

Berbieri touched his forearm. "Hey. I'm your partner. Right now, it's probably the best lead we have. We might as well go for it!"

He rather liked her brief touch. She studied his face for a moment and spoke again. "You look tired, Park."

"I am sort of crapped out. I guess I've been running on adrenaline all day. Don't worry. I'll still be able to take it up a few notches if we see our man."

The occasional buffeting of the helicopter made it hard to sleep, but Fealder managed to doze for a few minutes. The lights of Olympia passed underneath. The lights of Tacoma came into view with the contrasting curve of blackness that their pilot said must be Commencement Bay. They descended over the downtown area toward a huge hemisphere that Fealder recognized as the Tacoma Dome. Below, men with glowing guide wands motioned them toward the landing area. The pilot smoothly settled the R44 onto the tarmac of the parking lot and cut the engine. They were greeted by a plain clothes detective and two uniformed police officers showing TPD insignia and wearing a full complement of armored vests, Glocks, two-way radios, mace, and handcuffs. Introductions were quickly made. The pilot was to stay on the ground with the helicopter awaiting further instructions.

"Is the plan to halt the train or do we just board it and do our search as it rolls north?" asked the detective.

"We won't have time to search the whole train in the station," said Fealder. "I've cleared everything with AMTRAK security so we can board and ride it to Seattle while we check out the passengers. We'll have the chopper meet us in Seattle. How will you guys get back here?"

"I'll have one of the officers drive the squad car to the King Street Station in Seattle and meet us there," answered the detective. "If we make a collar, the perp will probably have to be jailed here or in Seattle anyway, until you can set up extradition."

"Alright. How much time before the train arrives?"

"It should be here any minute," the detective said. "We're only three or four minutes away. Lute, we'll run for the train while you're parking the car. Then you come down and watch the platform in case this guy tries to jump off right here."

"Here's a photo of the guy we're after," said Fealder passing the photo to the others. "It sounds like he's changed his appearance to look like a gray-haired, beardless, old man with a limp and a cane, but concentrate on the basic structure of the face. He's about five-eleven and medium build."

Townsend sat next to the window on the platform side as they entered each station along the way. So far, his trip and the stops at Kelso and Centralia had been uneventful, but he knew he had to remain vigilant. The train passed through a long tunnel and then continued its course close to the waters of Commencement Bay. It reduced its speed noticeably and, a few minutes later, rumbled slowly through an area of warehouses and machine shops on its way to the station. The train stopped and there was the usual commotion as people hustled their luggage down the vestibule steps to the platform. Townsend could see at least two dozen people on the platform obviously waiting to board. But, two cars ahead, he also saw a uniformed policeman and two other men and a woman without luggage. Then he recognized one of the men and the woman as Fealder and Berbieri. He instantly grabbed his shoulder bag and rushed into an on-board lavatory. He pulled off his sweater and topcoat and replaced them with a Seattle Mariners sweatshirt from his bag. He quickly pulled on a light brown wig and covered that with a Mariners ball cap. The cane was too long to fit in his bag, so he had left it on the floor under his seat.

How could they possibly have known I was on the train, he asked himself. He had included in his bag the one additional simple disguise, but he had no plan to avoid his pursuers if they stayed on the train. He tried to concentrate: should he get off or try to bluff his way through by staying on the train? He feared that Fealder and his team would remain on the train and perhaps even try to talk to every passenger. The time had come for some inspired improvisation. Townsend got off the train, mingling with the last few to disembark.

The officer the detective had called Lute, after parking the car, had turned an ankle while rushing down the first flight of stairs. He stopped for almost a minute trying to soothe the excruciating pain in his ankle, then hobbled down the second flight to the platform. He looked toward the rear of the train where the last few passengers were boarding. Fealder, Berbieri and the two Tacoma policemen had crowded onto the train at Car 3 ahead of those waiting to board and were out of Lute's sight.

Berbieri and the detective immediately began walking slowly through the cars looking over every passenger. The uniformed officer checked the luggage areas and snack bars on the lower level of the cars while Fealder sought out the conductor.

Townsend had walked quickly along the platform toward the locomotive. An idea had come to him. It was a long shot, but he had no better alternative and he still entertained a faint hope of catching the plane to Atlanta. Fortunately for him, the engine was far enough forward to be out of the bright lights. Equally fortunately, Lute had just started down the first flight of stairs at that moment. Reaching the locomotive, Townsend grabbed the ladder rungs on its side and pulled himself onto the ladder. He climbed to the cab door and knocked forcefully on the window. The engineer looked out with surprise and lowered the window.

"What are you doing?" he asked heatedly of the stranger in the ball cap. "You're not supposed to be up there. We'll be leaving in a few minutes. Get down!"

"Please, Sir. I'm a passenger headed for my chemo at the Fred Hutchinson Cancer Center in Seattle. They say if this last phase of chemo doesn't work, I've only got two or three months left. All my life, I've wanted to ride in a locomotive. I suppose that sounds kind of silly, but I was hoping… . I mean, I'm running out of time and I thought 'it can't hurt to ask'."

The scowl on the engineer's face softened. "Christ, I'd be breaking sixteen different rules. Oh, what the hell! I'll open the door. You can only ride to the next stop. That's Tukwila. And don't tell anyone or they'll have our jobs!"

Townsend scurried inside the cab and the engineer shut the door.

"I'm Terry and this is Mike, my fireman," the engineer said, nodding toward the other man in the cab.

"Hi. I'm Dave. I can't tell you how much this means to me! And I won't tell a soul."

The engineer and fireman started explaining the controls and gauges to Townsend. Four minutes passed and the engineer eased the train out of the station.

On their first pass down the aisles of the cars, Berbieri and the Tacoma detective had spotted eleven older men. Six of them appeared to be with their spouses. They found two more older men, alone, in the dining car and the lounge car. Six of the unaccompanied older men had grey hair and the other one was bald. Three of those six looked far too short. That left them with three possibles. They huddled to study the photo again and then resumed their reconnoitering. They identified three more single, older men on the return walk, two of them balding. They assumed the additional possibles had boarded at Tacoma and taken their seats after the team's first pass. Meanwhile, the uniform reported to Fealder that there was no one in the baggage car or the luggage areas and no one even close to Townsend's description in the snack-bars. Fealder and the conductor checked every restroom to no avail. He thanked the conductor for his cooperation. Fealder contacted Berbieri on his cell phone and asked her and the Tacoma detective to meet them in the lounge car.

"He's not hiding in any of the lavatories or the baggage car," Fealder summarized. "So he must be just lying doggo among the passengers. What'd you guys see?"

"Unless he's cozied up to some woman, we think there are only four possibles," said Berbieri. "We've had a second, unobtrusive, look at those four and I think there's really only two that bear much of a resemblance. But you should look also."

"I will. Lead on. I'll look at all of the older men, even those sitting with women, but use hand signals to tell me when we approach those two."

They walked through and Berbieri gave the signals. Fealder studied all of the faces carefully. One of the men had fallen asleep and was quietly snoring as they passed his seat. At the end of the train they stopped.

"You're right. I want to talk with those two where you signaled," said Fealder.

They strolled casually back toward the front of the train. Fealder stopped the group and sat down in the empty seat next to one of the men. The man looked up at the group with a puzzled expression. Fealder flashed his badge and said, "Excuse the intrusion, but we're looking for someone and need to ask you a few questions. May I know your destination?"

The man answered with surprise, "Everett. Why do you ask?"

"Where did you board?" asked Fealder, ignoring the man's query.

"I got on at Kelso. I've been to see my daughter and son-in-law. I'm no villain!"

"Do you ever use a cane?"

"No. I don't need a cane. I'm a little stiff if I sit too long, but I do not use a cane."

Fealder was listening to the timbre of the man's voice and concluded he was probably as old as he looked and was not Townsend. To be sure, he asked, "May we see your ticket?"

The man reached into a carry-on bag. Fealder watched his hand intently and noticed that Berbieri slid her hand to the gun in her shoulder bag. The man

produced a ticket and handed it to Fealder. It confirmed a Kelso to Everett trip. Fealder apologized for
bothering the man and they continued their walk. The
next person Fealder wanted to question had a young
man sitting next to him. The group stopped in the
aisle and some of the passengers looked at them curi-
ously. Berbieri braced herself against a seat back as the
train swayed on a curve. Fealder leaned over and whispered in the young man's ear and he quickly excused
himself. Fealder sat down as the older man looked at
him apprehensively. Again, Fealder flashed his badge.

"We're looking for a fugitive we think may be on
this train. Please tell us where you got on and where
you are going."

The man broke into a grin. "A fugitive? I hope you
don't think it's me. I haven't robbed a bank for at least
six months!" he announced with a cackling laugh.

"Do you ever use a cane?"

"Hell no! I may be an old cuss, but I can still get
around okay."

Fealder was almost convinced this was, indeed, an
older man with nothing to fear, but he was not quite
ready to let it go. Townsend had proved to be a re-
sourceful perp and might be a consummate actor as
well. "Glad to hear it. But you didn't answer my question. Please show me your ticket."

The man reached into a patch pocket of his sport coat
where Fealder could see the top of the ticket. He handed it
to Fealder. It showed a trip from Eugene, Oregon, to Seattle.

Fealder looked at the liver spots on the man's hand as he passed the ticket over. This was genuinely an older man. He again apologized and led the group back to the lounge car. He asked Berbieri to fetch the conductor. While they waited, he said, "The grey haired man with a limp does not seem to be among the people we've seen. Even if the man with the limp isn't Townsend, we can't presently account for him. We do know the men we've seen either don't fit the description at all or are really older guys and not Townsend."

Berbieri arrived with the conductor in tow. Fealder smiled at him and said, "I should've asked you this when we first boarded, but we were focusing on the lavatories and I forgot. You should have had a few people board at Vancouver. Could you tell us the seat assignment of the older man we're looking for?"

The conductor frowned. "Not offhand. Sometimes I can really recall everyone's place, especially when the train isn't so full, like tonight. But darned if I can clearly recall this man or where he was seated. I'm pretty sure a couple of people from Vancouver are in car five, but that's all I can say. However, I can show you the tickets-sold listing and that will narrow it down to the seats assigned to those who got on at Vancouver."

"That'll be fine," said Fealder.

The conductor went to his mini-office and returned a few minutes later. "Here's the listing. There were four Vancouver passengers all together and three of them were seated in car five. I'll show you all their seats"

They followed the conductor and checked all four locations. There were persons in seats at each of the locations except one seat in car five. Fealder looked in the overhead ledge and saw nothing had been left. They were leaving when Berbieri stooped to look under the seats. "Wait!" she called. "Here's the cane!"

"Damn!" exclaimed Fealder. "So he *was* here! Somehow he got off, maybe even before Tacoma."

He pulled an evidence bag from his pocket and lifted the cane by its lower end. He placed the bag over the handle and secured it with a rubber band. He was willing to bet they would find Townsend's prints on the cane.

Fealder turned to the Tacoma detective. "Can you notify your commander? It's probably 'way too late by now, but maybe your boss will be willing to mount a hotel check. I have one extra photo and I'll give it to you. Berbieri and I will continue our search in Seattle. I'll call the Seattle police and see if we can get permission for our helicopter to land at the parking lot next to Century Link Field. If they okay the landing, we'll hoof it the few blocks from the train station.

Townsend had sounded appropriately grateful and enthused as the engineer explained dozens of details and told anecdotes about driving locomotives, getting through switchyards, and experiencing close calls on the rails. In spite of his desperate situation, he did find the conversation interesting. When the train arrived in Tukwila, he thanked the engineer and the fireman effusively and dismounted from the cab. He was relieved that they had not seemed to notice that he had brought his shoulder bag with him. He walked back in the direction of Car 5 in case the engineer was watching. Then he quickly joined the cluster of people heading away from the tracks. He saw, by the clock on the wall of the simple waiting room, that he was right on schedule since he had intended all along to get off at Tukwila. Leaving the train at Tukwila made the trip to the airport much shorter and quicker. For what it was worth, he hoped the booking showing him going to Seattle would further confuse Fealder and Berbieri. He immediately hailed a cab and was on his way. Not a bad improvisation, he told himself.

Fealder had had to contact the Federal Aviation Administration, as well as the Seattle Police, for permission to land the helicopter, but finally received a clearance. He called the pilot who said he would be there waiting for them. Fealder was hugely frustrated. The disappearance of the 'limping man' convinced Fealder that he had been right and that Townsend had slipped through their fingers even though he had been on the train for a while. Feeling discouraged and fatigued, he found an empty seat and fell asleep. Berbieri sat beside him and dozed a little herself. She awoke when the train slowed to a stop. Thinking it was Seattle, she turned to wake Fealder. She held back when she saw a station sign that read "Tukwila". She was unfamiliar with that town, but correctly assumed they were still en route to Seattle. She was half-asleep as she looked out the window and did not notice a man of medium weight and height, and wearing a ball cap, leave the platform.

23

Townsend approached the ticket counter for Delta Airlines and joined the queue with three persons in front of him. He tried to suppress the need to constantly check his watch and look over his shoulder. He finally had his turn at the counter. The woman in the Delta uniform looked cheerful and alert considering the late hour. His guess that the red-eye flight would have available seats was correct. He asked for a round-trip ticket to Atlanta. Townsend knew that the terrorist profile included having little or no luggage, paying cash for the ticket, and only flying one-way. He was reluctant to spend the extra money, but – since he had to pay cash and only had a shoulder bag – he wanted to avoid the third triggering condition. The woman looked up at him questioningly as she counted the cash.

"Got lucky in a big poker game a few hours ago and I don't want to carry so much cash around in Atlanta," Townsend explained with a grin.

That seemed to relax the woman. "Well, I hope you bought a lottery ticket as well! May I see two pieces of ID?"

Townsend passed her his new driver's license and passport. She studied them and keyboarded in some information. "So, going abroad from Atlanta?"

Townsend wished she were less conversational. "Probably not. I just have a few quick days of family business to attend to. But, I've got a brother-in-law down there who likes the Bahamas. Last time, he talked me into staying a few days longer and we went over to Nassau. I have to admit, we had a pretty good time. He said, in case we do it again, to bring my passport. I guess these days you need one to come and go anywhere, even to Canada."

"Yes. This post-nine-eleven world is a whole different place, isn't it?" She gave him his boarding pass. "Well, have a good time. You'll be boarding through Gate A-twelve."

Townsend entered a men's room before he reached the security-check area. He debated with himself whether or not to dispose of the blue sweater and black coat that were now inside his shoulder bag. If Fealder and Berbieri had followed him onto the train, they also might have circulated particulars about his appearance to the security screeners in Seattle. He had nothing in the bag that would look suspicious at the x-ray station, but there was still a random chance that the bag would be opened and its contents examined. On the other hand, he reasoned, if he left the sweater and jacket under used paper towels in the lavatory waste bin, the custodians might report the unusual find. Then security would alert Fealder that he, Townsend, had presumptively been at the airport. He decided to leave the clothing in the bag and take his chances.

Townsend's luck held and the Transportation Security Administration screeners had no interest in opening his bag. He proceeded into the gate area and saw that boarding would begin in thirty-five minutes. There were plenty of available seats, but he chose to sit next to a teenage boy who also wore a Mariners cap. He hoped that a seeming affinity of interests could support a casual conversation. Engaging in conversation, however mundane, would ease his nerves and would make him appear innocent and relaxed to any watching eyes.

Berbieri woke Fealder as the train rolled into the King Street Station in Seattle. "Hah!" he said. "I was out like a light! Did you get any shuteye?"

"Just a little. I woke up when we stopped at Tukwila."

"What? Are you kidding? Tukwila's that golfcourse community down around Woodburn isn't it?"

"You've got me on that. I'm not a golfer. No, it was just the last stop before Seattle."

Fealder sat up straighter. "There was a stop in between Tacoma and Seattle? I didn't realize that."

He frowned as he thought the Tukwila stop might have been closer to the airport than downtown Seattle. He wondered if he should have told their pilot to meet them there instead, in order to make a quicker hop to the airport. Then it occurred to him that Townsend might have done that also. Townsend's ticket was good all the way to Seattle, but what if he had purchased it that way to obscure his real intentions? Well, in any case, Fealder thought, Townsend had somehow left the train at Tacoma or an earlier stop, so this new information was beside the point. The AMTRAK Cascades shuddered to a stop in the station.

Fealder faced another choice: to continue with his fall-back plan to try to close the net at the airport or to admit defeat and head back to Portland. He reasoned that the abandoned cane somewhat supported his disguised-fugitive-on-the-train theory. We've come this far, he told himself, no point in quitting now. They were into extra innings.

Their helicopter, as promised, was waiting for them beside the vast bulk of the stadium. Fealder told the pilot to fly them to the airport. The pilot radioed the control tower to clear his landing and refueling.

Fealder phoned his contact at Sea-Tac security to arrange speedy transport from the helipad area to the United gate area. Twelve minutes later, they were shaking hands with two men from airport security.

"We're almost certain the tricky bastard was on the train for Seattle. We boarded the train at Tacoma, but somehow he gave us the slip. There's no guarantee he'll head here. We're just playing the odds. The first flight I want to focus on is the United flight to Los Angeles. We're so close to boarding time, we probably should go straight to the gate area. If he's here, he will recognize Detective Berbieri and me from afar, so it'll be better if you two scout the area first. Here's a photo of what he actually looks like, but he seems to have changed his appearance to look like a much older man with gray hair, no beard, no glasses, and a limp."

They climbed onto a six-seat, electric utility cart and silently motored past jet-ways, fuel trucks, baggage carts, and caterers' vehicles as they moved toward the United hub. A light fog had settled on the runway, blurring the exterior lights and turning them into murky way stations. A stiff breeze drove a chill into their bodies. Berbieri gave an involuntary shudder. They agreed on a radio channel and Fealder laid out his strategy.

"While you men are having a quick look around at the gate area, Berbieri and I will check the United ticket counters and show the photo to all the customer-service reps. Hopefully, that will help them tell us if they've sold him a ticket for either the Dallas-Ft. Worth flight or the L.A. flight. If that doesn't lead us any-where else, we'll try to join you a few minutes before they start the boarding process for this flight. At that point, we don't care so much if he spots us since we can have a better shot at keeping him in the gate area."

"Is this guy armed?" asked one of the security officers.

"He isn't licensed to carry a gun. Of course, that doesn't mean he isn't carrying, but somehow I doubt it," offered Berbieri.

"I'm still not real comfortable with confronting this character in the gate area. Even at this time of night, there'll be quite a few people there."

"I share your discomfort," said Fealder, "but, unless we have the numbers to do a person-to-person search over the entire airport – which we don't -- this seems like the most efficient way to close in on him."

"Okay. Let's get started. The United counters are back at the main terminal. I'll get one of our Sea-Tac security guys, Dave, to drive you over there and get you back out here past the TSA security check."

Berbieri zipped her jacket tightly under her chin and leaned a little against Fealder on the ride back to the main terminal. Inside the terminal, the two detec-tives, helped by the presence of the third uniformed Sea-Tac security officer, bypassed the few waiting pas-sengers as they moved up to interview the two cus-tomer service representatives. Both said they had not seen any person resembling the photo, even allowing for some cosmetic changes. Fealder's radio crackled to life.

"Yes, Fealder here. Over."

"There's nobody in the first United gate area that looks like your man in terms of appearance. They're going to board in about five minutes. Can you make it back here in time? Over."

"We're done here. We had no luck at the United counter. See if you can delay the boarding just a few minutes. We're on our way!"

They entered the gate area and unabashedly looked at the face of every male standing in the pre-boarding line or sitting in the lounge area. Fealder knew they had drawn a blank. "Let's get over to the Delta counter," he said to Berbieri. Looking at the airport security men, he said, "Let's handle it the same way as we did for the United flight."

"Okay. Dave will take you to the Delta check-in counter. We'll survey the gate area."

There was only one customer-service representative, behind the Delta check-in counter. Fealder flashed his badge and thrust the photo across the counter top. "We're hunting for this person and we think it's possible he'll try to leave the city by plane tonight. Has he, by any chance, checked in with you this evening?"

The woman stared at the photo. "I don't think so, but the face does sort of look familiar. What time would it have been?"

"Probably sometime in the last hour or so."

"Well, there *was* a guy who looked sort of the same that bought a ticket. Paid cash for it as a matter of fact... said he got lucky in a big poker game. He didn't have a beard and his hair was longer. I don't think he wore glasses either, but I'm not sure about that."

Berbieri and Fealder exchanged glances when the woman mentioned a cash purchase. Berbieri said, "He may well have changed his appearance. Shaving off a beard would be an easy change to make. Take another look and try to imagine the face without the beard."

The woman picked up the picture and studied it thoughtfully. "Yes, it could be the same person. It definitely could."

Fealder's pulse raced. "Where was he going?" he asked.

"It almost had to be Atlanta. We only have a couple of flights leaving this time of night: Atlanta and Boston. Yeah, I remember now. He talked about maybe going to the Bahamas with his brother-in-law, so it *was* the Atlanta flight."

"Do you remember how he was dressed?"

"Not really. I'm kind of spacey by this time of night. I remember he was wearing a cap, though."

"May we have the name on the ticket and the seat reservation?"

"Just a moment". She referred to a duplicate in her drawer and then verified something on her computer. "Yes. The name is David Markley. Seat twenty-four-C."

"When are they boarding?"

"That plane is on time. They should be boarding around eleven-forty-five."

"Thanks! You've been a great help," said Fealder as they hurried away.

Fealder radioed the two security officers checking the gate area. "There's a good possibility he's on the Delta flight. Over."

"Hold on a second," followed by several seconds' pause. "Sorry about that. I needed to walk away from the gate 'cause these two-ways are a little loud and I forgot to use my earphone. We haven't seen anyone yet who really fits the description, but he may be delayed for some reason. Over."

"We don't think he had any luggage other than a good-sized shoulder bag. Maybe he's killing time in one of the bars. Over."

"Shall we start to check them? Over."

"No. Not just now. Berbieri and I will come to the general area. Is there someplace close enough to see the people in the gate area without ourselves being there? Over."

"There's a little newsstand-bookstore just across the main aisle that might work. Over."

"Okay. We'll be over there. Don't come to us unless we have to take immediate action. You can do a big arms-over-the-head stretch to show you see we're in position. Over."

"Roger that. Out."

Ten minutes later, Berbieri and Fealder were ostensibly browsing books. The security officer standing near the gate gave a big overhead stretch. The newsstand proprietor asked them to please hurry and make up their minds as she was closing at eleven-thirty. Fealder whispered in her ear and she left them alone. There were no more than fifty people lounging or trying to sleep in the rows of padded, leather chairs at the gate. Fealder put the book he had been holding back in its rack and produced a small digital camera with a zoom lens from his pocket. He got Berbieri to look as though she were posing for a photo, while he actually used the camera as a crude telescope. Only two men attracted his attention and one of them was sitting beside a teenager and was engaged in an animated conversation. In the camera's viewer, Fealder saw that both of the men that had caught his interest had the same general facial features as Townsend. The first man he focused on – the one engaged in conversation – wore a sweatshirt with some image on the front and had a ball cap covering most of his hair. Fealder saw the second man had grey hair under a golf cap and wore a yellow sweater over a collared shirt. Fealder turned to Berbieri.

"I want a closer look at a couple of these guys. I'm going to stroll down the center aisle."

He pocketed the camera and walked into the center aisle. There was a bank of television monitors suspended from the ceiling eighty feet down the corridor.

Fealder walked there and appeared to consult the monitors. Then, he walked slowly back toward the newsstand.

"I can't be sure," he whispered to Berbieri. "They both are possibles. I did notice that the man in the sweatshirt has some kind of a bag tucked under his seat. Let's leave the area and hang out further down this corridor. We'll come back in ten minutes when it will be almost boarding time. Then I'm going right up to them both and I'll check all the other men too, in case he came to the gate at the last minute. You will have to be ready to cover me if we have a situation."

They walked away from the area, laughing softly and seemingly engaged in their own personal conversation. At eleven-forty, they started back to the gate for the Atlanta flight. There had been no radio contact from the security officers during their absence. Entering the gate area, Berbieri took a seat near the main corridor and Fealder walked right past the man in the sweatshirt. He could hear enough to tell that the man and the boy were discussing baseball and he saw that the printing on the older man's sweatshirt said "Seattle Mariners". There definitely was some likeness in the man's clean-shaven features and the voice sounded quite like Townsend's, but he wanted to check out the second man before making a move. He kept walking, but something was nagging him about the first man's appearance. The man's eyes were the wrong color, but that was not it.

Fealder was, by then, nearly abreast of the second man. He stopped and studied the man's face. He was reading a paperback novel and looked up questioningly. Fealder saw the man had a scar on his left cheek and had more wrinkles on his face than Townsend could possibly have manufactured.

"Sorry," Fealder said, "I thought for a moment you were an old friend."

The man nodded understandingly and went back to his reading.

Fealder had resumed walking when it hit him. The shoes! The man with the scruffy Mariners sweatshirt was wearing tailored slacks and expensive, black tassel-loafers. Exactly the shoes Townsend had been wearing each time they interviewed him! Fealder glanced back across two rows of chairs at the man in the sweatshirt and discovered that the man had stopped his conversation and was staring directly at him. Townsend hesitated only for an instant and then leaped out of his chair and sprinted toward the central corridor.

Fealder yelled, "It's him! The guy with the baseball cap!"

Heads turned at the outburst. Berbieri drew her gun and yelled. "Stop! Police! Stop or I'll shoot!"

Townsend turned as he reached the corridor and ran even faster. Fealder saw three people in airline uniforms coming toward them in the corridor beyond Townsend. Firing a shot was out of the question in those circumstances. The two security officers had both managed to end up on the same side of the gate area, away from the side Townsend was passing through in his effort to escape. Fealder was poised to give chase, but he had noticed that the teenager had been idly tossing a hardball from hand to hand. Fealder knew what he had to do, but the memory of that late-August day in Memphis nearly paralyzed him. Then his vision cleared and he sucked in a breath. He snatched the ball and threw it as hard as he could at the fleeing man's back. The baseball hit Townsend between his shoulders and he collapsed to the floor. Fealder hurdled a row of empty seats and sprinted into the corridor. Townsend had regained his feet and was breaking into a run when Fealder tackled him. Berbieri was close behind with her Glock still in her hands.

"Stay down! Face on the floor! I have you covered!" she shouted.

Townsend thrashed under Fealder's weight for a moment and then lay quiet. In the tussle, his cap and wig had come off. The security men completed a perimeter around the prone man and one of them handed Fealder a set of handcuffs. Fealder yanked Townsend's arms behind his back and attached the cuffs.

"Nice throw, Detective Fealder!" said one of the officers.

"Yeah, well, that's one of the few things I happen to be any good at," responded Fealder with a chuckle.

"Geez, you really nailed him!" chimed in the other officer.

Berbieri read Townsend his rights. Many of the passengers, after being frozen in place by the unexpectedly loud and violent action they had witnessed, were now coming toward them to get a closer view. The Sea-Tac security officers ordered them to get back to their seats and assured everyone that the danger was over.

Fealder rose from kneeling over Townsend and grinned at his partner. "We got him, Tami," he said.

24

The Sea-Tac security officers stood on either side, gripping Townsend's biceps. Fealder dusted off his slacks and walked over to a disconsolate Townsend, his head down and his now-grey hair disheveled from their struggles.

"How did you get off the train?" Fealder asked.

"I'm not going to answer any questions without an attorney," said Townsend sullenly.

"I'm not asking about what you may have done to Warburton or Mayfield. I'm only asking about your escape from Portland to the Seattle airport."

Townsend shook his head, negatively. Fealder removed a small recorder from his pocket, showed it to Townsend, and handed it to Berbieri. He asked the two security officers to release their grips on Townsend, saying he wanted to take a short walk with the captive and would take full responsibility. They backed away and the two men walked a short distance away.

"This is off the record," said Fealder in a soft voice. "You know I'll find out sooner or later. Suppose you and I just discuss how a hypothetical person trying to escape a train search on the northbound Cascades might go about it."

Townsend studied Fealder's face for a long moment, and then nodded ever so slightly as if acknowledging a worthy adversary in a chess match. "Such a person might consider moving to a forward car, might try to become an unconventional passenger."

Townsend offered nothing further. He turned and walked back to the waiting security officers. Fealder returned the baseball to the wide-eyed teenager. The young man asked him to autograph the ball. Fealder grinned and obliged him. The security staff summoned Sheriff's Deputies who promptly took Townsend downtown to a holding cell at the King County Jail. Fealder called Beth Saunders at her home and told her of their capture of Townsend. Next, he called the Lieutenant who headed the Portland Homicide Detectives Unit, relishing the thought of his call waking James from a sound sleep. The phone rang six times and the message machine had started to kick in when James finally picked up the receiver.

"Yes? What is it?" he mumbled.

"It's Fealder. I thought you ought to know that we just captured Townsend at the Seattle-Tacoma International

Airport. He was minutes away from boarding a plane for Atlanta when we flushed him."

" You actually got him! Well, I must say, that was good work, Fealder. Where is he and where are you?"

Fealder was gratified and somewhat amused that James could not help but bestow a compliment on their capture of the fugitive. "He's on his way to the King County Jail until Saunders can file the papers for extradition. Berbieri and I and Stewart, our pilot, are going to check in at an airport hotel and fly back in the morning."

"On the expense account, I suppose?"

"Yes sir. We're all a bit tired at this point."

"I see. Well, you can report to me tomorrow."

Fealder and Berbieri agreed to meet for breakfast in the hotel coffee shop at 9:30. Fealder had ordered a wake-up call at 8:45, but he was awake by eight o'clock. He vaguely remembered dreaming about someone jumping off a train. He was at the basin splashing water on his face when he had his first inkling of what Townsend might have meant by his cryptic answer to the "hypothetical" question. Still in his briefs, Fealder searched in his notebook for the number of AMTRAK security. He got through to Dispatch and asked for the name and phone number of the engineer on last evening's Cascades. Minutes later, he had awakened Terry McMahon and explained why he was calling.

"We caught our man at Sea-Tac and we know he was on the train. We boarded the train in Tacoma and couldn't find him. I've been asking myself how he got to the airport. I keep coming 'round to the fact that he had to get close to make the timing work. Tacoma seems a little too far away even with a speedy taxi. I'm guessing he stayed on until Tukwila or maybe even Seattle. So where was he? I wonder if you could help me here? If maybe you had an extra person in your cab?"

There was a long silence at the other end. Finally, the man cleared his throat. "Detective Fealder, you put me in a very awkward situation. There are FTSB and company rules against anyone but operating personnel in the locomotives."

Fealder sensed he had solved Townsend's puzzle. "Mr. McMahon, I'm a homicide detective. I am not a federal inspector or a railroad dick. It's very unlikely that any details about his attempted escape will need to be made public even if the prosecution goes to trial. Why don't you tell me what happened last night?"

"Lord, we certainly didn't know he was a murderer or was making an escape. He told us he was a cancer patient and had only a couple of months to live. Said he'd always wanted to ride in the cab of a real locomotive. I guess we're suckers, but we fell for it. This was in Tacoma. I told him we'd allow it, but only to our next stop in Tukwila. He said he was on his way to Seattle, so when he got out, we assumed he went back to his passenger car."

"Thanks for your candor, Mr. McMahon. Assuming we don't find anything to suggest you two knew each other or that you accepted money from him, you'll probably never hear from me again."

"Well, we're safe there. Neither my fireman nor I had ever laid eyes on him before last night. And, believe me, he didn't offer us money. That would've tipped us off right then that he wasn't on the level!"

The man's statement had the ring of truth, thought Fealder. "I can respect your trying to do a good deed for a dying man. You don't deserve to get in trouble for that. Thanks again for talking to me."

It was late Monday morning when the helicopter landed Fealder in Vancouver. Berbieri said she would ride back to Portland in Fealder's car. Fealder grinned at her in the seat beside him as they crossed the interstate bridge into north Portland.

"You had quite a baptism into the Homicide Unit," he said.

"Believe it! But I had a terrific partner. Watching you sort through all the suspects in this case and smoke out Townsend was the best OJT I could've hoped for."

"Ah, thanks. But you pulled your own weight from day one, Tami. I think we're going to make a good team!"

Her lips formed the slightest of smiles as she turned to face him. "Thanks for saying that, Park."

Monday afternoon, Fealder received a call from Andy Delikoff. He offered Fealder hearty congratulations for closing a double murder case and began an update on the work of the criminalists at Townsend's cabin.

"You'll be interested to know that my guys checked that outdoor fire pit and guess what? They found evidence that a lot of paper had been burned. They found two partial pages that had been scorched, but not consumed by the fire. We'll need a handwriting expert to look them over, but it's pretty clear that they're part of some clinical records dealing with depression."

"Great!," said Fealder. "All the hard copies of the records in the depression clinic that Townsend ran at the medical school – one of the places where they were doing the drug trials – were stolen in a mysterious break-in. We were pretty sure that Townsend himself stole the records to make it easier to suppress the data on the suicides. He must have needed a way to destroy the hard copies and taking them up to his cabin and burning them was probably the easiest way to do that."

"There's more, Park" said Delikoff. "Remember the duct tape?"

"Sure, I asked your guys to see if there was a match on the tear boundary."

"Well, there was a perfect match! And our tire tread casts showed a match to the tires on Mayfield's car."

"Great! But not so conclusive on the tires, huh? With so many of the same size and make?"

"Generally, that's true. But Mayfield's tire had some damage … a gash in its tread that matched right up to the cast. It's still not totally conclusive, but, statistically, it makes it highly probable that his car was there. And finally, we found Mayfield's prints on the paper that had the driving directions"

"The A.D.A. will appreciate all of that. Every piece of converging evidence just makes her case that much stronger. How about those license plates? Were they ever found?"

"They sure were! About twenty-five feet from the car. We found them buried just under the surface, maybe three inches down."

"Glad to hear it. They weren't too important since we had the VIN number off the chassis, but it's nice to tie up the loose ends."

Mark Holloway, the FBI agent working with the FDA, called Fealder that same afternoon to tell him that Bradley Pharmaceuticals had agreed to withdraw Zolane from all further testing. He also said that, when they decoded the matrix and other trial data, they saw that all three suicides had been in the group that received Zolane.

Two days later, a handwriting expert matched the entries on the two scorched pages to the handwriting of two of the counselors in the clinic. That same day, Berbieri spoke to one of the clinicians who had been on vacation when Hokanson and Schultz did the first round of interviews. The clinician confirmed she occasionally had been responsible for dispensing the capsules containing the Zolane or the placebo and that she had never been told not to administer those capsules to the persons who committed suicide. The following day, Fealder learned that the fingerprints on the cane recovered from the train matched Townsend's prints. He also received a call from his contact at AMTRAK security wanting to know what had become of the search by Fealder and the Tacoma police. Fealder told them the man had eluded their search and left the train, but that they had later caught him at the airport. He was not questioned further and did not elaborate. Fealder procrastinated dealing with Patty Lawson's breaking into the affirmative action office. He finally called the Chief of Campus Security and told him what they had learned. He was never officially told what became of Ronald Talbourne or Professor Lawson. Months later, at a holiday-season open house, he was introduced to Adam Warburton's friend, Bruce Faraday, who said that Lawson had been dismissed for cause after an acrimonious hearing on the campus.

Three weeks after his arrest, Townsend waived extradition and was transported to Oregon where he was remanded to the custody of the Multnomah County Jail. He was quickly indicted for two first-degree murders. He pled not guilty at his arraignment and bail was denied. Ten months passed before he was brought to trial. The jury convicted Townsend of the first-degree murders of Adam Warburton and William Mayfield. Beth Saunders and Clay Osborne asked for the death penalty, but the verdict was for life imprisonment. The evidence of guilt was strong, but circumstantial and, without an eye witness, the jury was not willing to sentence Townsend to death. Fealder found that to be ironic. By his reasoning, the more carefully one planned a murder, the more secretive was the act itself so that there was almost never an eye-witness.

Upon their return from Seattle, James *did* assign Fealder and Berbieri to the homicide in Northeast Portland involving a drug dealer and they quickly identified the murderer. James had the decency to ask Fealder if he were satisfied to have Berbieri as a permanent partner. Fealder said "yes, we seem to make a good team." Fealder then took two weeks of vacation, part of which he spent in his woodshop finishing the cradle for his newborn niece. While on his vacation, Fealder thought about his throw that felled Townsend at the airport and decided that perhaps he had exorcised the specter of his own guilt over the incident in Memphis.

Berbieri experimented with several new recipes in her kitchen and spent several off-duty weekends fishing the Clackamas River with considerable success.

Paul Stranglund, the University Counsel, called Fealder to tell him that the Promotion and Tenure Appeals Committee had reversed the denial of tenure for Howard Callison, held that two additional referees should review his publications, and sent the case back to the Provost for reconsideration. Fealder had long ago decided that he had nothing to tell any

University administrators about the scholarship of Norman Plaget, so that name did not come up in their conversation.

The Seattle Mariners had earned a spot in the post-season play-offs, but were eliminated when they lost their first series. Even without the Mariners or the Cardinals playing, Fealder watched much of the World Series on television and reflected upon how very much he liked his new career.

ACKNOWLEDGEMENTS

Many thanks to those who read early drafts and made truly helpful suggestions: my wife, Joyce; Kathy Brault, Phoebe Smith; the late Bob Miller; Melinda Casby and the late Jerry Casby; Peter Mellini; Pierre VanRysselberghe; and the late Jon Jacobson. And special thanks to my superb proof readers Kathy Brault, Del Thomas and Suzy Sivyer.

Made in the USA
San Bernardino, CA
19 September 2016